SHADOWS OF THE PAST

Port Carin
Tarium
Lone Bay
Tarium
Bridge of Sorrows
Sea of Kings
Fincastle
Sterling River
Bakea
Sternz
Cedar Town
Broken Point
Redoak
Crixaria
Xanica
Roughstone
W
Brooksville
Vetin
Helahm
Lewisburg
Rockport
Roughstone Mountains
Schel
Kirnton
Hoiduhn
Malgen

lia
Petelia
Northern Wastes
Suasa
Colubra Bay
Azara Cradle
Azara
Azara
Serpent's Pass
Ricina
Xarul's Rage
Entella
Wraith Island
Nobun
Vor-Dual
Crowned Mountains
N
W
E
S

Shadows of the Past
Copyright © 2020
Luther Salyers

ISBN: 978-1-948679-89-3

Cover art by Reuben Lane
Map design by Aaron Drexler
Cover treatment by Jonathan Grisham for Grisham Designs

Published by WordCrafts Press
Cody, Wyoming 82414
www.wordcrafts.net

The Unbroken
Book 2

Shadows

OF THE

Past

Luther Salyers

WordCrafts Press

Xanica
Evalon
King's
Cradle
Harpsburg
Bakea
Treasure River
Cedartown
Chinon
Roughstone
Keep
Bamberg
Travert
Lake
Bayeux
N
W   E
S

1

A harsh icy breeze swayed the branches of the thick elm trees in the forest. A young human girl dressed in warm furs walked toward a stream carrying a small wooden bucket. She knelt by the stream and dipped her bucket in the frigid water. She heard a dull thud, and felt water flow over her feet. The sight of an arrow piercing the side of the bucket caused her eyes to widen, and tore a scream from her throat. She rose, and started running; fast—faster than she ever had, as fast as her spindly legs could propel her.

She risked glancing right and left and behind her, trying to spot the attacker. She stifled the cry that welled up within her, unwilling to give her position away, if indeed her attacker did not already know her position. She stumbled on a large root protruding from the ground, tumbled to the ground, twisting her ankle and smashing her knee against an unforgiving rock.

Blood poured from the gash, drawing a whimper of pain from the girl. She clamped her hand over her mouth and scanned the shadowed woods for any sign or sound of her pursuer. There was no movement, no sound—other than the whistling of the wind through the trees.

The girl regained her feet and hobbled forward as quietly as possible. At last weariness exceeded her fear and she sat with her back against the tree to rest. She examined her bloodied and swollen knee, flinching in pain when she tried to touch it.

Movement caught her eye. Fear paralyzed her mind. A Wraith of Colubra stood above her.

Clad in tight, black leather armor, his face obscured by a hood and mask, the scale tattoos on the Wraith's bare arms marked him for what he was.

The Wraith knelt before her, fixing her with his hollow-eyed gaze as he placed a single finger over her lips. With infinite economy of movement the Wraith slipped his dagger from its sheath, and just as deftly sliced through the girl's throat.

The girl's fingers clasped hard around the open wound. Warm blood rushed between her fingers, over her hands, and down onto her body. Her eyes never wavered from the Wraith's hollow-eyed glare, even as her life-blood flowed out. She was still gazing into his eyes when life faded away.

The Wraith wiped his dagger on the girl's fur clothing, then returned it to its sheath. If he felt any remorse, it did not show in his eyes.

The sound of elves on horseback drew his attention from the dead girl. The Wraith bowed low to honor the approach of Prince Domatin. Mounted on a black horse and attired in his accustomed dark blue scale armor, Domatin was armed with only a simple wooden bow. Behind him road five more Wraiths and 20 Praetorians in their heavy, white scale armor and soft cream colored masks.

Domatin noticed the dead girl, and a smile crept across his face. His gaze, however, was fixed on the village in the distance. He pointed at it as he addressed the elves gathered behind him, "This human village has been confirmed to harbor and aid members of the Xanican resistance. Make an example of them so that all will know not to defy us. Spare no one. Not the women, the old, or the infirm, not the children. Kill them all. Burn their village to the ground."

The Wraiths ran through the snow toward the village, the Praetorians followed at the slower pace, and Domatin waited at the edge of the forest to watch. The first dwelling sparked and caught fire. The fire skipped across to the next dwelling. Soon the village was ablaze and the screams of its inhabitants pierced the night sky. Domatin caught a snowflake on his tongue and let out a soothing breath before returning his gaze to the carnage.

Out of the corner of his eye, Domatin saw a young human boy, perhaps eight years old, running as fast as he could toward the forest. A wicked gleam shone in Domatin's eyes. He spurred his horse into a gallop through the frigid air toward the small boy.

The boy looked over his shoulder once, then laid down in the snow, overcome with fear.

Domatin spurred his black steed faster. The boy didn't make a sound as the horse plowed over him. Domatin reined the horse in, turned, and trotted him back to where the boy's battered body lay.

"Perhaps I should have done that to Liam those years ago," he muttered to himself.

2

Walking in the gardens at Sternz, Kaia raised her hand to shield her eyes from the vivid winter sun that glared down upon her. Her eyes adjusting from the brightness, she watched Bethany chase Alyssa around the statue of The Hero of Aclia.

Out of breath, Bethany paused and said to Kaia, "I think it is your turn to chase our sister. Alyssa never seems to run out of energy."

Kaia laughed as Alyssa jumped on Bethany's back. "Or both of you could chase me!" Alyssa said. "That way it would be twice as much fun."

Kaia stopped at the rectangular pond in front of the statue and asked, "I thought you two were going to play in the gardens?"

"We were," responded Bethany. "But Alyssa decided to try and splash water on me, so I've been trying to throw her into the pond."

Alyssa gasped as she felt Bethany's grip tighten around her legs. Bethany laughed as she walked toward the pond with Alyssa squirming to try to get off her back. Kaia smiled at her two sisters as Bethany fell backwards into the pond, drenching them both in icy water.

"Princesses!" came a shout from behind the gate.

Kaia looked behind her to see Jaclyn rush past her to help Bethany and Alyssa out of the freezing water. Both were shivering so much their teeth chattered. Jaclyn stripped off her own fur coat and wrapped it around the children as they huddled together for warmth.

"What were you two thinking? We have to get you inside before you catch your death of a cold—or your mother finds out and scolds all of us," Jacelyn admonished.

Kaia lowered her head and muttered, "Mother wouldn't care. We seldom even see her anymore."

Jaclyn chivvied Bethany and Alyssa back toward the citadel as she addressed Kaia. "Your mother is busy, you know that. Since your father's death she has been trying to run this country and build up an army to be able to attack the elves. These past three months have been hard on her, but I promise she isn't ignoring you on purpose."

"I miss papa," Alyssa whimpered.

Bethany pulled Alyssa close. "We all do. But at least we have each other. Kaia and I don't plan on leaving you anytime soon." Bethany turned to Kaia and joked, "Unless a certain someone takes her away from us."

"Who is going to take her away from us?" Alyssa demanded.

Bethany continued to tease as Kaia's face blushed scarlet. "Do you not remember that handsome man she has spent a great deal of time with?"

Alyssa grinned. "You mean the man with the big green orc?"

"That's right," replied Bethany.

Alyssa smiled up at Kaia with approval. "I like him. He seems nice."

Kaia returned the smile. "Vernon is a very kind and handsome man. Now if only we could find someone for Bethany."

Bethany scoffed, "That'll be the day."

They arrived at the door leading to the citadel and Jaclyn allowed Bethany and Alyssa to step inside before addressing Kaia. "Speaking of that handsome man, this came for you."

Jaclyn pulled a sealed envelope from her sleeve and handed it to Kaia. Kaia snatched the envelope.

"Thank you Jaclyn. I still don't know why mother doesn't want me to read these."

"Queen Alezzia probably just doesn't like the fact that a man is becoming a part of your life," Jaclyn replied.

Jaclyn followed the two princesses inside, leaving Kaia alone to read her letter.

"My dearest Kaia.

How are things back in Sternz? Or rather Crixaria. It may have only been a month since I departed but Xanica is a cold and unforgiving country. The forests here are much larger and thicker than the ones we are used to, and the snow hasn't helped.

Almost everyone is doing fine here. Konar is still drinking but slowly cutting down. Kassandra—well Kassandra is Kassandra, there is no slowing her down. Liam, however, has been even more quiet than normal, and he seems to be in a sour mood. Konar thinks that Liam is just tired, so we will see how he shapes up..."

As Kaia neared the end of the letter, her smile flipped to a frown, and she started running toward the front of the citadel. She passed soldiers and common people alike, greeting neither, oblivious to their salutes and salutations. She paused only briefly at the front gate to catch her breath, then entered the citadel and made her way to the throne room where Queen Alezzia sat in her chair listening to General Izak, Vicar Matthew, and Benjamin argue.

"Why are you even here?" Izak shouted at Benjamin. "You have nothing to offer that could help us."

Alezzia answered for Benjamin. "Benjamin is my new head advisor. He will be here during all discussions involving the state of Crixaria."

Vicar Matthew chimed in. "I agree with General Izak. We should send our armies as soon as we can. Within three months I will have 300,000 paladins ready to march toward the elven homeland of Azara. With your new army of 100,000 we can at least force the elves out of Xanica."

Alezzia remained silent and allowed her gaze to flow from Benjamin to Izak to the Vicar. "Benjamin and I believe it would be best to wait for Vetin's reply. If they join us we can add another

200,000 to our army. We can't take the war to the elven homeland unless we have Vetin's support as well as the dwarves continuing their war."

Izak tilted his head in annoyance. "In Xanica there are only 35,000 elven soldiers. They have their 15,000 occupational force and the 20,000 that King Dylenn allowed to leave. Most of those are still nursing wounds from the siege. If we were to send even a small contingent of troops, we could retake Xanica now."

Benjamin barked a short laugh. "And what about the weather? It has begun to snow in Xanica, are you not worried that our forces could freeze to death if they got stuck somewhere? We should wait until the winter has passed before we send our armies east."

Matthew glared at Benjamin. "If we were to take Xanica back from the elves we would have a better staging ground to prepare for the march across the Eacru wastes. And we would have the support of Xanican people."

Kaia, who had been listening silently, now cleared her throat to draw attention to herself. All eyes turned toward her. "I apologize for interrupting, but I have some news that may be of value."

Alezzia took a deep breath and motioned for Kaia to continue. Kaia pulled out Vernon's letter and said, "One month ago The Unbroken volunteered to go to the aid of the Xanican Resistance. This letter is from Vernon Regnier. It says they haven't made contact with the resistance yet, but his news gives us reason enough to send some sort of aid."

Alezzia glared at Kaia,. "A letter from Vernon Regnier? I thought I made it clear you were not to write to him. For all you know that could be an elf trying to give us false information or draw us into a trap."

Before Kaia could respond, Izak interrupted. "What does the letter say?"

Alezzia shot Izak a withering glare, but nodded for her daughter to continue. "Vernon said that the elves have begun to burn entire villages again. The Unbroken have only been in Xanica for two weeks and have come across four villages that have been massacred and burned to the ground. They think the increased pressure from the Xanican Resistance has made the elves take desperate measures to quell them."

"Surely that news is enough of a reason for us to send aid," Matthew interjected. "To my knowledge this is the first time since the elves invaded 15 years ago that they have butchered entire villages. These are not only fellow humans who are being slaughtered, but fellow believers in The One. We must send whatever aid we can."

Alezzia pondered for a moment before turning to her advisor. "Benjamin and I will go over the finances of Crixaria one more time before deciding on a course of action. Raising an army while rebuilding the wall is expensive. I would not waste money where we don't need to."

Izak tried, but failed, to contain his annoyance. "Take too long to respond and there might not be a Xanica left to liberate," he prophesied.

3

The Unbroken rode through the solemn forest, each wearing dark brown cloaks covering their new armor, gifted by the Vicar of Tarium.

Vernon's chainmail and surcoat had been replaced with a mixture of plate and leather armor. His chest, shoulders, and hands were protected by finely smithed plate armor. Beneath, Vernon wore a heavy, dark purple, wool coat, black trousers, and a soft cowl of black fur that hung from his neck and draped down his back. His feet were shod with dark brown, leather boots.

Kassandra's new armor provided protection without sacrificing mobility. New leather boots and leggings covered her legs, while a tight, dark brown, leather vest rested over a long-sleeved, white shirt. Smaller pieces of plate armor shielded her breasts, shoulders, and forearms.

Liam's new armor was made entirely of charcoal black leather, matched with leather boots, vest, and gloves. Liam had removed much of the steel plating.

"I hate being in the middle of forests," Kassandra complained while riding her spotted grey horse.

Konar, resplendent in his new armor which was fashioned similarly to paladins from Tarium, with heavy grey plate armor beneath a purple cloth tabard, trimmed in yellow with Crixaria's emblem, a golden bear head in the center, sighed. "You've said that every day for the past two weeks. Complaining about it won't make it any better."

9

"You two have been at each other's throats more than normal," Vernon snapped. "If I had to guess, your constant bickering is what has been putting Liam in a bad mood."

All three turned around to look at a sulking Liam.

"I'm fine," was the only reply they got from him.

Kassandra let out a deep sigh and shook her head. "I thought maybe given some time you'd at least *try* to open up. Especially after we all survived Sternz. To be honest I would even accept you lying with an, *I'm cold*, or *I'm tired*, but all you ever say is, *I'm fine, don't worry about it, leave me alone*."

"Perhaps we need to accept that maybe Liam is always going to be like that," Konar said. "Quiet and ready for battle."

Eyeing Konar, Kassandra replied, "Don't you think in his state of mind he is going to get himself killed?"

Vernon joined the conversation. "Kassandra, we all know that out of the four of us Liam has the best chance to survive. He singlehandedly killed three Praetorians, swung off the damn wall, and even beat eight Tarians to a pulp without any weapons."

Kassandra, more annoyed than ever, bickered, "The best chance of survival? Liam has the least! Anytime something related to Prince Domatin pops up he shuts down and focuses on only that." Kassandra directed her ire at Liam. "One of these days you are going to get so caught up with him that you'll run off with no one to watch your back, and Domatin will defeat you."

Liam held Kassandra's gaze for a long moment before dropping his gaze to the large black wolf beside him. "Blaster will always watch my back."

Soft white flakes fell from the sky as they pressed their horses deeper into the forest. A soft breeze echoed through the barren trees. Clouds darkened the sun. Konar studied the sky and said, "I had hoped that it wouldn't snow again for at least another week."

Vernon allowed the cold flakes to pile up on his hand. "This isn't snow," he muttered. "It's ash."

The Unbroken halted, their focus turned to the woods. They

sat quietly searching for any sign of movement of where the ash might be coming from. Blaster's ears perked up as he shifted his attention to the left of the group. With a bark Blaster stared into the woods, alerting everyone else to that part of the forest.

Vernon dismounted, drew his longsword from within his cloak and began to creep into the woods. The rest of the team followed stealthily, watching for signs of a threat.

The hushed tone of the woods put Kassandra more on edge than the others. A branch snapped to her left. Without hesitation, she turned and released an arrow toward the area of the noise. The arrow thudded into a large tree a few feet away and Kassandra just stared at it. A hand holding a simple sword appeared from behind the tree followed by Liam, who stared right back at Kassandra with a heated gaze.

Kassandra forced an apologetic smile to her face as she mouthed, "I'm sorry."

Liam pointed his sword to where Vernon, Konar, and Blaster were walking and the two of them rejoined their team.

They soon heard the gentle flowing sound of water and came upon a small stream. Konar spotted a bucket pierced by an arrow and whispered to himself, "I hope we find at least one survivor this time."

Vernon led the way across the stream, and they continued down a small trail. Blaster sniffed the air and darted off in front of them. Liam yelled out, "Blaster! Get back here."

Liam ran after Blaster and found him sitting by the corpse of a young human girl. The rest of the team approached more cautiously. They could all see the look of pain on the dead girl's face as a trail of dried blood ran from her slit neck to the ground below. They exchanged grim looks then continued up the trail while Konar paused to close the young girl's eyes.

At the edge of the forest they stumbled upon a burnt village, its once welcoming wooden buildings now turned to burnt ruins and piles of ash. They walked toward the village with their weapons ready. Fires still crackling and the stench of burnt flesh assaulted their nostrils. Vernon knelt and touched a pile of ash. "It's still warm—perhaps 12 hours."

Out of the corner of his eye Konar spotted a slight movement. He turned to see the body of a child, face down on the ash pile. In a hushed tone he said, "I think we have a live one over here."

Konar crept slowly toward the child, knelt, and offered words of comfort as he turned the child over. "It's alright now. We are here to help." But then Konar saw that this child's throat had also been slit.

Another movement from the pile of ash drew his attention. He eased the child's body back down, then slowly moved forward.

"Konar, are you alright over there?" Vernon called.

Konar raised his right hand signaling for silence, then wiped away at the top of the pile of ash. No movement. He brushed more ash from the pile. Again, no movement. Konar stood and uttered to himself, "It must have been the wind."

As Konar turned back toward the group, a Wraith of Colubra leapt from within the pile of ash and onto Konar's back, her dagger tearing through the air toward Konar's throat.

The Unbroken dashed toward him as five more wraiths appeared from within the charred remains of the village, surrounding them. One, wrapped in cloak, attempted to throw a spotted brown cobra out of his sleeve, but Kassandra predicted his move. Her arrow pierced the cobra's head then sank into the heart of the wraith.

Vernon, Liam, and Blaster engaged the nearest wraith, as the first wraith desperately tried to pierce Konar's throat, but Konar managed to grab the hilt of the wraith's dagger and forcefully turned the point of the dagger upward. With his other hand, Konar grasped the wraith's collar. Inch by inch Konar pulled the struggling wraith closer and closer to her own dagger, until it finally pierced her chest. The elf's lifeblood flowed over his hands and onto his chest. Konar tossed the body away, gripped his hammer, and stood.

Vernon and Liam had dispatched the wraiths they were engaged with. The two remaining wraiths turned and fled toward the woods.

Kassandra loosed an arrow after them, but missed. Liam whistled for Blaster. "We've got it," he said, then ran off after them into the woods.

Blaster hurtled over roots and stumps as he gained ground on one of the wraiths. The wraith was fast, but not fast enough. Blaster planted his feet on a tree stump then leapt into the air, crashing down on the wraith's back. Razor sharp teeth ripped at the wraith's neck. He was dead before he hit the ground.

Liam caught up to the remaining wraith. Rage overcame him and he let out a roar and tossed his swords aside. He hurled himself onto the wraith knocking them both to the ground. He clasped his fingers around the wraith's neck and squeezed with all his strength. The wraith struggled to get free, pounding and punching, each strike weaker than the last. The wraith's legs began to tremble uncontrollably. He struggled to gasp for breath, any breath. At last, he stopped moving, but Liam continued his death grip, lifting the wraith's inert body by the throat and slamming it back to the ground. With his rage at last spent, Liam loosed his grip. He flexed his fingers to relieve the cramps from strangling the elf. As he was retrieving his swords, Blaster rushed to his side and barked twice.

Liam gazed about him in response to Blaster's warning. In the distance he heard a horse neigh and turned to see a Praetorian galloping away. He shook his head in frustration, then made his way back to the ruined village

"The last two wraiths are dead," he reported to Vernon. "But there was a Praetorian in the distance. He spotted us and rode off."

Vernon nodded. "It was only a matter of time before they discovered we are here."

Kassandra spat in disgust. "But why were the wraiths here in the first place?" she demanded. "This is the fifth village we've come across like this; massacred without mercy."

"I suspect the elves destroy the villages, and leave the wraiths behind to ambush any resistance fighters who search for survivors."

Konar asked, "How much farther until we reach the resistance headquarters?"

Vernon pulled a map of Xanica from his belt. "If Makay's information was correct, the resistance is set up in Harpsburg. That's only a day's ride from here. Let's get there as quick as we can and hope the elves haven't found their way there yet."

4

Their breath condensing in the cold night air, two elven soldiers stood guard at the double doorway to a large wooden manor that sat atop a hill overlooking much of the Xanican countryside. Dozens of braziers scattered around the manor illuminated the surrounding area.

Shivering in the cold, one asked, "Did you hear about the village that was burned last night?"

With her spear resting on the door, the second elf quickly rubbed her hands together for warmth while replying, "I heard that it harbored at least 20 resistance members."

"Twenty! I heard that it was only four or five."

The second elf leaned forward on her spear and whispered, "Between you and me, I have a friend who is a Praetorian. He said they found intel that said the resistance leaders are meeting in Harpsburg tomorrow."

"Why aren't they telling anyone about it? We should deploy and wipe them out," the first elf stated.

"What good would that do? The resistance would know we were coming. By allowing them to think we don't know about their meeting, we can ambush them and wipe them out in one fatal attack."

Marching footsteps in front of them announced someone of importance approaching. Both elves focused on the road until they could make out three figures on horseback, followed by a large column of elven soldiers and Praetorians. The female elf raised her clenched fist to the door behind her and banged on it twice.

As the three figures on horseback dismounted, both guards bowed at the waist. The first elf said, "Welcome to Provincial Manor. Prince Domatin, Imperator Leontina, and Legatus Tauriel. I hope your ride up the hill went well."

With her teeth chattering Tauriel muttered, "Besides this blistering cold it was fine."

The two large doors to the manor opened as a skinny young elf with long curly blond hair, dressed in an elegant blue and white robe encrusted with gold pedals, extended her arms. Smiling, she exclaimed, "Domatin, my dear cousin! It's been too long."

Domatin returned her smile and rushed to hug her. "Phyra! I feared that being away from home this long would bore you to death."

Phyra laughed, "You must be joking? Being the Governess of this forsaken country has been the most fun I've ever had."

"Despite the constant attacks from the human resistance?" Leontina interrupted.

Domatin cringed at the sound of Leontina's voice. He turned and glared at her before announcing, "Phyra, I would like for you to meet Imperator Leontina, the Dwarven Blight."

Phyra passed by Domatin and skipped up to Leontina. She smiled as she studied her face, then said, "I have heard so many things about you. I never thought that I would actually meet one of my role models."

Leontina's eyebrows raised. "Me? A role model?"

"Of course!" Phyra exclaimed. "If it wasn't for you, Azara would've fallen to the dwarves decades ago."

Leontina bowed and said, "Thank you Madam Ophidian."

Phyra walked beside Leontina and hooked arms with her, "You may call me Phyra. We are all friends here. And besides it's not everyday a girl can say she is visited by family and such honored guests for dinner."

Phyra stopped and looked over at the chattering noises she kept hearing to her left where she saw Tauriel slightly hunched over rubbing her arms. "A little cold are we?"

Tauriel nodded her head before her gaze stuck on Phyra's bare feet on the freezing ground. Tauriel asked, "Madam Ophidian are your feet not cold?"

Phyra glanced at her feet before answering. "Oh, not at all. I've been here for almost 16 years, so I'm used to the cold. Now come along you three, dinner should almost be ready."

Phyra, still locked with Leontina, led them into the warmth of the welcoming manor. Lavish blue and white linen curtains draped across the floor. Leontina and Tauriel saw many decorations that reminded them of home—tiny cherry blossom trees in corners and several small statues of the snake god, Colubra. They even spotted Phyra's albino Cobra coiled up at the base of a cherry blossom tree.

As Phyra led them through the manor, she noticed Leontina's and Tauriel's observations and said, "This manor may have been built by humans, but I tried to make it more elvish."

They arrived at a short, square table with a steaming, succulent, roasted boar ready to be served along with a bounty of vegetables and rice. Phyra turned to her guests, "Human architecture may be dull, but I have to admit they sure know how to cook a fine roasted boar. Let's dine and drink on Azara wine."

The four of them sat on short, cushioned chairs as young human women in simple blue gowns served food and wine. As they were eating, Tauriel asked, "Madam Ophidian, how is it that at barely over 190 years old, you were picked to be the Governess of Xanica?"

"I like to tell people it is because of my charm and welcoming personality," Phyra quipped. "But between us, I think it's because no one else wanted the position. Everyone talked about how boring the human kingdoms are, just a whole bunch of dull trees and grass—but I saw deeper into the country as well as the bounty of human women to sleep with."

"Human girls?" Tauriel asked.

Phyra winked at one of the human servers as she answered, "Well of course. For starters most of the human girls who look my age can barely remember what it was like to live without us elves; and secondly if I for some reason fall in love, I only have to wait around 40 or 50 years before she dies and I can find another one!"

"So, Leontina, I've heard that you will be taking command of the forces here in Xanica," Phyra said, changing the subject. "Tell me, how do you plan on dealing with the resistance?"

Leontina took a sip of her wine before replying. "To be honest with you, I am not here to fight the resistance. Empress Julianna ordered that if Crixaria made a move to retake Xanica, I was to secure Roughstone Pass."

"Roughstone Pass?" Phyra said, confused. "Why there?"

Leontina continued, "The Empress fears that the humans will try to attack us in Azara and Roughstone Pass is the only way for a large army to pass between Xanica and the Eacru Wastes."

While plucking a bite of pork off her fork, Phyra giggled, "The humans? Attack us? Why that's just absurd. Even if they took the pass they would have to cross orc lands, which we could easily just pay to constantly harass the humans. And they would more than likely get lost in the desert anyway. But none of that is going to happen, because, well, Crixaria doesn't have reason to attack us, and even if they did, their army is too small."

Leontina cleared her throat. "The part about the Eacru Wastes may be true, but Crixaria is no longer alone. Tarium has joined, and they are probably trying to coerce Vetin to join as well. And they now have more of a reason to hate us than ever before." Leontina turned and stared directly at Domatin as she continued, "King Dylenn Allister was poisoned when he was offered peace, a peace offer that was supposed to be genuine."

With an annoyed grin Domatin waved his hands in the air. "That wasn't me, no matter how many times you imply it."

Leontina's glare of contempt didn't falter. "Your Praetorians were there. You could have given them orders to poison the wine."

Domatin lowered his hands. "Don't you think if I did it, I would be bragging about it all the time? Besides, if you hadn't lost the siege in the first place none of that would have happened."

Phyra and Tauriel stopped eating as the tension between Domatin and Leontina escalated, while Phyra appeared to be enjoying the situation. Leontina took a long deep breath before replying, "I wouldn't have lost if you had told me that the Vicar and his army were approaching. Instead, you just ran off with your tail between your legs."

Now even the human servants paused at the insult. Everyone in the room stared at Domatin. With a sudden clap of his hands, Domatin looked at one of the humans and demanded, "Pour me more wine."

With her hands trembling the young girl walked toward Domatin's outstretched hand and carefully poured the red wine into his goblet. Domatin raised his glass in her direction and with a smile said, "Thank you my dear."

As the girl hurried from the room, Leontina said, "I honestly thought you were going to take your anger out on that poor girl."

Domatin set his glass back down on the table and resumed his dinner, talking while he chewed, "Why do you hold me in such low regard, Imperator? I have never caused you harm in any way."

Leontina shifted uneasily in her chair. Domatin spoke again, "There are no wrong answers here. Everyone knows how you feel about me. I just want to know why."

Leontina pondered her words for several moments before firmly replying, "Because of you, your brother Tiberius was killed. You created Tantabus. You are the reason we lost the siege at Sternz. And, quite frankly, you are a monster."

Picking up the napkin in front of him, Domatin wiped his mouth and leaned back in his chair. "Tiberius sacrificed himself for me, and believe me when I say I miss him every day. As for Tantabus that problem will be rectified very soon."

"Rectified?" Phyra interrupted, "I thought you killed Tantabus a few years ago?"

Domatin gave Phyra's question no attention as he continued to address Leontina. "Exactly how was Sternz my fault and not yours? Let us recall who did what in those days. You failed to make sure our mages survived. You may have managed to open the gate but failed miserably in keeping it open. And despite you blaming me for the arrival of the Vicar, what was I supposed to do? Your troops were exhausted, and if you had deployed to face the Vicar, the humans inside the city would have figured out what was happening and regained hope. By me not telling you, the elven army had a chance to perhaps take the city and use the walls to defeat the Vicar's army. I, on the other hand, successfully extracted information from a human officer, which Legatus Tauriel failed to do, I might add. I am the one who came up with the idea on how to breach the human walls, while all of your plans failed."

Leontina squinted her eyes at Domatin and replied, "You will still always be remembered as a monster."

"A monster? Exactly how am I a monster? I guarantee that out of the two of us I have killed far fewer people, both directly and indirectly. Take The Unbroken for example—those humans and that orc are the real monsters, killing anyone and anything in their path. For a fact, I know that Liam has killed a few hundred and that's not including the ones he has killed since he returned to human lands. Yet they are viewed as heroes, as symbols of hope, even though they have and will kill more people than I. No, I think it is my methods that scare you and everyone else, because I'm different. I don't conform to the normal way of doing things. You can torture someone by beating them, threatening them for hours and not get anything. But you gave me ten minutes with that officer, and I had her telling me what we needed to know. You're scared because my methods are more effective than yours."

Domatin turned to Phyra and asked, "Phyra, wouldn't you say it is more civilized to scare someone into submission for a few minutes rather than beating them for hours?"

Phyra sat speechless in her seat, so Leontina answered, "You frighten people because they think you enjoy war, that you enjoy hurting people. Some even say that you hope this war will last as long as you live to fight in it."

"What is wrong with war? War is a necessity. And the people who say the world would be a better place without warfare are clearly too simple-minded to understand its purpose. War brings families, towns, countries, and races together for a greater purpose. War advances civilization faster. War shows people's true natures. War is the greatest test of all."

As an uneasy silence draped over the room, a Praetorian entered and approached Domatin. The Praetorian whispered something in Domatin's ear and then immediately withdrew. Phyra took a long drink of wine, "So, what was that about?"

Domatin returned to his meal, "None of your concern."

"Oh, no no no, not that again," Leontina snapped. "Last time this happened the Vicar and tens of thousands of paladins showed up a little later."

Domatin finished a bite of pork, then said, "Four robed figures killed the Wraiths that I left at the village last night."

"That's it?" Leontina interrupted.

Domatin smiled as he finished. "Four robed figures—and a large black wolf."

Tauriel set her glass on the table before turning to Leontina, "Surely that means Crixaria and Tarium plan on attacking us. We should try to quell the resistance as soon as possible."

Clearing his throat Domatin informed them, "I've already sent a small force to attack the resistance headquarters."

Phyra clapped her hands three times, and the human servants cleared the table. Leontina grabbed a map of Xanica from a side table and flattened it out on the dinner table. She pointed to the top area of Xanica and said, "We are here. Our army is here at Roughstone pass," moving her finger to the center of the Xanica and Eacru Waste border. "We should gather all the elven forces in Xanica, along with the humans that are loyal to us and move them to the pass. As long as we control the pass, we can halt the humans from advancing. Roughstone Keep and the mountains to our back will give us aid when and if a massive human army tries to take it."

Domatin pointed to a spot on the map with only trees for markings. Looking at the group, he smiled and said, "As long as we can draw the humans to this spot, I will be content with whatever plans we make."

"Why there?" asked Phyra. "Nothing of importance is there, only a small forest."

Domatin looked back down at the map and with a malicious grin answered, "If you want The Unbroken to break,—lead them here."

5

Kassandra glared at the barren trees and asked, "How much farther until we arrive at Harpsburg? I'm ready to get out of all this forest."

Konar sighed. "We all know your sister disappeared in a forest, but you've got the four of us to help make sure you don't get lost. You don't have to complain every five minutes that you don't enjoy being in forests."

"Quiet down you two," Vernon insisted. "I'd rather not have to ask Liam to shut you both up."

Kassandra raised an eyebrow. "You really think Liam could beat both of us?"

"You don't think I can?" Liam questioned.

Konar turned toward Liam and said, "Even for you that might be a stretch. But let's say for a moment you had to defeat any of us. Do you even have a plan?"

Without hesitation Liam answered, "Konar, I would take out your legs. Without your mobility you wouldn't be able to defend yourself. You'd be stuck in the mud. Kassandra, without your bow you may be able to fend off common soldiers, but anyone with training would give you trouble. I'd take away your bow, and then I could easily beat you. As for Vernon, all I would have to do is attack him fast enough and relentlessly enough for his confidence problems to take hold of his mind. With that hesitation I would finish that fight in a matter of seconds."

All of them, shocked and speechless, stared at Liam in astonishment and slight horror. Konar was the first to speak. "You've thought about this before, haven't you?"

Liam muttered, "I knew how to beat each of you when we rescued Kaia on the first day of the siege. It's nothing personal. It's just what I learned to do."

"Where in the world did you learn to do that?" asked Kassandra.

Liam took a deep breath before answering. "You remember those three scars on my back? When Domatin would make me fight in the arena, if I ever came close to losing or even had a little trouble with an opponent he would take a sword and carve down my back."

"Domatin really did a number on you, didn't he?" Vernon asked.

Before any more words could be said, Blaster lowered his body and began to growl, gazing off into the forest ahead of him.

Konar looked to Vernon and asked, "How far away is Harpsburg?"

Vernon pointed to a hill. "It should be just over that ridge."

They pressed forward at a more rapid, yet stealthy pace. When they crested the ridge, they heard the sounds of battle. From the top of the hill they could see the resistance in a large village surrounded by a meadow, fighting a much larger elven force. Vernon peered over to the village center and spotted a familiar face, "Look over there!" Vernon shouted. "That looks like Makay."

Konar surveyed the village and said, "We need to get down there and help as fast as we can."

"Agreed," replied Vernon. "Konar, you and I will ride up the street directly toward the center. Kassandra, you, Liam, and Blaster go toward the chapel on the right side of town. The elven forces seem to be concentrating there."

With a quick nod they all galloped toward the village. Vernon leaned over and grabbed his kite shield from the side of the horse while drawing his longsword from his side with his right hand. Galloping beside him, Konar reached behind his head and pulled out his mighty war hammer. Both were ready to fight their way to Makay.

Vernon and Konar plowed their way to the center. They noticed that the fighting was not just in the streets but in the wooden buildings of the village as well. They reached the center to see Makay along with dozens of other resistance soldiers covered in blood and mud fighting off the elven forces.

Makay turned to see Vernon and Konar approaching him. He yelled, "You beautiful bastards! I don't think I've ever been as happy to see a foreigner as I am right now."

"How bad is it?" Vernon demanded. "Where do you need us?"

Makay took a few moments to catch his breath before replying, "By the looks of it we almost have the situation under control, the elves underestimated our numbers. Did you see anything when you arrived?"

"To me it seemed as if the elves are trying to get to the chapel," Vernon replied.

"The chapel?" Makay asked, turning his gaze toward that structure.

Before Vernon could reply, Makay turned around and shouted, "Everyone fight to the chapel. We can't take the chance on one of those bastards getting a glimpse."

Vernon turned to Konar, "We can get there sooner than they can. Let's go."

Riding toward the chapel Liam, Kassandra, and Blaster hurried past the fighting. Approaching the chapel Liam pulled the reigns on his horse and dismounted while grabbing his two short swords from his saddle. A confused Kassandra shouted, "What are you doing?"

Liam ducked under the swing of an elf as Blaster clamped down on the elf's throat. Liam stood back up and yelled, "I can barely ride a horse, let alone fight on one."

Kassandra spurred her horse toward the chapel. She readied her bow and began to release arrows toward the elves fighting around the chapel. Not all of her arrows made contact with her targets as her horse fidgeted, startled by the clashing of steel. Kassandra slowed her horse to a halt as Liam and Blaster rushed past and began to fight around the chapel.

Blaster jumped on an elf, sinking his fangs into the neck. Liam swung down with his right sword across an elf's face while stabbing another on his left. Vernon and Konar soon arrived, and at the sight of the five of them together a cry of terror rose from among the elven forces. "It's—its them, from Sternz."As more elves fell their onslaught, a number of the elves started to flee toward the hill.

With the revelation that The Unbroken were in the battle, the elven forces quickly crumbled and fled from the fighting. Enthusiastic cheers rang across the village as the last of the elven forces exited the village.

A panting Makay arrived and hunched over to catch his breath. Then he pointed to the chapel and asked, "Did you see anyone leave the chapel?"

"I didn't see anyone," Kassandra replied.

Makay turned to some of his fellow resistance fighters. "Does anyone know where Malum is?"

A strong voice replied from within the chapel, "I'm in here Makay."

Everyone's attention turned to the doorway of the chapel as an aged man with narrow brown eyes and short black hair, armored in a slightly rusted Vicar's Chosen armor stepped outside. His mace and shield dripped blood as he said, "None of the elves who saw our plans made it out alive. I made certain of that."

"We've got a live one over here!" shouted a female resistance fighter. Malum looked toward the young woman, her dark, black hair covered in blood. She pushed the elven soldier on the ground.

Malum walked toward them and said, "Thank you Jenna,"before squatting down to the enemy soldier and asking, "Now tell me exactly how the elves knew that we were here? Was it the spies you have, or something else?"

As the soldier stared back, Malum became impatient and picked up a muddied dagger from the ground. With one hand firmly wrapped in the elven soldier's hair, he jerked his head back and stuck the edge of the knife into his right nostril. "Tell me how, right now," Malum commanded.

The soldier spat in Malum's face. Enraged, Malum pulled the tip of the dagger through the nostril, then stuck the blade under the soldier's nose and started sawing upward, cutting the soldier's nose completely off. The soldier cried out in pain as blood gushed down his face and into his mouth. Malum got right in his face and screamed, "How?"

"A human village was raided, and a letter was found."

"What did the letter say?" asked Malum.

The soldier shook his head side to side. "I do not know. The elves keep the important information to themselves."

Konar turned to Vernon and whispered, "He said that bit as if he wasn't an elf."

Malum heard this and replied, "That's because he isn't." Malum dropped the dagger and pulled the white hood back from the soldier's head, showing everyone that the soldier was human.

Looking around, Vernon noted that none of the resistance fighters, not even Makay, are surprised by this revelation. He took a step forward and cleared his throat. "My name is…"

"I know who you are," Malum interrupted. "Makay and the rest of resistance fighters who fought at Sternz have told us about you. And to be honest, I'm not impressed."

Kassandra's face soured, "Not impressed? We didn't save your ass just to impress you."

Malum glared at Kassandra and said, "It's easy to rise to the occasion when the city you are in is besieged, and you don't have a choice. How about when for 15 years your country has been subjugated, when harboring resistance fighters means your entire village will burn to the ground, and all your neighbors and family will be killed? Or when friends you've grown up with join the elves against you? None of the people here were forced to be here. They all joined because they wanted to."

Vernon raised his hands and tried to calm the situation. "We meant no offense in being here."

In silence, Malum turned and walked back into the chapel. Makay clapped his hands together and said, "Alright now everyone, the show is over. Go see where you can helpful, especially to the town folk, and be ready to leave soon, I doubt we will stay here much longer. And Jenna, you know what to do with the soldier."

Jenna kicked the ribs of the bloodied soldier and dragged him away.

As the resistance fighters moved through the streets, Makay turned his attention to Vernon. "I apologize about Malum's words. He isn't very fond of outsiders, even if they are trying to help."

"Why?" Liam asked.

Makay shrugged. "Look around you. The only person that isn't a native of Xanica is Malum. He feels that the rest of the human kingdoms abandoned Xanica, and since we've been on our own for 15 years, he thinks that we can do just fine without any help."

Konar peered into the chapel and asked, "How did he get the armor that the Vicar's Chosen wear?"

"He used to be one," Makay replied. "After word reached Tarium that Xanica had been overrun, he wanted Tarium to join the war immediately and come help, and when no aide was sent, he simply left. It took a year or two before he started to talk normal and another three after that until we heard him laugh, but he's only done that four times"

"And the Vicar just let him leave?" Vernon asked.

"Oh no," Makay replied. "He was hunted by his old comrades. Apparently, breaking an oath to the Vicar's Chosen results in your death. He even had to fight a few of them off himself on his journey. But thanks to him, the resistance has survived and grew. He taught us how to fight, ambush, and spy on the enemy. To be honest with you, if he hadn't shown up, the resistance would be a memory by now. In the first weeks of the invasion all was lost, our army defeated, and all of the Knights of Xanica slain."

"The Knights of Xanica," Kassandra said with a reminiscent smile,

"My father would tell my sister and me of their many exploits when we were children."

"I've never heard of them," grumbled Liam.

"Not surprising since you grew up a slave in Azara," Makay said. A look of wonder crossed his face. "The Knights of Xanica were the most revered fighting force in all of Aclia. Vicar's Chosen, Praetorians, Zealots—no one could beat them in a one-on-one fight. Their entire purpose was to Xanica and its people. Xanica would have fallen countless times throughout history if they had not been here to protect us. On top of being well trained in battle, they spent much time devoted to studies of the faith of The One, politics, philosophy, and history. There are even accounts of Knights being able to out-debate the nobles of Xanica. I could talk for days about them."

"If they were so great, how were they all killed?" Liam asked.

Makay's happy reverie faded. "No one really knows for sure. In the first and only major battle of the war, at Chinon, the entirety of the Knights of Xanica lead the countercharge against the elves. None came back. You ask someone loyal to the elves, they will say the elves butchered the Knights and that it wasn't even a fight. You ask any one of us, or anyone loyal to the Resistance, we know that the Knights had to have almost won singlehandedly against the invading army, otherwise they wouldn't be so quick to try and make everyone forget about the Knights."

A loud *crack* came from the chapel, and Malum screamed, "Damn it!"

Makay ran into the chapel. The Unbroken followed, but remained outside. From the doorway they could see the bodies of elves littering the pews. Malum and Makay stood over a broken table with sheets of paper scattered about. Makay pointed to the Unbroken and after several seconds of hesitation, Malum nodded his head once. "Alright you five, come on in here," Makay called. "Malum would like to ask you something."

As they entered the chapel the stench of death assaulted their nostrils. Flies had already started to swarm the bodies. Malum asked, "What do you know of the town of Bakea?"

Vernon, Kassandra, and Liam look confused, but Konar spoke up. "I passed through it when I traveled to Crixaria, but I arrived at night and left the next morning. I only spoke to two or three people."

"So, you know nothing." Malum stated bluntly, his voice laced with sarcasm. "Why did you even bother answering?"

Makay, sensing the tension rising again, butted in, "Bakea is one of the newest, but also one of the biggest, towns in Xanica. Built 10 years ago by order of the elven Governess, Phyra. She built it in the center of Xanica to try and bring the people, both human and elf, together."

"And it's working," Malum scowled. "Everyday more and more humans are joining the elves. Children too young to remember the takeover have been growing up in a country where the elves are the top class. They think that if they join the elves, they too could share in the wealth. Now the men and women who have been fighting their oppressors for years are having to fight their neighbors, friends, and sometimes families."

Vernon looked down at the sheet of paper detailing a town, the name at the top of the map was Bakea. He asked, "What can we do to help?"

Malum snatched the paper away from Vernon as Makay continued, "Before the attack here today we had planned to capture Phyra Ophidian as she attended the annual festival she created to celebrate the anniversary of the day that the elves seized control of Xanica. The festival, which lasts one week, starts in four days. We had hoped to take Phyra hostage as a way to bargain for Xanica's freedom. Being a member of the royal elven bloodline, she is quite valuable."

Malum pointed at the papers scattered around the room and fumed. "But now I'm missing several pieces of paper detailing the plan. There's no way to carry it out now. One of those elven bastards must have slipped past me, or even worse, it could be one of the many spies the elves have in the Resistance. The plan was to attack her convoy either when she entered or exited the village. But now, we don't know for certain if the elves know our plans. If we continue, we may be walking into an ambush."

"Why do you want to capture this Governess? Wouldn't the elves just replace her with another member of the Ophidian family?" Vernon asked.

"Phyra has *become* Xanica," replied Makay. "She continues to steal more and more humans away from their families as her popularity grows each day. No stories about her have ever been negative, and each day she remains in control of Xanica the more powerful the elves become. You can't replace someone like her if you are the elves. We know that Crixaria and Tarium plan on taking the war to the elves sometime in the future. For all our sakes it will be much easier for us if the majority of Xanica thinks Phyra somehow betrayed or abandoned them."

Makay took a long look at Malum before turning to Vernon and saying, "It doesn't seem like Malum is going to ask, so I will. Would it be possible for you to take your group and somehow capture her? I know it's a lot to ask, but if you could manage to do such a thing we would be in your debt."

Vernon looked each member of The Unbroken. Each one nodded. Vernon extended his hand to Malum and said, "We will find a way."

Malum seemed pleased as he shook Vernon's hand. He said, "Go now. If you ride with haste you can make it to Bakea in three days. Makay, tonight we will leave Harpsburg. The elves will come back to murder the villagers so we need to take them with us."

Vernon nodded once at Malum, then turned to lead the way out of the chapel. As they walked out of the doorway and to their horses, Konar asked Vernon, "Just how exactly do you plan on capturing this Governess?"

Vernon shook his head. "I have absolutely no idea."

6

Kaia sat on the bench under the statue of the Hero of Aclia watching Alyssa chase Bethany with a tiny mouse through the frigid evening garden. Captain Tori stood beside Kaia in full uniform.

"Those two sure do sound happy," Tori said.

Kaia looked at Tori's motionless eyes and replied, "Ever since Alyssa was bitten by the cobra, she and Bethany have gotten along much better. I think Father's death and the realization that Alyssa could die made Bethany rethink her attitude."

Bethany shrieked at the mouse as Alyssa managed to get the mouse mere inches from her face. Tori used her hands to guide herself to sit down beside Kaia. Then she slid her hand across the bench until she found Kaia's hand and laid her own hand on top of it. "Princess, I want to thank you for helping me these past few months."

Kaia rested her other hand on top of Tori's and replied, "Tori, if it wasn't for you I would be dead right now. You bought me time to make it back to the citadel, and I can never repay you for that."

With a soft smile Tori closed her eyes and lowered her head, "Of all the people to help me through this, I never thought you would be one of them."

"You saved my life, and not only that but you've become a good friend these past few months. I've even heard rumors that you are learning to fight again, is that true?"

Tori chuckled to herself. "Well, it is resulting in a lot of bruises, but Sir Gregory has been helping with that."

"How does he do that?" Kaia asked.

"It was hard at first. I usually ended up getting hit or knocked off my feet, but I soon noticed that with my sight gone my hearing has become better. And ever so slowly, I have been learning to listen to my sparring partner—the pivoting of his feet or which side of his body makes more noise."

Kaia's tone turned serious. "Let me ask you this; would you be my personal bodyguard?"

Tori pulled back her hand in surprise, her breathing quickening. "Why would you want *me* to protect you? I may have memorized the layout of many places in Sternz, but if you take me somewhere new I won't be useful to you at all."

Kaia looked at how uncertain Tori had become. She took Tori's hand again and with a gentle tone replied, "Because I trust you. When we go to war I will need someone I can trust beside me."

"You plan on going with the army?"

"Why wouldn't I? With my magic I can help."

Finally Tori smiled and said, "I guess that means you do need someone to look after you. I will do my best to try and keep you from burning yourself with fire."

They laughed as the gate to the garden opened, and Jaclyn stepped out into the garden. She paused for a moment to watch Alyssa chasing Bethany through the thuja trees. Walking down the pathway she looked at Kaia and said, "I thought you should know that your mother has called a meeting with Benjamin, Vicar Matthew, and General Izak. I believe she is announcing her decision about sending aid to Xanica early, and I thought you would like to know."

Kaia stood and thanked Jaclyn, then turned to Tori, "Would you like to come with me? I may accidentally set myself on fire," she joked.

Nodding her head, Tori stood and began to walk straight ahead, toward one of the trees. Kaia reached for her and wrapped her arm around Tori's arm, leading her away from the tree. Tori sighed. "I was about to run into something wasn't I?"

Kaia giggled. "You see? This will work out perfectly. You keep me safe, and in return I will make sure you don't run into anything."

Kaia steered them toward the citadel and then into the throne room where she observed Alezzia sitting in her throne with Benjamin standing behind her while General Izak and Vicar Matthew stood below on the stairs. Captain Harrison was also standing beside the Vicar. After they took a few steps into the throne room, Tori stopped and whispered to Kaia, "I may be an officer, but I do not think what is being discussed is meant for my ears. If it is alright with you I think it would be best if I stayed here by the door."

"I understand. I will be right back. I hope this doesn't take long." Kaia started walking closer to the group. She saw Izak cringe and heard him say, "That simply won't be enough."

Benjamin stared down at Izak and responded, "It will have to be, General. That's all we can afford."

"Just who do you think you are?" Izak snapped.

Kaia could see her mother and Benjamin scowl. Alezzia closed her eyes and took a deep breath before replying to Izak. "Benjamin is my head advisor. You know this."

Not backing down, Izak responded, "It doesn't make any sense your highness. He is a doctor, and you've known him for only two years. He has no military experience that we know of and most likely has no knowledge about how to run a kingdom."

With her glare unrelenting Alezzia stated, "General, that is enough."

Izak seemed not to hear Alezzia's command as he continued, "We don't know where he was born or where his loyalties lie."

"I said enough!" Alezzia screamed as she slammed her fist on the arm of her throne.

An uneasy silence consumed the room. Kaia watched closely as her mother regained her composure. "Now, Vicar Matthew, what is the situation of your army, and how many paladins can you send with our force tomorrow?"

The Vicar turned to Harrison before saying, "Due to an increase in raiders attacking some of Tarium's ports, I had to send the majority of the army back to help secure the coast. Out of the 10,000 remaining here, Captain Harrison has volunteered to lead 5,000 of them with your force tomorrow. As well as Zafrinia and her 2,000 volunteers."

Izak grunted at the news and even though he tried to hide his frustration everyone could see his anger. "So with that 7,000 plus our 8,000 we have around 15,000 to liberate an entire country."

Benjamin snapped back, "General if you do not wish to be in command of Crixaria's forces any longer, I am sure plenty of officers will gladly take the mantle."

Izak's hands balled into fists, and his teeth begin to grind as he replied, "We know for a fact that the elves have at least 20,000 troops in Xanica—as well as Imperator Leontina, since King Dylenn allowed them to leave. That's not counting the 15,000 they have as an occupational force that has been there for almost 16 years, or even the possibly of loyal humans that are joining the elven army, which we know not the number."

"But you will also have the resistance's help," Benjamin interjected.

Captain Harrison raised his hand to his chest and said, "No disrespect if I speak out of turn, but we also don't know their numbers. For all we know they could 500 or 5,000."

Vicar Matthew jumped to Harrison's defense, "I'm sorry about that your highness. The Captain here was just leaving."

With a smile Alezzia replied, "There is no need for that. Captain Harrison spoke with respect in his voice, and I do not mind when I am talked back to unless it is with a rude tone." Alezzia then turned back to Izak and said, "So even if you don't get very much help from the resistance it shouldn't matter about how many elves are there. Only three months ago we defended the inner wall with only 30,000 against an army over 200,000."

After several seconds of deep breaths Izak responded, "The elves have better weapons, better armor, and perhaps hundreds of years more experience than we do. If it wasn't for the Vicar's arrival the city would have fallen. Time and time again the elves have defeated us on the open battlefield. The only reason we were able to survive those few days was because we had Sternz's walls."

"Ah, but those battles were without my paladins," Vicar Matthew pointed out.

Alezzia sighed, closed her eyes and said, "Kaia my dear you have been standing behind everyone for a while. What is it that you want?"

As everyone's attention turned to Kaia, she replied, "I was just curious about when we were planning on leaving."

Alezzia leaned forward in her throne and asked, "We? What do you mean, *we*?"

Kaia could feel her heart racing as her mother's unflinching gaze focused on her. "I intend to leave with the army to Xanica," she said.

Alezzia let out a small laugh as she leaned back into the throne and waived Kaia's remark away. "You most certainly will not."

Kaia matched her mother's gaze and asked, "Why not?"

Alezzia stopped smiling and replied, "Because you could get hurt. Need I remind you about that scar on your face?"

Unflinching in her stance Kaia replied, ever louder in her response, "Yes I may have gotten a small scar, but my magic helped our forces during the siege while you stayed here, hiding from the enemy. You have never allowed me to go beyond the outer walls, and I am tired of being a prisoner because of who I am."

Alezzia rose to her feet, "And what happens when you get killed from your curiosity?"

Kaia took a step forward, "This war isn't about me anymore! Father's death turned this war from one of protecting just me to a war about justice for him and all who have grievance against the elves. It shouldn't matter if I die anymore, this new war will still go on. I can do more out there, in the field, than I can being trapped here. Like it or not I am leaving with General Izak for Xanica."

7

As the sunlight gave way to the night's darkness, an owl's sudden hoot caused Kassandra to jerk in the saddle. "It's just an owl," she said to herself. "Just a harmless, cute, little owl."

Humored, Konar said, "When you complain about it, it's annoying, but it still hasn't gotten old seeing you startled by every noise in the dark."

Peering into the forest left and right Kassandra asked, "Vernon, why couldn't we have stayed at Harpsburg tonight?"

Leading the way through the forest, Vernon held a map of Xanica in one hand as he planned their route and wasn't listening to their banter. Kassandra tried to whisper, but it came out as a yell, "Vernon!"

"Sorry, what was the question?" he asked.

Kassandra continued to search for movement as she stared into the forest, "Why didn't we stay the night at Harpsburg? We could have had warm food and comfy beds. And how do you expect to see an attack from the enemy with all your attention on that map?"

As he looked away from the map to gain an idea of their location, he replied, "The earlier we get there the better, more time to plan. And I would be quite impressed if the elves ambushed us with Blaster here to alert us, as well as you scanning the woods every two seconds."

Konar turned to look back at Liam. "Still alive back there?"

Before Liam had a chance to say anything, Kassandra interrupted. "Wait I've got this." Clearing her throat she spoke in an exaggerated deep voice, "I'm fine."

Liam ignored her and mumbled, "The sooner we get out of Xanica the better. I hate this country."

Kassandra smiled, surprised that Liam said more than two words. Then she remembered that this was where Liam was from. "Which village are you from?" Without pause she turned back to Vernon and asked, "Vernon can we go to Liam's home? Maybe that will cheer him up?"

"Or make him more upset," Konar mumbled.

Kassandra huffed at Konar before turning back to Liam. "So where is it?"

Liam ignored Kassandra and directed his attention Vernon. "Any ideas on how we will take Phyra?"

"Ugh," Kassandra muttered. "You were starting to open up while we were in Crixaria, but as soon as we got here, you're quieter than you were the first day we met you, and I'm getting tired of it."

Konar laughed, "Just as we are getting tired of all your complaining."

Foreseeing yet more bickering between Kassandra and Konar, Vernon slowed his horse to a halt and said, "Alright you two, settle down. It's getting too dark to travel. Let's make camp for the night before any elves can hear your arguing."

They wasted no time setting up camp while there was still light. Each grabbed several blankets from their horses, and Vernon started a small fire. After they had tied their horses and prepared their bedrolls, they gathered around the warm flames.

Kassandra broke the comfortable silence. "Who is cooking supper? I'm hungry."

"I think all we have left is jerky," Konar replied as he passed around the dried meat. They ate in silence, then began to settle in for the night.

Vernon gazed at the stars, frowning as he pondered the coming days. Konar noticed the pensive look on Vernon's face and asked, "What's got you so down?"

Vernon sighed, "I honestly don't know how we are going to capture Phyra. She will almost certainly be surrounded by hundreds of guards. And I bet even most of the people in Bakea would stand against us."

Liam joined the conversation. "What about outside of the Bakea, either before or after the festival?"

"I've thought about that, but when she is out of the village is when the elves would most likely suspect an attack. The resistance has been trying to get to her for years, and they haven't succeeded. I doubt the five of us could do it if Malum and hundreds of fighters couldn't."

"Malum was an asshole," Kassandra proclaimed. "Someone needs to teach him some manners."

Konar chuckled. "He was, but he seemed to have a lot of experience. I doubt you would want to fight him."

Turning on her side to face Konar, she declared, "I've faced tougher."

"Like who?" asked Vernon.

"Sophia Lati, or as we in Vetin call her, Vetin's Maiden. A noble's daughter from Vetin, she has to be the best horse rider I've ever seen. She wields a spear in one hand and a mace in the other while reining the horse with her teeth. I've never seen anyone ride like her. One day when we were sparring, she decided to dismount and fight me on foot. She had me on the ground in less than 30 seconds. Not to mention the fact that she is five years younger than me."

Then Vernon asked Konar, "What about you? Who was the toughest person you've ever had to fight?"

Konar's expression turned sad. "I never knew his name. He was the leader of the band of blood mongers who killed my family. When I found them I became so enraged that I barely remember the fight. All I remember is that it was the longest fight I ever had. We both lost our weapons and fought with our fists until I broke his neck."

Kassandra looked over to Liam. His eyes were closed and Blaster was snoring beside him. "Still awake Liam? I think it's your turn."

Liam opened his eyes and looked at Kassandra, then just closed his eyes again. Kassandra smiled as she said, "I'm not going to let you go to sleep until you tell us."

With his eyes still closed Liam mumbled, "It's too long of a story."

Konar stretched his arms above his head and said, "We've got plenty of time, I don't think any of us are really that sleepy yet."

"Please," Kassandra begged. "You must have had several tough fights when you were a gladiator."

Liam kept his eyes closed but began to talk. "Almost 16 years ago I was taken by Domatin, but I was not the only one. In total there were seven of us from different villages. We were taken back to Domatin's private estate to be trained as gladiators for the amusement of the elves. Seven years after our capture, seven years of bonding with each of them, fighting beside each other, a special event was planned for Empress Juliana's birthday. After an entire day of fighting, what we thought was the last match was about to begin. Usually the crowd picked the top two fighters of the tournament to duel each other, but this time was different. All seven of us were taken to the arena and Domatin announced that it was to be a free-for-all between us, and that the winner would be given a chance for freedom.

"The people that I had considered my brothers and sisters soon turned on each other, on me. The elves laughed and clapped, and children tried to mimic our actions until only two of us were left—myself and an older girl named Maggie.

"Maggie was the kindest person I ever knew. She always wore a yellow ribbon in her hair. Of all the kids taken I was the youngest, but Maggie always made sure I had enough food in my belly, or if the other kids picked on me, she would always stop them. Sometimes I wonder if she let me beat her, because I know she was the best out of us all. As she bled out in my arms, the crowd roared in applause, but it was not over. Domatin proclaimed that now the true final event was about to begin. The gates to the arena opened and through them out walked Salzor, an elf who was imprisoned for stealing, and had been the reigning champion for over 200 years.

"This wasn't supposed to be a real match but instead a symbolic showing of the mighty elven race over the bickering human kingdoms. A 400-year-old elf versus a 12-year-old child, no one even considered that I could win—but I did. Fueled by my rage I let go of my shield and grabbed Maggie's sword. I remember the look on Salzor's face as I caught him off-guard, moving faster than he could have predicted and after several long minutes I managed to slit his throat. And ever since that day, I have fought with two swords.

"But I wasn't granted my freedom as promised. I was forced back into chains for another six years before I escaped. Six more years of fighting."

As Kassandra, Vernon, and Konar sat in silence and shock, Liam rolled over on his side, facing away from the fire. He was finished talking.

With only the sound of the fire around them, the quiet soon became too much for Kassandra. "Well that was informative. Vernon, I believe it is your turn."

Vernon raised up on his elbows and began, "To be totally honest it has always been my father."

"Your father?" Kassandra asked.

Vernon smiled as he continued. "Any time we sparred with each other he always beat me. No matter how old I get, he will probably always beat me."

Konar chuckled. "Of course he will. He is your father and has witnessed you grow from a baby. Until he gets too old to move, he will probably still beat you."

A sudden loud crackling of branches from the woods caused Kassandra to startle. Konar and Vernon laughed at her, but she gritted her teeth and whispered, "It's not that funny!"

"Yes, it is," replied Konar. "I could throw a rock at a tree in broad daylight, and you'd still get startled."

"I thought you said you had moved past your sister's disappearance?" Vernon asked.

"Yes, I've moved on. What bothers me is that we never knew what happened to her. Her body was never found, and it just makes me wonder what happened, that something could have jumped out of nowhere and taken her."

"Well, now you have us," replied Konar with a smile. "Between of all us it would take quite the assailant to snatch you from the woods."

Kassandra tilted her head and smiled, "Aw, you'd be my gallant knights in shining armor?"

As Vernon was about to say something, Blaster interrupted with a low whine. Each of them, knowing why, looked over to Liam, who was sweating profusely, and tossing and turning in his fur blankets.

Vernon sighed, "He has had nightmares every night since we arrived in Xanica."

Kassandra's looked at Blaster as he rested his head close to Liam's feet. "I wish there was something we could do."

With a smirk on his face Konar suggested, "Why don't you go cuddle with him?"

Looking at Konar, Kassandra replied with a serious tone, "I don't cuddle."

Vernon yawned and said, "Alright you two I think it's time we get some rest. We've got a long ride ahead of us tomorrow."

8

Hints of light flickered across the hallway as Phyra and Tauriel strolled side by side through the manor. A whiff of something caught Tauriel's nose and she asked, "Madam, is that cinnamon?"

"Why yes, it is," Phyra replied. "Cinnamon is Domatin's favorite scent, and I thought that he might like to be reminded of home. Especially since his cobra froze to death."

Tauriel stopped at one of the wooden tables against the wall and inhaled the stalks of burning cinnamon before asking, "If it's not too much to ask, how well do you know Prince Domatin?"

"Quite well," answered Phyra as she leaned in close to Tauriel. "He may be 50 years older than me, but we still get along like chocolate and strawberries."

Tauriel turned to face Phyra but, as soon as she realized how close Phyra was standing to her, she jumped back a little. "Sorry Madam Ophidian, I didn't realize you were so close."

Phyra smiled and replied, "It is quite alright dear. I'm just looking you over."

"Looking me over?" asked a surprised Tauriel.

Phyra stepped to within an inch of Tauriel's face. "I'm just curious to see if you would be a good match for Domatin."

Butterflies were building up in Tauriel's stomach as she felt Phyra's soft touch halfway up her inner thigh. Phyra leaned in

43

and seductively whispered, "Or a good match for me," and then she placed a brief kiss on Tauriel's lips.

Phyra giggled at the shock on Tauriel's face. As Tauriel struggled for words, Phyra said, "Just because I'm an Ophidian don't feel pressured at all. I won't be distraught if you say no. But if you feel the same, or are just curious, my bed is always open to you. And if there is someone else in it that night, we can make some room for you."

Tauriel, still standing in surprise, grew more uncomfortable by the second due to the silence and Phyra's unyielding smile. As she finally started to reply, Phyra grabbed her hand and said, "Come along now, you're embarrassing both of us with your silence. Let's go find Domatin and Leontina and see how the plans are going."

With Phyra leading the way they continued along their original path through the hallway. As they turned the final corner, a shadowy figure caught them off-guard as it approached.

"Oh my," Phyra exclaimed. "I've never seen a Wraith of Colubra with hair before, or one as enticing."

The wraith walked toward them with slow menacing steps. Almost everything about her was the same as other wraiths except she had short strands of dark raven hair draping over her face, and instead of one cobra hilted dagger she had two, one on each thigh, and a small, black, leather cape covering her right shoulder.

Phyra and Tauriel stood still, but Phyra whispered, "Would you look at her build. Those thighs, her chest." As the wraith walked between them, Phyra turned to Tauriel with a smile on her face and said, "If I could get you two in bed with me at the same time, I could die with no regrets. Do you know who she is?"

Tauriel watched as the wraith turned away. "Yes, that was Isila Fendrel. She is the leader of the Wraiths of Colubra, but if she is here, that must mean the conflict is about to escalate. If I had to guess, Prince Domatin and Imperator Leontina will use her skills in ways we can't even begin to think about."

With an eager smile on her face Phyra replied, "As long as both of you are around, I will be quite the happy girl."

Suddenly they heard Domatin's voice call out from the doorway behind them, "Phyra, Tauriel come join us!"

They both turned around to see Domatin waving them toward him. They walked into the dining room to see a stressed Leontina rubbing her face as she stood above a small map on the dinner table. As Domatin closed the door to the room, Tauriel walked to Leontina and asked, "What is the leader of the wraiths doing in Xanica?"

Domatin clapped his hands when he overheard Tauriel and replied, "Isila is going to be half of the head of Phyra's security force."

Phyra's smile widened at the news, before a confused Tauriel asked, "Half?"

Domatin turned his attention to Tauriel. "Yes half. Isila will take care of any threats from the shadows, and you will be in charge of her personal bodyguards while she attends the festival in Bakea."

"Me?" Tauriel questioned. "Why me? Why not Legatus Conra or Legatus Dezipie?"

"Because the imperator seems to believe you are her best officer."

A squeal of glee escaped from Phyra and she clapped her hands in excitement. "I can't wait. This is going to be so much fun!"

Tauriel turned back to Leontina and asked, "Why do you seem so stressed?"

For the first time since they entered the room, Leontina looked up, "Fighting the resistance will be tiresome work. They are part of the country, part of its people. We can't simply fight them in an open battle when we don't know who is or isn't a part of it. And if that wasn't bad enough, The Unbroken are somewhere in this damn country, so that probably means Crixaria and Tarium will attack soon."

Domatin replied, "I told you not to worry about them. I made it clear that when The Unbroken show themselves again, I will deal with them. You focus on the resistance."

9

With the morning sun warming their faces, Kaia and Captain Tori walked down the hill away from the comfort of the citadel toward lower Sternz. They walked side by side and many citizens greeted them with, "Good morning, Princess Kaia," or a whispered, "Look how beautiful she is!"

Easily recognizable with her long, fiery red hair and dark purple dress, Kaia smiled and greeted the citizens of Sternz. Tori's hand rested on Kaia's arm as she whispered, "It sounds like you are everyone's favorite."

Kaia waved at a mother and child, "To be honest, I think the people favor me over Bethany. She isn't known for being polite. But Alyssa is without doubt the people's favorite. She always runs up to people and gives them hugs, and I've never seen her be rude to people—just like mother used to be."

Hearing the sadness in Kaia's voice at the last phrase, Tori tried to comfort her. "I never met Queen Alezzia before she contracted Cormorden, but I'm sure even if she acts differently now she still wants what is best for you and you sisters."

As they approached the bridge Kaia replied, "I know, but it's hard to see her like this. She used to be so gentle and welcoming, almost like a grown-up Alyssa, but now she is a different person. I don't think she's cried once since father died."

"Perhaps she is being strong," answered Tori, "strong for you and your sisters. Especially now since you are leaving all of them."

Kaia paused and turned to look back at the citadel. She gazed upon the towers she used to run through as a child and said, "I can do more good out with the army than I can hiding here."

Tori nudged Kaia and joked, "Or is it because you want to be reunited with your one true love."

Kaia's soft, white cheeks turned to bright red. "I have no idea what you are talking about. I don't love Vernon."

Tori leaned in closer and whispered, "Maybe not yet anyway."

After only walking a short distance into lower Sternz, Kaia was amazed at what she saw. Tori felt the change in Kaia's mood. "You got awfully quiet. What is it that you see?"

"It's just breathtaking how quickly lower Sternz is being rebuilt. I was here only a week ago, but so much work has been done since. All the buildings now have roofs, and even some windows have glass in them."

As they continued to walk through lower Sternz, Kaia described in great detail all that was around them, commenting on the fresh wood being used and the happy smiles on people's faces.

Almost at the gate, the sound of stones being placed on top of each other echoed around them. Kaia noted that the section of the wall that fell there was already a fourth of the way toward being rebuilt.

"Who are we meeting at the gate?" asked Tori.

Kaia turned her attention to the open gate. "General Izak. He asked me to meet him here this morning. But he isn't alone. I can see him with Captain Harrison, Zafrinia, and even Sir Gregory, all gathered on horses, with what looks like two for us. It looks as if they are waiting for us."

General Izak spotted Kaia and Tori approaching and greeted them. "It's good to see you two."

Zafrinia muttered, "A little late, aren't we?"

Completely ignoring Zafrinia, Kaia led Tori to her horse and helped her into the saddle. As Kaia grabbed a rope and tied one end to her saddle and the other end to Tori's, Zafrinia strained to contain her laughter but failed. "Oh, this is precious. In all my days this is the cutest sight I have ever seen. The bodyguard being cared for by their protectee."

"Zafrinia," Harrison scolded.

However, as Kaia pulled herself up onto her horse, Zafrinia continued, "This is why I love you Crixarians so much, you're just so pitiful. No wonder we Tarians had to save you."

"That is enough Zafrinia!" Harrison's tone was sharper this time.

"Alright everyone," Izak said. "Now that we are all here, it is time we leave. The army is gathered by the outer eastern wall and I'm sure they are anxious to leave."

Izak turned his horse and led the way out of the city with Gregory by his side, Kaia and Tori directly behind him, followed by Harrison and Zafrinia. The sounds of the city faded behind them until all they could hear was the crackling of the frosted grass beneath their horses' hooves.

The peaceful quiet faded when Zafrinia said, "So tell me this. What would happen to a blind rider if the rope attaching her horse to her guide were to become untied or cut?"

Before anyone else could respond, Gregory yelled out, "I would have to guess the same thing that will happen to you if you don't shut up."

Izak stopped his horse, turned, and shouted at the top of his lungs, "Enough! All of you! I don't care if you can see or are blind, rich or poor, young or old—we have a job to do. We are the leaders of this force, and it is our responsibility to free those who have been subjugated by the elves for too long. If we cannot get along with each other, how do you expect the men and women under our command to get along? Xanica is on fire. The elves are burning human villages and slaughtering their people. More and more innocent people who just want to have a peaceful loving day with their families are being dragged into a war they had no choice but to become a part of. Now if you don't want to come, fine. Stay here and follow when the main army sets out in a few months. But I am going to Xanica and do my best to help liberate them."

Without waiting for a response, Izak spurred his horse onward again toward the outer wall, and everyone followed in silence. They approached the top of a hill that seemed familiar to Kaia. She looked around trying to remember what seemed so familiar to her before finally spotting it—several large rocks protruding out of the ground. They were the same rocks that months earlier she had taken cover behind from the elves with Vernon, Konar, and Kassandra as they made their way back to the inner wall during the siege. Her heart filled with sadness as she scanned the now empty fields around them that were once filled with the dead and dying. Kaia watched as Tori listened to the chirping of birds overhead. She reached over and touched Tori's hand. "I can't say it enough but thank you for saving me."

Tori smiled and said, "Don't thank me just yet. Who knows how long I can keep you safe?"

Clearing his throat, Harrison asked, "General Izak. Do you have any thoughts toward the liberation?"

From the front of the line Izak replied, "My thoughts on the matter are pretty simple. A human army numbering around 15,000 marching into Xanica will not go unnoticed by anyone. Hopefully the resistance will hear of our arrival first and send someone to guide us. If not we may have to fight a force larger than 35,000 strong."

"We faced worse odds during the siege. Why are you so worried now?" Zafrinia's question dripped with arrogance.

"We had a 100-foot wall helping us then," Gregory answered.

Before the bickering could resume the group reached the top of the final hill and saw the gathered army below. The armor of the paladins glimmered in the morning light, while the Crixarian soldiers sat by their fires wrapped in their heavy brown coats. Neither the purple and gold bear banners of Crixaria nor the white and gold eagle banners of Tarium blew unfurled in the wind but dripped with icicles instead.

They heard horses galloping up behind them, and to everyone's surprise when they turned around, they saw four Vicar's Chosen, wearing their heavy, plate armor and faceless hoods, surrounding Alezzia who was mounted on a white steed, with Bethany on a smaller horse at her side. Alyssa sat in Bethany's lap. As they approached Alyssa lifted her arms in the air and shouted, "Kaia! Kaia! Mama said that we are all going to come with you."

Kaia's brows drew down. "Mother, this doesn't make any sense. Not even you should be coming with us. I can at least protect myself if need be. What happens if the elves get to Bethany or Alyssa?"

Alezzia waved her concerns away as if they were annoying gnats. "I thought that it was time for all of us to go on a trip together. And perhaps if the good people of Xanica see the royal family of Crixaria leading the fight to save them, then more people will be willing to join the fight."

"No, no, no, no!" Izak protested. "This fight will be hard enough as it is. Now I have to worry about keeping all of you safe from harm? And what about the diplomats from Vetin? Don't you think they will be offended that the Queen who invited them just up and left?"

The fake smile faded from Alezzia's face. "Vicar Matthew and Benjamin will stay and attend to that business."

Izak gripped the dark leather reins until his knuckles turned white. "I don't trust Benjamin," Izak said through his teeth, "Something is wrong with him. I have always said that."

"Your trust in Benjamin has no effect on my decisions. All you need to worry about is the liberation of Xanica. The Vicar and Benjamin are more than capable of handling the diplomats from Vetin as well as the dwarves."

"The dwarves?" Kaia asked. "I didn't think we had sent them any messages."

"A week after your father died, I sent them an invitation to come here and discuss the possibilities of a joint assault against the elves," Alezzia answered Kaia, then turned back to Izak. "And before you ask, yes, Benjamin was the only other person to know about this. In fact, it was his idea. The dwarves should arrive within the week. Now if it's not too much trouble, I would like to begin our journey. I am quite eager to finally end this war and return order to this world."

10

"Vernon and Liam have been gone too long," Kassandra complained. "Shouldn't we go look for them?"

Konar finished tying the horses to a tree, "It's only been an hour. They'll be back soon. In the meantime, why don't you stop looking for shadows in the woods and find something useful to do?

"What if they have been captured?"

"I seriously doubt that." But Konar could tell that Kassandra was getting really worried, so he walked over and put his hand on her shoulder. "And even if they were spotted, I have a theory as to what might happen."

"What?"

"Picture this. They get spotted and the garrison of the village chases them. Maybe 50 or 100 soldiers would follow them into the woods. One of two things would happen. Either all three of them would stand their ground and fight, or Liam and Blaster would try to hold them off and give Vernon enough time to come and get us."

A familiar voice called out from behind them, "Luckily, neither of those things happened."

Vernon, Liam, and Blaster walked out of the woods. Blaster ran toward Kassandra, and she bent down and hugged him. "Did you miss me that much?"

"How did it look?" Konar asked Vernon.

Vernon and Liam set their weapons down as Vernon responded,

"It'll be tough, but I think I have an idea on how we are going to pull this off." Vernon pulled out a small, hand-drawn map of the village and explained, "After being spotted at the burnt village a few days ago as well as Harpsburg, we have to assume that the elves know we are here, and they will be looking for a group of people matching our description. So only three of us will be going in."

"Just three?" Kassandra asked as she looked at the map. "That's quite a large city. Maybe we could all go in and then split up or something."

Shaking his head, Vernon replied, "Theoretically that could work, but as soon as they see a large, black wolf following one of us, our cover would be blown. And not to sound rude, Konar, but I doubt there will be many, if any, orcs at the festival."

Konar smiled. "No offense taken my friend. That is a good point. I'm sure Blaster and I will get along well." Konar turned to Blaster, "As long as he doesn't try to hide anything." Blaster barked once and wagged his tail.

Liam petted Blaster and then looked back to Vernon. "What about us three? You saw that they are taking weapons from every-one as they entered the gate."

"I will go in first. Since I no longer have the armor resembling a soldier in the Crixarian army I will pose as a mercenary looking for work. Kassandra, you and Liam are going to pose as a couple to be married within the month and…"

Before Vernon could finish, Konar started laughing so hard he fell backwards and rolled on the ground.

"And what exactly is so funny about that?" Kassandra didn't see the humor in the situation.

Wiping the tears from his eyes but still chuckling, Konar said, "You and Liam a happy couple? I'll be surprised if you don't sleep with at least three men in the village, and Liam? Well Liam hasn't looked happy since we got to Xanica."

Liam looked at Vernon, "I agree with Konar. I doubt I could pull that off. Why don't you and I switch?"

"If you went into that village alone you would get into a fight within an hour."

Kassandra turned to Liam and said, "Vernon does have a point. He could probably stay neutral the best out of all of us and with you as a reminder to me and I to you, we should be able to make it work. Besides all I have to do to make you smile is sing your favorite song."

Liam gave Kassandra a firm look. "Don't you do it," Liam said.

"My darling, My dear."

"Kassandra don't!" Liam snapped.

"See. I can cheer him up," she said with a grin.

Vernon shook his head and continued, "So I will go in and find a tavern where I can stay while I get to know the rough side of town. Unfortunately for you two, you will need to leave your weapons and armor here, so you won't arouse suspicion. Find a more reputable inn and stay there. Make friends with the more welcoming folks."

Konar stood to stretch his arms as he asked, "So Blaster and I will just be sitting out here in the woods for a week?"

Pointing at the map, Vernon replied, "On our way to scout the village, Liam and I saw what looked like a statue of the Hero of Aclia. It's about a mile away from Bakea and will be a good place for you and I to meet when we need to discuss things. While the three of us are inside Bakea, we will gather information on the garrison and escape points. I need you to watch the town and take note of guard shifts and patrols outside."

Looking at the supplies on the horses, Konar said, "As long as you occasionally bring me some wine I'll be fine."

"I can do that." Vernon turned back to Kassandra and Liam, "While we are in Bakea it would be best that we didn't speak to each other unless it is absolutely necessary. I will be going by a different name, and I suggest you do the same. I will head into Bakea and get started this evening. It is up to you two when you go in. It could either be later today or even tomorrow morning when the festival starts."

"Does it matter to you when we go?" she asked Liam.

"No."

"We'll go tonight."

Konar studied the map. "Let me get this straight. You three are going into a town that you have never been into before, to capture the Governess who will probably be guarded by hundreds of soldiers."

"Sounds about right," Vernon replied.

Konar looked over at Blaster and said, "I think we got the better end of this deal."

Taking one final look at his friends, Vernon rolled up the map and handed it to Konar. "Alright everyone. Stay safe, stay hidden, and before we know it Phyra will be captured, and we will be back with the resistance."

Without another word Vernon started walking toward Bakea. It didn't take long for him to come to the large dirt road that led into the town. The dirt path was empty now, but Vernon noticed the many tracks of wagons and horses leading into the town. He finally approached the entrance to Bakea. A 10-foot tall wooden palisade served as the town's wall. Vernon took note of the many guards, armed with bows, who were patrolling the top and surveying the woods.

When he approached the gate, one of the two guards outside the palisade raised his arm and shouted, "You there! Stop and tell us what business you have in Bakea."

Vernon stayed calm and replied, "I am a mercenary looking for work. I figured since the festival is to start soon, Bakea would be a good place to find someone in need of my services."

The guard motioned with his hand for Vernon to approach them. As Vernon closed in, the guard pulled out a piece of paper along with a feather dipped in ink and said, "Name and where you are from, please."

Looking at the guards patrolling the palisade Vernon replied, "My name is Jake. I grew up in Tarium."

The guard wrote down the information and then looked Vernon over from head to toe. "Tarium, huh? Makes sense considering your armor I guess, a little too nice for you to be from anywhere else. Alright, you are free to go in and out of Bakea, but you must relinquish your weapons here at the gate."

Vernon unstrapped the leather sheath around his waist without argument. "Seems like a lot of guards for the festival?"

After putting the scroll away, the guard took Vernon's sword and shield and replied, "Not particularly. If you are looking to find work right away you may want to start at Harper's Hall. Just keep walking straight once you enter town, and it'll be on your right. It's a loud place full of all sorts of people. Enjoy the festival."

Nodding, Vernon walked through the entry way, taking note that the two large, wooden doors were able to be opened and closed by pushing from the inside of the palisade. Now focused on the town ahead, Vernon observed everything around him. Large buildings with foundations of stone led up to dark brown wood for the second or third stories. The town of Bakea was alive with everyone getting ready for tomorrow's festival. Happy faces from both humans and elves of all ages surprised Vernon as he walked through the large town. Children from both races were chasing each other around the dirt streets, while older citizens were decorating. Blue and white streamers hung above the streets, while elven banners—rectangular with a white background and a dark blue cobra head in the center—hung from many windows and merchant stands throughout the streets. Vernon saw a group of elves dressed in casual, warm furs getting their instruments ready to play melodies during the festival.

He soon saw a shingle with a freshly painted mug of ale hanging over a door inviting everyone to Harpers Hall. Vernon figured he was at the right place. From outside he could hear glass mugs breaking, and shouting, and slurred singing. He took a deep breath and opened the door.

Once inside, Vernon noticed how the drinking area was

segregated. The elves sat on the right side looking disdainfully at the humans sitting on the left side. However, in the middle of Harper's Hall, the largest section, humans and elves were sitting and drinking with each other.

"How can I help you young sir?" Vernon turned to see a greasy older man around his height, but overweight, cleaning a mug.

Vernon cleared his throat. "Do you have any rooms available for the week?"

"Of course I do! I always have rooms available. Would you like to stay in the area reserved for humans or the mixed area?"

Looking around the dimly lit hall, Vernon pondered for a moment as he caught some welcoming and some scornful looks from elves. "It doesn't matter to me," Vernon replied. "Which ever works best for you."

The greasy man smiled showing his rotten teeth and replied, "Welcome to my establishment, young man. You may call me Mr. Harper if you need anything." Harper reached below the table and grabbed a small, metal key. Looking back at Vernon he said, "I will need your name and 25 elven rupees—five for each night of the festival. But if you plan on staying past that, the rate will go back down to three per night."

Vernon began to sweat, "I apologize good sir. I am a mercenary, and my last job was in Crixaria. Crixarian florins are all I have right now."

Vernon's anxiousness grew by the second as Mr. Harper considered his words. Vernon's hands became clammy, and he started craving some Eacru root.

Then Mr. Harper smiled, "Well young sir, the elven rupee is worth more around these parts, so if you are paying with Crixarian florins that will be 50 for the entirety of the festival."

Knowing he had no choice in the matter, Vernon reached into his pocket and counted out 50 florins to pay for the accommodations. "My name is Jake. If you hear of anyone who needs a mercenary, please send them my way."

Mr. Harper slid the key to Vernon and said, "It's good to have you here Jake. You will be in the mixed area directly at the back, last door on your left. If you have any problems just let me or one of my seven daughters know, and we will take care of you." Mr. Harper leaned in close to Vernon and whispered, "Just between you and me, I have heard rumors that the elves are always looking for humans to hire as mercenaries. You may want to start there for work—but be warned. It's said that they have been hiring orc warriors as well, and they aren't too fond of competition."

11

On a wide dirt path in the heart of Xanica, a large elven patrol rode south toward Bakea. The sun shining down on them did little to warm them up as they guarded their Governess. Phyra Ophidian, still dressed in her robes but now with a heavy fur cloak, rode her creamy white horse with Tauriel to her left and Isila, the leader of the wraiths of Colubra, to her right. Fifty elven soldiers and 10 elven praetorians led the way, and 10 more elven praetorians and 50 elven soldiers brought up the rear.

With a cheerful smile Phyra looked back and forth between Tauriel and Isila. As Isila surveyed the thick forest around them, Tauriel made eye contact with Phyra and asked, "Madam Ophidian, is there any certain reason you seem extra happy today?"

"I am traveling to my favorite town for a week-long festival full of drinking and celebrating while being personally guarded by two irresistible women."

Tauriel awkwardly smiled at Phyra and said, "Well, I'm glad you are excited that we are going."

"Are you not?" asked a surprised Phyra.

Tauriel turned to look at the troops behind her, making sure they are all still there, before responding, "I'm just nervous is all."

"Nervous? How could you possibly be nervous?" asked Phyra, "We are perfectly safe, both here as well as in Bakea. You are free to enjoy yourself no matter what that entails," she said with a wink.

Still nervous, Tauriel peered over at Isila. "Then why is the leader of the wraiths here? Her presence doesn't comfort me. Not that she unnerves me, but if Prince Domatin asked her to be here then he must suspect that something bad might happen."

Phyra turned to look at Isila, who was keeping her eyes on the forest, and whispered, "As long as I can get one of you in bed with me, I don't care what happens." Biting her lip at Tauriel, Phyra winked again, trying to gain a sexual response from her.

Tauriel looked away, but that didn't stop Phyra. "Alright I have to know. Is it that I'm not pretty enough for you, or do you have someone else back home?"

Tauriel was at a loss for words but before she could reply, and to everyone's surprise, Isila replied in a dark tone, "Legatus Tauriel was assaulted by eight humans while she was held prisoner inside Sternz."

Tauriel and Phyra sat stunned in shock. Neither of them had ever heard a wraith speak. "Isila I had no idea you could even talk. I thought all wraiths had their mouths closed by scarring," Phyra commented.

Isila reached up to her face and pulled the black cloth mask covering away to reveal her mouth, that had once been scarred closed, was now open. They gawked at the mouth for a few seconds before Isila pulled the covering back up and said, "The leader of the wraiths must be able to communicate."

Still surprised, Tauriel finally muttered out the question, "How did you know about what happened in Sternz?"

Isila resumed her survey of the forest. "It's my job to know everything. Just like I know you were saved because a human, known as Liam, fought off your attackers and carried you back to the rest of the prisoners."

"Is that true Tauriel?" Phyra asked.

Tauriel nodded. "Yes, it's true."

"Do you know why he would save you?" Phyra questioned.

"No, I don't. I think the other humans thought he might enjoy what they were doing, but as soon as he saw me he, he was enraged and put at least five of them in the infirmary. I sometimes find myself wondering why he would help me."

"Isila, what do you know about this human named Liam?" Phyra asked.

"Very little, and that worries me."

"You? Worried?" Phyra asked. "I didn't think the leader of the wraiths could *get* worried."

Isila made sure no one but the three of them could hear her as she quietly explained, "Liam is a part of a group of what the humans call The Unbroken. My spies have gathered information on all the members except him. Their leader, Vernon Regnier, is a Crixarian noble from Redoak who is currently courting the human Princess, Kaia Allister. Kassandra Verbeck, a Vetin noble, is known for her upbeat personality as well as her appetite for men, and for doing whatever she wishes. Konar Qal, an alcoholic orc, traveled to Crixaria after losing his family during a raid on his village. All the information we have on Liam is that he arrived in Crixaria almost three years ago with a black wolf and started wreaking havoc against our forces. Some of my sources even say that he is the best fighter they have ever seen, but I plan to test that personally."

Tauriel had seen first-hand Liam's warrior skills and said to Isila, "You must be well trained in combat to be in the position you are, but I have seen how devastating Liam can be. I've never seen anything like it."

Intrigued, Phyra appraised Isila's slim and fit figure. "I'm sure Isila can take good care of herself. I suspect she is among the best of the elven warriors."

Peering back out into the woods, Isila's voice turned cold. "That title belongs to Prince Domatin."

"Prince Domatin?" Tauriel sounded surprised. "He refused to fight during the Siege of Sternz. If he is that good of a warrior, why didn't he fight?"

"If the prince chose not to fight, he had his reasons." Isila turned her attention back to the woods.

As Tauriel grew more confused by this revelation, an upbeat Phyra asked, "Did you know Domatin before the war with the humans, Tauriel?"

"No. The first time I ever met him was at Sternz. And pardon my words, but I was taken back by his manner and attitude."

"I love my cousin and I always have, but he has changed since Tiberius's death. Did you ever get to meet him?"

Tauriel shook her head.

Phyra leaned in close and continued in a hushed tone. "Most people don't know this, so please keep it to yourself. Domatin always looked up to his brother, was always trying to be like Tiberius. The two were inseparable, but all that changed the day Domatin was abducted, around 200 years ago. Domatin was taken prisoner by a group of human mercenaries. I don't know how—it was all very hush-hush. They demanded an absurd amount of money for ransom, and while Empress Juliana was negotiating with them, Tiberius grew impatient, eager to get his little brother back. Against Juliana's wishes Tiberius left alone. He tracked the mercenary band down and rescued Domatin, but he was wounded in the process. Contrary to what you've heard, Tiberius didn't die from a random fever. He died from infection. Juliana didn't want the news that some rag-tag band of human mercenaries were able to kidnap one of the Royal elven children and kill another, so they concocted that story about Tiberius getting sick. Empress Juliana has tried her best to keep Domatin's name out of the ordeal, but a few of us know the truth."

"Why are you telling me?" asked Tauriel.

Phyra gave her a playful wink. "There shouldn't be any secrets between future lovers."

12

Konar looked upon the ruins of the statue of the Hero of Aclia. Unlike the one in the gardens of Sternz, this one had been overtaken by the forest. A tree had sprouted from underneath, cracking the base. Dirt and grime covered the statue, but Konar wiped away enough to read the inscription.

Here stands a monument to the savior of all races,
leader of the free peoples,
The Hero of Aclia.
From cruelty and anguish a single spark gave hope to all
When out of darkness she led, wielding holy fire.

Konar gazed into the face of the hero and wondered what it was like to live during her time, during ages of despair and loss, not knowing if you would live or die on a daily basis. His thoughts were interrupted by Liam fussing at Kassandra, "You wanted to go tonight. Are you ready yet?"

"Almost."

Konar stood and turned to see Liam leaning against a tree with his arms crossed. He was clothed in his black cotton shirt and pants, and a soft fur coat, but without his usual black leather armor.

Kassandra emerged from behind the tree wearing brown leather pants and a heavy white cotton shirt. She was also draped in a fur cloak.

"Which horse should we take?" Liam asked.

"Mine," she answered.

Konar untied the spotted grey horse and walked it over to them. Liam knelt down to Blaster to scratch his head. "Promise you'll be good, and don't annoy Konar too much."

Blaster looked at Konar and barked once only, making Konar suspicious. Blaster turned back to Liam and licked his face. "All right settle down," Liam said while nudging Blaster back to the ground, "Do you remember the three main rules you have to follow?"

Blaster lowered his head and puffed once, then looked Liam in the eyes. Reaching down to rub Blaster's neck, Liam continued, "Remember, don't eat any fruit you find. You know fruit goes straight through you. Don't stray too far from Konar, and don't explore any caves this winter. If you wake up a bear like you did a few years ago, you're on your own."

Blaster whined and puffed but then barked once. Liam smiled at Blaster as Kassandra walked to the horse. "Ready to go?"

"I guess so."

Pointing her finger at Liam, Kassandra fussed, "You know that you are going to need to smile at least once or twice while we are in town."

Liam took the reins. "We are going into an enemy town without any idea what we are going to do and without our weapons. I'm *not* excited about this."

Kassandra walked away and headed toward the village. Konar laughed as he shouted, "You're walking in the woods alone. Aren't you afraid something will snatch you?"

Even though she didn't reply, they noticed her pace slowed. Konar put his hand on Liam's shoulder, "You are going to be alone with her for a week. Why don't you tell her how you feel this time?"

Kassandra yelled over her shoulder, "Liam let's go! The sun has almost set."

Konar pushed Liam forward, "You've got this. It's really easy. Just tell her."

Liam caught up with Kassandra and together they walked toward Bakea, leading Kassandra's horse behind them. When they reached the dirt path, Kassandra wrapped her arm around his arm.

"What are you doing?" he snapped.

"We are an engaged couple, remember? It would look weird if we were walking so far apart from each other."

"I guess so," Liam muttered.

Kassandra tried to tickle his ribs, "Oh come on. This will be fun. It's a week-long festival."

Liam squinted his eyes and replied, "A festival that celebrates the elven invasion and the start of this war."

As they continued on the path, Kassandra spotted the entry way to Bakea, the same one Vernon entered. Guards patrolled the palisade. After a few seconds of observing, Kassandra whispered, "Alright, since it doesn't seem like you are going to be very cooperative, I will do the talking. Just keep a small smile on your face and act happy."

"Fine." Liam forced a small smile.

They felt many sets of eyes glaring at them as they approached the gate. One of the two guards outside raised his hand. "You two, hold for moment." With the guard walking toward them, Kassandra whispered, "Just be calm, and don't make him think you want to kill him."

"Please state your names, where you are from, and what business you have in Bakea."

Without hesitation a cheery Kassandra replied, "My name is Mary and this is my love, Allen. We are here to celebrate the Unification festival, and I also need a wedding gown." As the guard wrote the information down on his sheet of paper he looked at Liam and noticed the sour expression on his face, "Are you alright sir?" he asked. "You look... ill?"

"Just curious is all," Liam replied. "This is the first time either of us have been here."

The guard smiled. "Well then, I welcome both of you! I promise you'll enjoy it. Despite her young age, the Governess really knows how to bring people together. Now all I need is where you are from."

Kassandra answered first, "I am from Middleburg, a small village in Vetin."

The guard turned to Liam, "And you sir?"

Liam looked at the guard and replied with a deadpan tone, "Jonesburg in Xanica."

The guard took a step back and then called out to his fellow soldiers on the palisade. "Do any of you know where the village of Jonesburg is?" They all shook their heads.

"None of us have heard of it before. Which part of Xanica are you from?"

"Just one of those small villages in the middle of nowhere," was all Liam said.

The guard nodded his head, finished his notes, and said, "If you need accommodations there are several taverns and halls, but I'm guessing since you two are soon to be married you would like your privacy. I would suggest avoiding any of the crowded and dirty places, especially Harper's Hall—it's full of nothing but criminals and mercenaries. There is a simple, clean inn by the name of The Elven Whisper. Just follow the street on the left after the gate and you'll see it."

"What about our horse?"

"The stable is to your left as soon as you enter the gate, I hope you two have a pleasant stay."

Kassandra and Liam walked toward the gate, aware that the guards were watching them. After dropping their horse off at the stable, Liam grabbed their bags as Kassandra wrapped her arms around his once again. They walked down the street and watched the citizens of Bakea finishing up the last of the decorations for the festival.

"You've got to admit," Kassandra said, "The town does look quite nice, all the ribbons and flags. I'm actually kind of excited."

Liam carefully studied everyone they passed on the street, "That makes one of us."

"Of course *you're* not." Just then a thought popped into her head and she turned to look at Liam. "Liam, where did you get the idea for the name Jonesburg?"

"He asked where I was from, and I told him. Jonesburg was the name of my village."

Kassandra dug her fingernails deep into Liam's arm.

"Ouch," Liam cried. "What was that for?"

"Do you want them to know what we are up to?"

"Please let go of my arm."

Not realizing how hard she was squeezing, Kassandra loosened her grasp and apologized. Liam shook his arm as he replied through his teeth, "Thank you. And don't worry about Jonesburg, no one even knows where it is."

"Well that's depressing."

Just as the sun disappeared behind the horizon, they arrived at a small, two-story building painted a soft, cream color shining with torchlight. "Here we are."

They entered the warm building and Kassandra smiled as she looked around, taking in the sight of freshly painted, white walls festooned with all sorts of elven decorations. Cherry trees in full blossom stood tall under each window, while several patrons of both races sat around a large, blazing fireplace sharing stories.

They looked to an area that seemed to be near the kitchen and saw a short plump elven woman sweeping the floor. When she looked up and saw them, she exclaimed, "My goodness, this just makes my day!"

The woman was smiling from ear to ear, "You two have to be the cutest couple I've ever seen in my entire life," she said as she walked toward them. "Titus get in here! We have two new arrivals."

A scrawny, hunched-over, elderly elven man opened the door from the kitchen, wiping his hands on his apron. "Clara," Titus said, "I've got two pots of tomato soup boiling in the kitchen, and I need to finish the rolls before they burn." Titus stopped in his tracks when he saw the glowing smile on his wife's face. Then he saw Kassandra and Liam and smiled himself knowing how much his wife loved having young people to dote over.

Clara turned back to Kassandra and Liam. "I'm so glad you two decided to come here."

Kassandra's excitement multiplied. "Well now I am as well. The guard at the gate told us about this place as well as Harper's Hall…"

"Oh no, no, no, no!" Clara interrupted. "I will not have you two stay there. Not in a thousand years. That place is not for anyone with any decency. You will stay here, and that'll be the end of it."

Titus reached under a podium and flopped a heavy book on it. He dipped a feather in ink. "I will need your names and how long you are staying please."

Kassandra put her arm around Liam's back and answered, "I am Mary and this is my fiancé Allen. We plan on staying for the entirety of the festival if that is alright."

"Of course it is." Titus replied. "You seem like a nice, young couple, and we are happy you came to our establishment. Now if you will excuse me I need to attend to the dinner rolls—I think I smell them burning. Clara will take good care of you."

Titus disappeared through the kitchen door, and they could hear him fussing about burnt bread. Clara looked at Liam. "Are you alright young man? You seem slightly… confused?"

Liam tried to smile as he replied, "I'm sorry ma'am. I'm just tired."

"It's been a long journey here," Kassandra added. "I think we are ready to turn in for the night."

Clara closed the book and grabbed a key. "Follow me, and I will take you to your room."

Liam hesitated and asked, "Don't we need to pay you first?"

Clara looked around to make sure no one was within earshot before whispering, "Not for you. You will need all your money once you start a family together."

"Thank you," Kassandra whispered, and then motioned for Liam to follow them with the bags. Clara led them up a small stairway talking nonstop. "Titus and I met each other 600 years ago and have been side by side ever since. The humidity of Azara didn't agree with us, so when news reached us that the Governess wanted elves to settle here, we packed up immediately and built our new home; as did many elves. Countless of us traveled with the armies as they crossed the Eacru Wastes and have been here ever since."

At the top of the stairs, Clara handed the key to Kassandra and winked. "Your room is the last on the right and the walls are thick, so any noise you two might make under the sheets won't disturb a soul."

Kassandra laughed, and Liam became tense and cleared his throat, while Clara continued, "Supper should be ready soon if you're hungry, and breakfast is just after dawn."

Kassandra smiled at Clara. "Thank you so much for your hospitality. We didn't expect such kindness from an elf."

Clara laughed and started walking back down the stairs, talking as she went, "Human or elf, it doesn't matter. We all live in the same world and we might as well help each other rather than pick fights just because we look different."

Kassandra unlocked the door to their room, and they stepped inside. Coziness and comfort welcomed them—a large, fur rug laid in front of a small lit fireplace with plenty of wood stacked beside it for the cold nights. A single, large bed rested against the wall with a dresser beside it. Kassandra wanted to check out the view from the glass window that was between the bed and the fireplace, but she was so tired, she flopped down on the bed first. "I'm so glad we finally have a bed. Sleeping on the ground this past month hasn't agreed with me."

Liam set their bags down and walked over to look out the window down at the street below. Kassandra sighed in annoyance at Liam, "You need to stop being so tense all the time. It's not healthy."

"I'm not tense," he replied without turning away from the window.

"Yes, you are. Every time I grabbed on to you I could feel how tense you were."

Liam finally turned away from the window and began to unpack his bag, putting his clothes in one of the dresser drawers. "If you say so."

"I do say so," Kassandra insisted. "The bags can wait. I'm going to get some sleep, and I suggest you should do the same. Does it matter which side of bed you sleep on?"

Without replying Liam walked to the bed and grabbed a pillow. He tossed it down in front of the fireplace and said, "You can have the bed. I'll sleep on the floor."

"Are you sure? There is more than enough room for the both of us."

Without acknowledging her, Liam added a small log to the fire before resting his head on the pillow. Kassandra stared at him for several moments then crawled under the covers. Fluffing the pillow under her head she laughed as she said, "So honey, how was your day?"

She heard Liam grunt. "I'm just joking with you," she said. "No need to get feisty." Kassandra was silent for a few moments just listening to the warm crackling of the fire and the whistling of the frigid night air outside. Liam was drifting off when she spoke again, "Are you going to be able to do this?"

Liam didn't open his eyes but responded, "What do you mean?"

"You know," she said. "Are you going to be able to stay calm and happy during this week, or are you going to be your normal grumpy self?"

"I'll be fine."

Kassandra didn't know how long they had slept when she awoke to the sounds of Liam tossing and turning on the floor and making low groaning sounds. She raised up and looked at him wishing there was something she could do to help him stop having those horrible nightmares.

13

After a long day's march, the Crixarian and Tarian forces stopped to set up camp for the night. Kaia and Tori walked through the camp wrapped in multiple fur blankets. Everyone began to gather around warm fires. Along their path they saw a group of very young Crixarian soldiers trying to start a fire. "They can't be older than 16," Kaia observed. The young group shivered against each other as each attempt to start a fire failed.

"Why'd we stop?" Tori asked.

As Kaia and Tori moved closer to them, one of the soldiers spotted them and quickly stood up. "It's Princess Kaia!" he muttered through chattering teeth. The other soldiers immediately stood and Kaia smiled at them. "Having trouble starting a fire?"

Some of the soldiers nodded their heads in shame as they looked at the frosty pile of wood. Kaia let go of Tori's hand and walked to the pile of wood. Kneeling down, she extended her hand and rested it on one of the logs. After a few seconds, the log started to burn and Kaia heard sighs of relief coming from the soldiers. "Thank you Princess," they all said as they rushed to huddle around the comforting flames.

"You're welcome." Kaia walked back to Tori and whispered, "They are so young. How are they expected to fight if they can't even start a fire?"

As they continued their walk through the camp, Tori replied,

"You didn't hear? Your mother lowered the age to join the army from 18 to 16. Most of the Crixarian forces that are with us right now have never handled a sword in combat."

"Why would my mother do that?"

Tori took a long breath. "May I speak freely?"

"You can always speak freely," Kaia replied.

"I have three guesses as to why. The first is that she is now a pawn to the Vicar. Without your father to lead the country she could be desperate and looking for guidance. Everyone knows that the Tarians are oppressors, even over other humans. The Vicar could be trying to somehow gain control of Crixaria, and if once again our weak and insufficient forces need to be saved by the Tarians, that could prove to be the push the Vicar needs to secure sovereignty over our borders. My second guess is that she could be desperate and wanting to raise a decent sized army. After 16 years of war the number of men and women able to fight is very low. I remember as a child hearing about the four great generals of Crixaria, now there is only one left. Granted, after winning the Siege of Sternz more people will join our ranks. No one wants to join an army that has been slowly losing for 16 years, but now that we have the morale boost, we can raise an army. Even still, the bulk of our forces will be untested recruits who don't know the difference between a short sword and a rapier."

"And what about the third?" Kaia asked.

"The third?" Tori said. "Pardon my bluntness, but my third guess is that she is deliberately trying to make us lose this war."

"My mother wouldn't do that! What could possibly make you think that?"

"Twice during the siege of Sternz it was on your mother's orders to abandon her soldiers. The first time I was taken prisoner, along with over half the army. The second time the sections of the wall fell. After your father died, she quickly raised taxes to a level where the common family is barely able to survive. With the lowered age level to join the army she is ensuring that the youth of Crixaria will be slaughtered in this war. Even with the aid of Tarium and possibly Vetin we cannot hope to beat the elves in Azara unless the Dwarves are still at war with them. And one final thing—she hasn't apologized to any of the families of the soldiers she abandoned, not even acknowledging that she left them to die, further alienating her from the families who had to sacrifice sons and daughters to defend Sternz."

"You sound a little biased," Kaia sounded offended.

Tori lowered her head and muttered, "I'm sorry Kaia. But you asked what I think."

Kaia pulled Tori close and hugged her. "Don't be sorry," she said. "We are friends, and you can always speak your mind to me, no matter what we are talking about, and even if I disagree."

Deep in conversation, they hadn't realized their walk had led them to the edge of the camp. Tori moved her face side to side. "I can't feel the warmth of the fires anymore, are you taking me out of the camp?"

Kaia shivered as she replied, "I didn't even realize we were here."

The howling wind grew stronger, and they huddled close to each other for warmth. Kaia looked toward the sky, at the bright moon and stars. "I wish you could see the sky—it is so beautiful."

Tori remained silent and motionless, staring blankly ahead. Kaia nudged her. "Have you frozen to death?"

"Ssshh!"

Taken by surprise, Kaia whispered, "What is it?"

"I think I hear someone in the woods ahead of us."

Kaia scanned the edge of the woods. Chills went down her spine when she saw four figures standing at the edge, almost hidden in the shadows of the trees, staring back at her. Each of the figures wore a black sack hood with what seemed like white paint outlining and crying from the eye-holes.

From behind them they heard the unmistakable voice of Zafrinia cry out, "You're a liar!"

Kaia quickly turned around to see Zafrinia and Gregory walking toward them. When she turned back to the forest the figures had disappeared. "Can you still hear them?" Kaia asked Tori.

Tori shook her head.

After scanning the woods one final time, Kaia turned around as Gregory and Zafrinia walked closer to them. Gregory pointed his finger at Zafrinia and said, "I'm not lying. It's true, and you're just going to have to deal with it."

"What's going on?" Tori asked.

Zafrinia and Gregory came to a stop, but before either of them could reply, they noticed Kaia shaking and looking pale. "What happened to you?" Zafrinia asked.

"Just thought I saw something in the woods," she said. "I doubt it was anything to worry about."

Gregory looked behind her at the woods, scanning from side to side. "I wouldn't be so sure. There is no telling who, or what, could be lurking in the dark."

Tori decided to change the subject. "What had you so worked up, Zafrinia? I might want to aid in whatever that may be."

Zafrinia made a face at Tori, whose eyes weren't even looking at her. "You may be blind, but don't think for a second that I won't hesitate to put you down face first in the dirt if you give me a reason."

Gregory chuckled as he answered Tori's question, "General Izak has mapped out our path to reach Xanica, and we are going to pass by Black Marsh. Zafrinia doesn't like that idea."

"I wonder why," Tori's tone dripped with sarcasm.

Zafrinia turned and stomped back toward camp, shouting as she left, "I pray that all of you rot for eternity!"

As Gregory and Tori laughed, a confused Kaia asked, "What's so special about Black Marsh? Why doesn't she want to go there?"

Tori cleared her throat and replied, "Have you never heard the story about her?"

"I guess not," Kaia replied.

Gregory began to explain, "Long story short, Zafrinia was unfaithful in a relationship and abandoned the man who loved her more than anything else. She left that man a broken shell of his former self, and in his grief, he volunteered with the Crixarian army to fight the elves. He befriended the orc, Konar Qal, and he died at the battle of Black Marsh. Now Konar carries the hammer of Zafrinia's old love. I heard Zafrinia tried to find him and heal the scars, but she returned to his village to find his funeral. She has been fighting the elves ever since, in a sort of self-imposed punishment."

"That's heartbreaking," Kaia said.

As Tori started to reply, the screams of a woman pierced the freezing night air. Soldiers from every tent rushed out to see what was going on. Kaia grabbed Tori's arm and hurried toward the sound of the screams. "This might have something to do with those figures that were at the edge of the woods."

Tori pondered as she listened to the screaming before replying, "I don't think so. There is only one thing I know of that could cause someone to scream that much without stopping."

Kaia and Tori hurried toward the horrid sounds. As they turned a corner they realized the screams were coming from one of the Allister family royal tents—the one where Kaia and her sisters slept. Kaia took a deep breath and cried, "Please not again."

Tori placed her hands on Kaia's arms and said, "You should go in there on your own. I'll be fine here."

Kaia wiped the tears away from her eyes and pushed her way through the crowd that had gathered around the tent. Kaia entered the tent to see Izak, Alyssa, and Alezzia standing over four Vicar's Chosen holding a sprawling Bethany down on a table. Bethany's screams were so earsplitting that Alyssa's crying couldn't even be heard as she clung to her mother's nightgown. Kaia looked in horror at Bethany as even with Vicar's Chosen holding her arms and legs down, they seem to be struggling to keep her flat on the table. Bethany's bloody fingernails had already begun to dig into the table as the screaming continued.

Alezzia reached down and tore a handful of her nightgown off.

Rolling it into a ball she gently stuffed it in Bethany's mouth to muffle the screaming. Kaia quickly walked over and picked her little sister up, holding her close, trying to hide Bethany's suffering from Alyssa's view.

Alezzia turned to Izak and commanded, "Send a rider back to Sternz to get Benjamin. We will not move camp until he arrives to help Bethany."

Izak took one long final look at Bethany before walking out of the tent. Alezzia looked at Kaia and Alyssa, and said, "I don't think you two should be here. Cormorden is not something any of you should have to witness."

Still carrying Alyssa, Kaia left the tent in time to see Izak send a rider away into the night, toward Sternz and Benjamin. Izak yelled out to the gathered crowd, "Go back to your tents and get some rest. There is nothing you can do here."

Kaia tried to comfort Alyssa by gently rocking her back and forth, but Alyssa couldn't stop crying. With sorrow in his eyes, Izak said, "You two can have my tent while we stay here."

"Thank you," Kaia nodded her head and continued down the hill. Over Alyssa's sobbing, she could still hear Bethany's muffled screams of pain. All the while she wondered who it was that was at the edge of camp.

14

As the dawning sun caressed the chilled trees outside of Sternz, Vicar Matthew slowly opened his eyes, awakened from a deep sleep by a loud knocking at the door. The bitter morning breeze blew into the stone room through the windows as the sounds of the city increased. Yawning, the Vicar rubbed his eyes and bellowed, "By the One, calm down out there. You sound as if the city itself is under attack."

Benjamin's deep voice boomed from the other side of the door. "Your Holiness, the three diplomats from Vetin have arrived and are making their way to the citadel as we speak."

"This early? I didn't expect them to arrive until tomorrow." The Vicar pulled on his jeweled, white robes as he spoke through the door. "I'll be there shortly, Benjamin. You may go on ahead if you like."

Silence was the only reply from the other side of the door. Vicar Matthew finished getting ready for the day. He let out one final yawn before opening the door and looking at the two Vicar's Chosen guarding his door. "Good morning, soldiers," he greeted.

Without flinching the two Chosen replied in their monotone voices, "Your Holiness."

The Vicar walked down the stone hallway toward the main hall to meet the diplomats. Passing by servants, citizens, and soldiers, Vicar Matthew smiled and greeted each with enthusiasm and grace as he made his way to the throne room. Upon entering, he saw Benjamin standing among three stylishly dressed men in fine leather and colored cloth. On the left stood a tall, dark man with salt and pepper hair. The man in the middle was short and stocky, his light brown hair pulled into a braid. To his right stood another tall but fat man with long, stringy black hair. The Vicar bowed. "I am Vicar Matthew, Grand Priest of Tarium, leader of the One's disciples, and guardian of His word."

The tall, fat man muttered, "We know who you are."

Caught off-guard by the rude remark, Vicar Matthew stopped in his tracks. He stared blankly at the man for a brief moment, then forced a smile, and calmly replied, "Come now, you must have had a long few days as you rode here. We are all followers and children of the One, let us be civil."

The short man in the middle shot a quick, disapproving glance at his fellow diplomat before nodding to the Vicar. "I apologize for my colleague. Francisco isn't the most pleasant man to be around. I am Edek Verbeck, head councilman of the Vetin Republican Party. The rude man to my right is Francisco Abar, head councilman of the Freeborn Establishment, and to my left is Johnathan Yarl, head councilmen of the Sons and Daughters of Vetin."

Recognizing Edek's last name, Vicar Mathew extended his hand. "I know someone with the name Verbeck." As Edek returned Matthew's handshake, Benjamin interjected, "It's miss Kassandra. The young woman who is part of The Unbroken."

"Ah yes, of course," Vicar Matthew replied. "Any relation between you two?"

With a proud but slightly worried smile, Edek replied, "Yes your holiness, Kassandra is my daughter."

Vicar Matthew returned the smile. "You have raised an excellent young woman who, I have heard, is quite the marksman."

The overweight man with long, stringy, black hair interrupted, "Enough of greetings. We were summoned for a reason, and I for one would like to get this underway."

"I agree," Francisco said. "Where is Queen Alezzia Allister? I wish to speak with her on the important matters discussed in her letter."

Before the Vicar could answer, Benjamin, who was hovering near the conversation, replied, "The Queen has regrettably left with the advancing army into Xanica. I represent the kingdom of Crixaria in these discussions."

"You?" Johnathan questioned with a laugh. "Tell me how a person we've never seen or heard of, is capable of representing the Queen?"

Francisco crossed his arms and grunted, "How insulting! We traveled all this way in the middle of winter, and that woman has the audacity to not even greet us? This was a waste of time."

Francisco and Johnathan started to turn away, but Edek urged a different approach. "We traveled for six weeks to get here. I for one would at least like to discuss the matters at hand and see if we could agree on whether or not Vetin joins the war."

Francisco and Johnathan looked at each other and nodded. Benjamin extended his arm to the left. "Now if you would all please follow me, we will—"

The main doors to the throne room burst open and slammed loudly against the wall. A stocky, barrel-bellied, middle-aged dwarf, armored in heavy chainmail, stormed into the throne room. An elegant cowl of eagle feathers draped down his back and onto the floor. His fiery gaze fell upon them.

"Not only did I almost die from the cold, but my favorite axe broke when I fought off a pack of wolves. And on top of that I'm hungry!" announced the dwarf. "Where is your Queen, humans? I am here to discuss her letter."

Squinting in disbelief, Francisco gawked. "So first, the Queen fails to greet us, and now we are expected to share a table with a short, smelly dwarf?"

The dwarf pointed his finger at Francisco and yelled, "Aye! Say something like that again, and I'll rip your damn tongue straight out of your ugly mouth."

Vicar Matthew raised his hands as he tried to calm the situation down. "Come now, friends. You all have had many long days of travel. Do not let your weariness dampen your moods. Let's discuss current events over a warm breakfast before the serious talk."

The dwarf made his way forward, and to his surprise Edek extended his hand in greeting. "The Vicar is right. I am Edek Verbeck from Vetin."

The dwarf's rough hands clasped onto Edek's, and with a cheery smile he replied, "Well its finally good to meet a human with some manners. I am Ovkon Thorvor, eldest son of the Thorvor Dynasty, loyal servants to the Crowned Lord, Gothvar Mortaim."

While Edek and Ovkon greeted each other, Francisco and Johnathan turned away in disgust and motioned for Vicar Matthew and Benjamin to resume their path further into the citadel. Benjamin led the way and the others followed. After several turns and a flight of stairs, Johnathan asked, "What form of madness would come over Queen Alezzia that would make her think that talking to a dwarf could prove useful?"

Ovkon clinched both of his fists. "You human sack of shit," he muttered through gritted teeth.

Before the situation could escalate, Benjamin slammed a door open, drawing all eyes to him. "In here please," he instructed.

The room was furnished with only a small wooden table surrounded by several wooden chairs. Benjamin and Vicar Matthew sat beside each other, the three diplomats from Vetin took seats next to each other, and Ovkon slid into a chair with vacant seats on his left and right. An awkward silence prevailed.

At last Vicar Matthew turned to Ovkon and started a conversation, "So Ovkon do you have a family back home?"

"No," Ovkon replied. "I lost my wife and three children to the war against the elves."

Francisco smirked. "Better to be dead than to be a dwarf, I always say."

Ovkon Slammed his fist on the table, and leapt to his feet, knocking his chair over in the process. "I didn't not travel all this way to have my family's memory disrespected by a fat pig of a human," he shouted.

Yelling between Ovkon, Francisco, and Johnathan filled the halls of Sternz. While Edek attempted to calm the situation down, Benjamin leaned toward Matthew and whispered, "It might take longer than we thought to convince them not to kill each other, let alone come to an agreement on the war."

A loud knock on the door got their attention. "Come in!" Matthew yelled. Instead of their expected breakfast, a weary Crixarian soldier stumbled through the doorway and sought out Benjamin. "The Queen has requested your immediate presence at the camp sir."

"Why? What has happened?"

The soldier lowered his head, as if shamed to deliver the news he carried. "Princess Bethany has contracted Cormorden."

Benjamin retained his calm demeanor as he turned to Matthew. "I trust you can handle things here Your Holiness. I must go and try to ease the Princess's suffering any way I can."

"Of course," Matthew answered. "Go, and I will pray to the One that she survives that horrid disease."

Benjamin followed the soldier out of the room. The Vicar blew out a frustrated breath and muttered to himself, "This will not go very well."

15

Vernon rubbed his eyes and grumbled as he made his was from his room the inn's common area. The freezing morning air burned his cheeks, but the welcome smell of sizzling ham and sausage drew him onward. Mr. Harper called out from the kitchen, "Is that the handsome mercenary from Tarium?"

Vernon looked toward the kitchen area where seven greasy young women stood staring at him all googley-eyed. He gave them a little wave which sent them into giggling fits and whispering. Waddling out of the kitchen, Mr. Harper, with his mouth full of food, said, "I'm cooking breakfast if you'd like some."

"I'm afraid I must decline," Vernon replied. "I had a rough night's sleep and I think I'm going to go walk it off before I even think about breakfast."

Outside, the cold, fresh air sent shivers through his body. Up and down the streets, men and women of all ages were already enjoying themselves on the first day of the festival. Vernon passed by both happy and rather upset looking people. As he walked he took mental notes of his surroundings—how many patrols there were; how many soldiers were in them; how quickly they came in and out of an area. Making his way to the town center he saw the central gathering ground with a large wooden stage. Vernon walked toward a small wine stand being watch over by a simple-looking human woman.

Smiling at her, Vernon politely asked, "How much for two small jugs of your finest wine?"

"That'll be 20 elven rupees," the woman replied with a smile.

Vernon nodded his head. "I take it that means if I pay with Crixarian florins it would be 40?"

The woman set the two jugs in front of Vernon. "You'd be correct." As Vernon reached into his pouch and counted out 40 Crixarian coins, the lady added, "This isn't the first time you've had to do this is it?"

Vernon handed her the money and answered, "Unfortunately no, and at this rate I'll be out of money before the end of the day."

"Have fun at the rest of the festival," the lady said as Vernon walked away. After taking several steps, Vernon noticed an elven soldier with scruffy black hair standing in his path with his arms crossed and a smile on his face. Stopping in front of the elf, Vernon awkwardly smiled and asked, "Is everything okay?"

The soldier leaned forward to reply, "That depends on your answer. Why didn't you pay with elven rupees?"

Vernon became nervous and struggled to find a quick reply, "Uh I, I don…"

The soldier narrowed his eyes as he interrupted, "It couldn't be because you're a Crixarian spy is it?"

Before Vernon could react, the elven soldier erupted into laughter and hunched over gasping for breath. "You should've seen the look on your face."

Out of relief, Vernon began to laugh as well, albeit a forced one. The soldier stood up straight and after regaining his composure looked Vernon over head to toe and said, "I apologize for worrying you. It's just a little gimmick I like to pull when I spot a newcomer to Bakea."

"Is it that easy to tell that I'm new?" Vernon asked while trying to hide his fidgeting.

"Oh absolutely. If I had to guess, you don't even know much about the festival, do you?"

"Not really, no. I figured coming to Bakea during the festival would be a good place to find work."

The soldier extended his arms out as he proclaimed, "Then on behalf of all of Bakea, and the freezing weather, I Quintus Soelous, welcome you to the Unity Festival."

"Good to meet you Quintus. My friends call me Jake."

Wrapping his arms around Vernon's shoulders, Quintus led him through the busy streets as he explained the festival. "The first day of the festival is themed *harmony*, and you must spend time with someone from the opposite race and give them a small gift. Day two is a masquerade day, and you must spend the entire day preparing a costume for the night's feast. The third day continues the feast from night two, and you must drink and eat to your hearts content. Then, on the fourth day, the theme is *compassion*, and it's a simple day. While you recover from the feast you must show some form of compassion to someone of the other race. It could be a small hug, or if you've made a real connection with that person a passionate night is also acceptable. And finally the last day you must make plans with a person of the other race to meet sometime during the year for an activity."

"Sounds simple enough," Vernon answered as he noticed a group of at least 20 elven soldiers who looked like they had absolutely no interest in harmony, masquerader, or compassion.

Quintus paid no attention to them and asked Vernon, "I take it by your armor that you are a decently successful mercenary?"

Fearing that everyone knew the truth about him, Vernon nodded his head as he glanced at the group of elves who appeared be approaching them and said, "That's right. Just finished a job in Crixaria, and I thought I would try my luck here."

As the elves began to gather around Vernon, Quintus smirked, "During your time as a mercenary, have you ever be hired to hunt for spies?"

With his heart now racing, Vernon struggled to make something up., "Nothing like that," Vernon said. "Mostly just escorting the rich from place to place. Occasionally dealing with a band brigands."

Quintus raised an eyebrow and whispered, "If you were to give me one of those jugs of wine, I might be able to get you a meeting with someone who is in need of a good mercenary."

Looking down at the jugs Vernon noticed that his hands were shaking, but he faked a smile and replied, "I don't see why not. That seems like a fair deal to me. Why, we could even consider this to be our good deed for the first day of the festival, couldn't we?"

Grabbing a jug of wine out of Vernon's hands, Quintus smiled and said, "Now you're catching on!"

After taking a long swallow, Quintus wiped a drop of wine off his mouth and passed the jug to another elven soldier. "Alright everyone; let's get back to patrol before someone notices us slacking off. I think we've frightened this human long enough."

Vernon watched as Quintus and the rest of the patrol walked through the bustling street. Relieved that they were gone, Vernon looked around him and saw a dark alley. He slipped into its darkness, and as soon as he was sure no one could see him, he slouched down and placed the jug of wine on the ground at his feet and covered his face with his hands trying to slow his heart rate. Focusing on the fact that it was just a joke and that the elves didn't know who he really was, he slowly regained his composure, and his breathing and heart rate returned to normal. He watched the street to make sure no one noticed him, then picked up the jug of wine and headed back out into the busy streets of Bakea.

Nodding and smiling to humans and elves that he met along the way, Vernon made his way to the gate where he had entered last night. A different elven soldier stopped him, "Halt! Name please."

Vernon cleared his throat before replying, "Jake. You have my sword and shield, but I will not need them."

The elven sentry looked up from his scroll at Vernon and then out to the woods and asked, "You want to go out into the woods, by yourself, without any protection, just a jug of wine?"

"Had a rough morning," Vernon replied. "I just need a little while to clear my head, away from all this noise."

Eyeing Vernon up and down, the sentry took several moments before replying. "We all need some quiet time every now and then, especially now during the festival. Just don't take too long. You never know who or what can jump at you from the trees."

"Thank you."

Vernon strolled casually out the gate and walked along the dirt path until he was long out of sight of any guards. After walking some distance into the woods, he arrived at the statue of the Hero of Aclia to see Blaster sitting by a small fire with Konar beside him cooking something over the fire. Without looking up Konar greeted Vernon, "It's good to see you this soon. Would you like some eggs?"

Vernon smiled and set the jug of wine down beside Konar. "Yes, that sounds very good right now. Thank you. But how did you know it was me?"

Konar motioned his head at Blaster, "I figured that Blaster would have started to growl if anyone he didn't know approached. And thank you for the wine."

Vernon smiled at Blaster, who even for a wolf had a worried gaze on his face. "You miss Liam don't you?" Blaster's ears perked up as soon as Vernon said Liam's name. The smell of eggs cooking brought Vernon's attention back to Konar. He noticed the dark circled under Konar's eyes and commented, "I didn't get much sleep last night either. To tell you the truth I doubt I will sleep very much at all these next few nights. This whole situation is stressful."

Konar pulled two small, wooden plates out of a bag behind him and put three cooked eggs on each one and then tossed one to Blaster. All three savored every bite. Konar licked his fingers and then asked, "Not even an entire day yet and you're already stressed?"

Vernon rubbed his greasy fingers on his clothes and let out a long, deep breath. "You have no idea. First, I have stuck myself into probably the loudest and dirtiest tavern I have ever been in, and I'm certain the owner is going to try to get me to marry one of his daughters. Then this morning I was intercepted by an elven soldier who I thought could see through my ruse, but it turned out that he just wanted one of the jugs of wine I had with me. And to top it all off, I still have no idea how we are going to capture Phyra Ophidian. The patrols are too numerous to try anything inside the city, and outside the city walls is where they would most likely suspect an attack. What about you? How was last night out here?"

Konar looked at Blaster and said, "Neither of us got very much sleep. I had visions of the night my family was killed, and Blaster here was worried about me. Yourself?"

Vernon shook his head. "I tried to fall asleep, but I kept hearing people in the tavern drinking. The way they acted and talked reminded me of how I used to be, before my sister was raped."

"Troubled that you never found the man responsible?"

"Very."

Konar could see the anguish growing on Vernon's face, "Well now, I can't have you distracted by those thoughts. You need to keep a level head, that way you can go home to your family. And Princess Kaia."

"Fair enough," Vernon replied with a smile as he handed his plate to Konar.

Konar put the plates back in the bag and asked, "I know you said that the patrols are too numerous, but what about grabbing her in the night with darkness helping us?"

Vernon let out a sigh. "Even if there were fewer patrols at night there are still issues we would face. First, there is the gate. It is garrisoned by at least 10 elves and that's not counting the patrols along the palisade. They take all weapons at the gate, so we would have to smuggle weapons in, or you and Blaster could try to force your way in, but the alarm would be sounded before any of us inside Bakea could do anything."

Konar stroked his goatee as he pondered Vernon's words. "Let's say we figure out a way to get our weapons into the city, what then?"

"From what I can tell there are dozens of patrols that each number 20 soldiers. If we grab the Governess inside the city during the day, we will have hundreds of elves trying to kill us, so that option isn't going to work. And at night we might have a slightly better chance, but I still don't think we would be successful."

"What about outside the city? The elves might be expecting that, but maybe we could use it to our advantage? What if we try to grab her after the festival? Somewhere on the road a few miles away from Bakea when they set up camp or early in the morning?"

Vernon nodded. "That will probably have to be the way we do it. Even so, the Governess will have at least 50 soldiers or more guarding her at all times. And I know what you are thinking, but we can't ask the resistance for help. By the time we got them and came back, the Governess would be gone and we would lose our best chance to grab her."

Konar asked one last question. "What would you like Blaster and me to do in the mean time?"

"If you can do it without being spotted, try to find an area along the road where we could spring a quick ambush if necessary. And when I say quick, I mean quick enough where we can grab the Governess and be back in the woods within 10 to 15 seconds."

Konar grinned. "I take it I will be the one carrying her?"

Nodding his head Vernon joked, "Only if you don't think she will be too heavy for you."

Konar pretended to be offended. "I may be getting older, but I bet I could beat you, Kassandra, Liam, and Blaster combined in anything regarding strength."

They both laughed, but the snapping of a branch put them on edge. Blaster popped up on all fours, ready to fight. With only the soft whistle of the breeze making noise, time seemed stand still. They listened and watched for anything deep in the woods. Blaster sniffed the air several times before sighing and laying back down on the ground.

"Must have been a branch falling off a tree—or a deer—maybe." Konar groaned as he sat back down on the cold ground.

Vernon remained standing. "I am praying the elves need an extra mercenary," Vernon said. "If I could be hired on as extra protection, that could give us a much needed advantage."

"If they don't recognize you first," Konar added.

"That's why you're here, to watch my back." Looking up at the sun peering through the heavy winter clouds, Vernon decided he had been gone long enough. Any longer could arouse unwanted attention.

"I have to go," Vernon mumbled. "We wouldn't want the elves to send a search party for me."

"I don't suppose you've heard from Liam or Kassandra?" Konar asked as Vernon walked away.

"No, but considering those two, not hearing anything is probably a good thing. But who knows how much longer we can count on that. You and I might have to rescue them at some point."

16

Liam and Kassandra walked out of Elven Whisper into the streets of Bakea. The frosty morning air made Kassandra's hands cold, so she wrapped them under Liam's arm.

"It's not that cold," Liam griped.

Pulling herself in closer to him, Kassandra shivered as she replied, "Yes it is. It was cold all night last night, even with the fire, and it's colder now. All I want to do is go back to our room and stay under the covers."

"I thought I was supposed to be the antisocial one," Liam jeered as he weaved them through the crowded street.

Although it took several seconds, Kassandra's face brightened, "You made a joke! An actual joke."

Liam grunted as Kassandra jabbed him in the side. "I can't believe you made a joke."

"Will you stop it," Liam insisted. "I am trying to do what we came here to do."

"Oh, loosen up a little. We can do that later. Just relax and try to enjoy yourself. This is a festival after all. Be festive."

Scanning everyone and everything around him, Liam ignored Kassandra's last statement, much to her dismay. Annoyed that he had stopped replying to her, Kassandra decided to talk to Liam constantly, just to annoy him even further.

"So," she said, "What's going on in that head of yours?"

Liam ignored her.

"I don't think I've ever seen people this excited about a festival. But I have to admit, it is strange to see humans and elves getting along this well. I mean, I know that before the war, tensions were not the best, but now with the war, I'm just surprised that things are this well here. What do you think?"

"I guess," Liam murmured.

Kassandra smirked. "That's better than silence."

They walked together for some time with Kassandra rambling on about the cold, and the decorations, when Liam jerked to a stop. "What are you doing?" she asked.

Liam's face grew hard as he watched a small group of both human and elven children push a young girl with rosy cheeks and long hazel hair, who looked to be no more than eight years old, down onto the chilly ground. The children shouted harsh words at the young girl.

"Mongrel."

"Cur."

As the child's eyes began to well with tears, one of the human girls wrestled a simple, wool doll away from the girl and began to tear it apart.

Liam stepped forward and shouted, "Stop that!" As the gathered group of children saw Liam walking toward them, they quickly scattered in all directions, leaving the young girl behind, alone on the cold and muddy ground. Kassandra, both surprised and happy to see Liam act this way, walked over to Liam and the small girl. Liam knelt down and gently wiped away the tears from the girl's rosy cheeks.

"You're alright now," Liam assured her. "What's your name?"

"Ly-, Lyla," she said as she wiped her nose.

"My name is Liam, and this is Kassandra."

Concerned that Liam just used their real names, Kassandra pinched him as hard as she could without Lyla seeing. Barely flinching, Liam continued to comfort the girl.

Lyla looked up at Kassandra and saw the silver sun necklace. "That's a pretty necklace," she said.

Smiling back at her, Kassandra replied, "Why, thank you. It was my mother's a long time ago."

"Why were those kids being mean to you?" Liam asked.

Sniffing, Lyla looked down at the ground, then pulled her hazel hair away from her ears which were not as long or pointy as an elf's but not as small and round as a human's.

Kassandra couldn't keep the shock out of her voice, "You're part-human and part-elf?"

Lyla nodded and frowned, but Liam gently placed his hand under her chin and said, "No need to be sad. Now we should probably get you back to your parents. Do you know where they are?"

"Yes," Lyla perked up. She stood up, took them both by their hands, and started pulling them through the streets of Bakea.

Over the hustle Kassandra leaned over and whispered to Liam, "Just because you did something unexpectedly sweet don't presume that I won't fuss at you later for using our real names."

Once again Liam ignored her, but a hint of a smile appeared on his face. Kassandra considered it a sign of progress.

After turning several street corners they arrived at the edge of Bakea, where small wooden houses lined up row after row with elven soldiers walking in and out of them. Liam and Kassandra realized this was the part of Bakea where the garrison slept. Lyla led them to her house on the corner at the southeast area of the palisade. Without knocking Lyla opened the door and pulled them into her home, a small but cozy dwelling with a small living area, a kitchen, and two bedrooms.

"Lyla, sweetie, is that you?" a woman called from one of the bedrooms.

Lyla released her grip on their hands and ran into the bedroom. "Yes, Mommy, and I made new friends."

Lyla's mother extended her arms out to hug Lyla, then stepped out into the living area. She was a middle-aged elf who was wearing the white scale armor of a common elven soldier. Her flowing black hair rested on her shoulders.

"I am Numeri. Welcome to my home, as simple as it may be. We try to make it as comfortable as possible," she introduced herself while still holding on to Lyla.

"It's lovely," Kassandra smiled.

Looking down at Lyla, Numeri nudged her to the other bedroom and said, "You are absolutely filthy, go wash up and change into clean clothes."

"Yes, Mommy." Lyla hurried to her room.

Numeri motioned for Liam and Kassandra to sit. Liam took mental notes of his surroundings while Kassandra began the conversation. "I'm sorry if we are intruding on anything but we…"

"Nonsense," Numeri interrupted. "Lyla is normally an extremely shy girl, and it makes me happy to see her talking to people."

Lyla came running out of her room in a clean blue dress and jumped onto her mother's lap. "Mommy, they saved me from Rufus and Marcia and…"

"I thought I asked you to stop playing with them. They are always rude to you." Numeri's tone was scolding, but not too harsh.

The door to the house opened and an overweight human male with short black hair walked in carrying a small sack of potatoes.

"Daddy!" Lyla shouted as she hopped off her mother's lap and ran to the man.

He put the sack down, caught Lyla in his arms, and lifted her up in the air as she jumped toward him. "Well hello to you too, sweet girl." Spotting the two new guests in the house, he asked Lyla, "Are these two people friends of yours?"

"Yes, Daddy," she said. "This is Kassandra and Liam."

Smiling he said, "It's good to meet you. I am Clark, and I see you've already met my lovely family." Looking back at Lyla, he said, "Would you like to help me make some soup?"

Lyla's face lit up even more. She reached down for the sack of potatoes, but no matter how hard she tugged it is too heavy for her. Clark chuckled, picked up the sack, and followed Lyla into the kitchen area.

Numeri turned back to Liam and Kassandra. "Are you here for the festival?"

Not giving Liam a chance to say anything to the contrary, Kassandra replied, "Yes we are. But that's not the only reason we are here. Liam and I are getting married soon, and I hope to find a gown as well."

"Oh, how sweet. I bet you are so excited," Numeri said with a smile.

Liam changed the subject, "Do you know why those kids were bullying Lyla? I thought being part elf would mean she would be accepted by both races."

With a sigh of disappointment Numeri shook her head. "You'd think that, but sadly it's not the case. Both the humans and elves here consider half-elves to be the lowest of the low. I was almost thrown out of the guard for adopting her."

"So, she isn't yours?" Liam realized too late how rude that sounded.

Kassandra slapped him in the chest, but Numeri smiled and replied, "No she isn't. I don't exactly know for sure how old she is either, but she has been with me for eight years now and it's honestly been the best years of my life."

"Do you know what happened to her real parents?" Kassandra asked.

Repositioning herself in the wooden chair, Numeri began the story. "I was with the first elven forces that arrived in Xanica almost 16 years ago. After the first few battles, I was stationed around the new Governess to be a part of the garrison that protected her. Then eight years ago I was out on patrol one morning when we came across a burned-down house. Inside the rubble there were two bodies, charred beyond recognition. I found Lyla hidden in the bushes, behind what was left of the house, covered in soot and dirt. All Lyla has ever said about what happened is that two people, with eyes shaped like a serpent's, glowing as bright as a red sun, came to her house and ate her parents. If I had to guess it must have been some sort of wild animal that knocked over a candle that started the fire. Since she was a half-elf, the Legatus in command ordered us to bring her back to be sold into slavery, but I couldn't allow that to happen. I protested and eventually was granted permission to adopt her. I have been stationed as a guard at Bakea ever since. Then seven years ago Clark left the Crixarian army. We met and fell in love. We've been a happy little family ever since."

A forceful knock on the door drew everyone's attention as an elven soldier opened the door and walked in without waiting for an invitation. The soldier addressed Numeri. "I know you already went on patrol this morning, but you are needed at the front gate."

The soldier turned and left, and Numeri reluctantly stood and walked into the kitchen to say goodbye to her family. Liam and Kassandra also stood up to leave.

Kassandra smiled at Lyla and said, "Thank you for inviting us over. Liam and I had a wonderful time."

Lyla gave Kassandra a hug, and Clark said, "You both are welcome back anytime you wish. And if either of you need anything during your stay, feel free to come here or my whittling stand in the center of town."

"Where are you staying?" Numeri asked.

"It's a small bed and breakfast called Elven Whisper."

"We know the place," Numeri said. "We will catch up with you two sometime throughout the week. I'm sure that would make Lyla happy."

"Yes, it would!" Lyla exclaimed.

Smiling at them Kassandra nodded and replied, "Then of course we will. Thank you again for your hospitality."

Feeling the icy breeze as soon as they stepped out the door, Kassandra wrapped her arms around Liam, and they continued their walk through Bakea.

"I'm glad you helped her. They seem like a sweet family."

Liam's remained stoic and Kassandra started to nudge him in the side, but he whispered, "Shh, one second."

Liam scanned the crowds, but all Kassandra could see were normal, everyday humans and elves along with the occasional patrol of soldiers.

She whispered, "What is it? What's going on?"

Trying not to draw attention, Liam slightly nodded his head toward a couple of alleyways and whispered back, "The streets are being watched by more than just elven soldiers."

Kassandra glanced toward the alleyways. At first, she saw nothing, but then a sliver of a shadow appeared. Kassandra's eyes widened when she saw Wraiths of Colubra in alleyways, silently watching everyone and everything. But one wraith, different from the rest, stood out. This one had strands of raven hair draping over her face, two daggers, and a small cape resting over her right shoulder.

17

"A little nervous, are we?" Phyra joked.

Looking back at her with a blank expression, Tauriel replied, "Why would I be?"

Phyra giggled. "I'm pretty sure this has to be your first time. I'm glad it is with me."

"Why wouldn't it be?" Tauriel asked.

Phyra winked at Tauriel and said, "I promise everything will go smoothly, and that I will be gentle."

"You're making a big deal out of this," Tauriel replied as she looked around them.

Phyra's smile becomes even wider. "I make a big deal out of everything I do!" she said.

"I don't know why," Tauriel replied. "Just because this is the first time I've ever been to Bakea?"

Phyra slouched on her horse and puffed, "I was trying to role-play a little, but you ruined it."

"Role-play? Role-play what?" Tauriel's face turned bright red when she finally realized what Phyra was hinting at, but she managed to escape further embarrassment as the cheers around Bakea grew louder and louder.

The gates of Bakea opened allowing the elven soldiers and Praetorians to enter. The elven force separated into two lines on each side of the gate, giving room for Phyra and Tauriel to pass through the crowd without being bothered or attacked. Once Phyra passed under the gates and into Bakea, the cheers and applause erupted to an almost deafening level. Phyra raised her hands and waved while blue and white rose pedals began to fall from second and third story windows, carpeting the ground below.

Tauriel remained calm and collected as she scanned the crowds looking for any signs of discontent, but the only discontent and angry faces she spotted were from Isila and her wraiths that sulked in the shadows, but she knew that was only part of their demeanor.

"Easy girl," Phyra said to her horse as she brought it to a halt.

Tauriel stopped her horse as well and turned to Phyra. "Madam Ophidian I must protest."

Still smiling and waving at everyone, Phyra hopped off her horse and began to walk among the crowd. "You're more than welcome to come with me," she said with a smirk.

Scanning the crowd in front of Phyra, Tauriel dismounted and joined Phyra. The more people Phyra greeted, the more anxious Tauriel became. She kept a hand readied on the hilt of her sword and prayed silently to Colubra that they safely reach Phyra's personal estate in Bakea. One thing Tauriel noticed, however, was the relationship Phyra had with the citizens of Bakea. Even when traveling with Prince Domatin or Imperator Leontina back in the elven homeland, she couldn't remember a time when either of them had a crowd this large or as enthusiastic. Thousands of humans and elves waved their banners and threw rose pedals for Phyra.

After several more minutes of greeting, they finally remounted and made their way to Phyra's personal estate in Bakea—a large three story manor made with some of the finest and smoothest carved wood Tauriel had ever seen along with dozens of glass windows adorned with white and blue streamers.

As Phyra climbed the stairs in front of her manor she turned to address the citizens, "My friends! Thank you so much for this most gracious welcome. I am just as excited as I know each of you are for this week's festival. Now if you will excuse me for a little while to unpack and freshen up, I will rejoin you soon." Phyra blew kisses to the crowd, then walked through the doors to the manor.

After following her inside, Tauriel turned to one of Phyra's Praetorians and ordered, "I want 50 soldiers guarding the manor outside at all times, and 15 to patrol inside the manor day and night. The other five will continue to be by the Governess's side no matter what."

"An excellent idea," said a woman's low voice from the corner behind them.

Out of the shadowy corner, Isila stepped toward them. As soon as Phyra saw her, she clapped her hands together and exclaimed, "Isila! It's so good to see you again."

Isila's forehead scrunched together as she questioned Phyra's excitement. "You saw me just this morning."

"So?" Phyra smiled. "Can I not be glad to see such a beautiful woman again?"

Isila gave a blank stare at Phyra before she turned her attention back to Tauriel. "Did you see anything of concern in Bakea?"

Still startled by Isila's sudden appearance, Tauriel said, "I could've sworn I just saw you in the streets, not 10 minutes ago."

"You did," Isila replied. "But while it's your job to take care of the visible threats, like an unruly mob or upset citizen, it's my job to deal with what you cannot see, and to be one step ahead of both our enemies—and you."

Clearing her throat, Tauriel gazed back at Isila's unrelenting stare and replied to her first question. "No, I did not see anyone that posed a threat. Everyone I saw seemed happy that Madam Ophidian arrived. What about you?"

"My wraiths and I saw a few concerns," Isila stated. "But we will watch them and proceed as needed. I will leave six of my wraiths here to help watch over the Governess."

Tauriel surveyed her surroundings from the spiral stairway in the center of the manor to all the shadowy corners.

"What are you doing?" Phyra asked Tauriel out of curiosity.

Turning back to face Isila, Tauriel inquired, "Just exactly how many wraiths do you have in Bakea?"

Even under the hood and mask Tauriel could see a faint smile as Isila responded, "There are three wraiths for every Praetorian Phyra has."

Clapping her hands again, Phyra exclaimed, "See ,Tauriel. There is nothing to be worried about. You should just relax and enjoy yourself. Perhaps even in a bath with me tonight?"

Tauriel froze, not knowing for sure how to reply.

"Honestly, Tauriel, you need to relax. It was just an invitation. You can say no, but I would prefer a yes. You'll have plenty of time to enjoy yourself here. We are perfectly safe. This is my city, these are my people."

"I agree with the Governess," Isila added. "Twenty Praetorians, 60 wraiths, with the extra 100 soldiers that arrived with you this afternoon; that brings the standing garrison to over 6,000, and on top of all that, out of the 100,000 people who live in the city I estimate that around 80 to 90 percent would side with us in the event of an attack. In summary, the Governess is at her safest during her stay here."

A satisfied Phyra smiled and nodded. "See, perfectly safe. Now if you two goddesses will pardon me, I am going to go wash up and change before I attend the festivities." As Phyra skipped up the staircase she yelled out, "Tauriel you are free to join me if you wish. Isila, you as well. Preferably both of you!"

With a timid smile Tauriel shook her head, knowing now that Phyra would not stop her advances on either of them. "Isila," Tauriel asked, "do you know why even the humans love Phyra? I've been through towns back in Azara where not even Imperator Leontina or Prince Domatin got such a warm welcome. To be honest, even the elves here seem to love her more than any other Ophidian I've seen."

"Phyra Ophidian is without a doubt the most popular and loved leader in all of Aclia in the past 500 years at least. For one, her personality is one of friendliness, joy, and love. She is a member of the royal family, which provides a level of popularity in and of itself, but the fact that she is only eighth in line for the throne means that she isn't going to do any political maneuvering, and that she is genuine, which the elves here appreciate. The humans in Xanica love her more and more each day. I was curious to see how she would handle governing a country where over 90 percent of the population is human and consider her an invader. But in only 16 years she has become their most loved leader. She kept slavery out of Xanica, which the humans appreciate. She has allowed them to continue to worship their god, which again they appreciate. And she doesn't treat humans any differently than she treats the elves. For someone who is only 193 years old, she has done something no one thought possible."

Tauriel looked out the glass window at the crowd, but continued to take full advantage of the suddenly talkative Isila. "What do you know about the resistance? How large of a threat do they pose?"

"A small but persistent one. When our army first took control of Xanica, the resistance was a major threat, and several times almost drove us out. Then one summer evening, 14 years ago, they made a mistake. All their top officers were captured by the old headmaster of the wraiths. After they were publicly executed, we thought the resistance would fade. And it did—until a former Vicar's Chosen named Malum arrived and turned their operation around. A very strict and stern man, he has made the resistance a thorn in our side ever since. They don't have the numbers to launch a major attack, and we have plenty of humans loyal to us in their ranks. However, now that Tarium and Crixaria are inevitably going to come here, the resistance will pose a much larger threat. Thankfully, we don't have to worry about an assassination attempt."

"Why not?" Tauriel asked. "I know they have tried before, when she first arrived in Xanica."

"Because of her popularity. If the humans killed her, then Xanica would be in uproar. What they are more than likely to do is to kidnap her and try to gain some advantage, or make the people of Xanica feel abandoned. Even though we know the resistance has members here in Bakea, they wouldn't be stupid enough to attempt to kidnap the Governess. They most certainly won't try it outside of the city because that is where the most guards will be around her. If they have a death wish they can try to take her inside the city walls, but they would have to get past thousands of our soldiers, 20 praetorians, 60 wraiths—and finally myself."

18

Still gathered around the table with the others, Vicar Matthew took a moment to try to pray, but just as he closed his eyes he was interrupted.

"You arrogant pile of shit!" Ovkon said in disgust to Johnathan across the table.

Enraged, Johnathan kicked up from his chair sending it clattering across the floor. "How dare you! You think just because you are a guest here means you are safe? One word from me and our guards will cut you down, and we will simply say you never arrived."

Ovkon snarled, "I'll kill you and Francisco before anyone can stop me."

"Gentlemen please be civil," Vicar Matthew pleaded. "At the current rate we are going we will be fighting each other rather than our common enemy."

While Edek nodded in agreement with the Vicar, Francisco pointed toward Ovkon. "Why even bother with the dwarves? They are only half-beings—half the size, half as smart."

To the Vicar's surprise Ovkon doesn't yell back out of anger. Instead a malicious grin spread across the dwarf's face. He said, "Tell me fat man, under all your fat rolls when was the last time your wife could find your half-sized—"

"Enough!" Vicar Matthew shouted at the top of his lungs. Now that he has everyone's undivided attention, the Vicar rose to his feet and placed his hands on the table. "It is evident that you cannot, or will not, see past your differences and past grievances long enough to get along. I think it is time that we finally discuss the real reason we are gathered here. We have a common enemy—the Elves."

Turning to Ovkon, the Vicar continued, "If this meeting continues the way it is going, the Dwarves will end up at war with both the Elven Empire *and* Vetin. I doubt you want to deal with war on two fronts."

Turning his head toward the diplomats from Vetin, Vicar Mathew said, "Edek, I commend you on your behavior. But Johnathan, Francisco—I have never in my life been more disappointed by two people. If you do not understand that your constant derision of Ovkon and his people will lead you to war, then you are both fools. Vetin and Schelmar already have enough tension between you, and I promise you that if you go to war you will go alone. Tarium, Crixaria, and Xanica have their full attention on dealing with the elves, so you will have to fight alone. Quite frankly it seems to me that neither of you have any intention of finding common ground. If that is the case then you both may be excused while the *adults* finish the discussion."

As Vicar Matthew sat back down, the room that moments before was filled with tension and hate shifted to one of uneasy quiet.

Looking back and forth from Ovkon to the diplomats, the Vicar's stern gaze finally gave way to a calm smile. "Let us start over. And to begin, why don't we all be forthcoming with each other about the current state of affairs as well as our intentions?"

Clearing his throat Edek replied, "An excellent idea. We will go first."

Taken aback by Edek's quick response, Johnathan and Francisco gave him a stern look but Edek disregarded it. "To be honest, Vetin does not wish to go to war at all. We understand that our fellow humans have suffered because of the elves and wish us to join, but it is something we do not wish to do. As of now, our standing army is 300,000 strong, a mix of foot infantry, light cavalry, and rangers. But we are loath to enter a war against the elves and leave our southern border open to attack from the dwarves. Since Vetin was established, the dwarves have coveted our land. Our senate believes the dwarves will attack as soon as we send aid, which would leave our borders weakened."

As soon as Edek finished his statement, the Vicar raised his hand making sure that no further words were said, therefore keeping the tenuous peace. After a moment of silence Vicar Matthew addressed Ovkon. "Would you like to respond?"

Reluctantly nodding his head, Ovkon stared at Johnathan and Francisco. "You want the honest truth? Here it is. You do not need to worry about any dwarf attacking Vetin as long as we are at war with the elves. The Crowned Lord, Gothvar Mortaim, hates elves so much that unless provoked by Vetin he will not shift any of the dwarven armies away from the elven front."

Vicar Matthew looked at the diplomats from Vetin, hoping for a civil response. Instead, Edek broke the silence. "How goes your war with the elves?"

Ovkon shook his head. "That is something I am not allowed to discuss."

Johnathan shouted, "See. He is a liar. Now he knows about our army and our plans."

"Trust me human, if we wanted to take your country back, which is ours by right, we would," Ovkon sneered.

Before the situation could escalate, Vicar Matthew cleared his throat and said, "Gentlemen, please keep the conversation civil or leave. Now, Ovkon, I understand that you are not allowed to discuss details, but even the briefest of overviews would be helpful."

Ovkon considered, then nodded and finally replied. "Simply put, we are... concerned. The first 20 years of the war went extremely well for us. Victory after victory—it seemed like we might win, but that changed 130 years ago. The main elven force received a new leader, a woman by the name of Imperator Leontina. That accursed woman single-handedly turned the war around in favor of the elves. All the territory we gained was retaken by Leontina, inch by inch, town by town. Since we halted her advance 30 years ago the battle ground has stayed relatively the same, but there is a growing concern that the elves are about to attack us and wipe out our main army."

"Why is that?" Edek asked. "If you have been at a stalemate do you not think that it will continue?"

Everyone could see Ovkon's uneasiness. "We had hoped that the revelation of Kaia Allister's magic abilities would divert their army and give us the edge we needed, but it seems the elves have been toying with us. Since discovering her powers, the elves have raised new armies. Every time we gain any momentum, they use their mages to devastating effect. And there is this new leader on that front, Imperator Atica. In 30 years Atica has yet to lose an inch. We cannot break any of her lines. We fear they will unleash this enormous new army they have been raising to finish us off once and for all."

"You see gentlemen, this is why we need to co-operate," Vicar Matthew declared. "If what Ovkon said is what the elves are truly doing, then none of us will stand a chance. The only possible solution is for us to simultaneously attack the elves with all we have. All races have suffered far too long under the heel of the Elven Empire. It's high time to take them down. Each of you has a question to ask yourself. Will you do nothing and be forgotten? Or will you fight, and be remembered as men who brought down an Empire?"

19

As light from the dawning sun peeked over the rooftops of Bakea, Liam and Vernon snuck into a dark alley near Harper's Hall.

Still half asleep and not happy about being awake this early, Vernon's whispered voice sounded more like a growl. "Do you know how dangerous it is for us to be speaking right now?"

Matching Vernon's tone, Liam whispered back, "Do you know how dangerous it is for us to be here without a plan?"

Peering behind Liam, Vernon asked, "Where is Kassandra? Is she alright?"

"She's asleep," Liam answered. "Now, do you have a plan?"

Rubbing his tired face Vernon whispered, "For the most part I do."

Grinding his teeth Liam whispered back, "What does that mean, *for the most part*? We are here in the middle of an enemy city, and you saw how the citizens of Bakea reacted when Phyra entered. They will not let her be taken without a fight. So, its high time you think of a plan before you get us all killed."

Vernon raised his eyebrows in shock, but before he could say anything Liam took a small step back and apologized, "I'm—I'm sorry. I didn't get any sleep last night."

"Don't worry about it," Vernon said. "I'm not getting much sleep either."

Hearing the footsteps of a elven patrol approaching, they pressed their backs against the wall. Without making a sound, they watched the large patrol walk past, praying no one got curious and looked their way. After the patrol passed by Liam whispered, "So what's your plan so far?"

After taking one final look out into the streets, Vernon whispered back, "Taking her in the city would be suicide. They have far too many soldiers and Praetorians…"

"As well as wraiths," Liam interrupted.

"Wraiths? Are you sure? How many?"

"Yes, I'm sure. But I don't know exactly how many. My guess would be at least 10, maybe more. Does that change your partial plan?"

Shaking his head Vernon replied, "Not really. If things stay the way they are then on the fourth night of the festival I will head out to meet up with Konar. He has been scouting a place along the main road where we can grab her. The plan is for Konar, Blaster, and I to ride in on our horses, kill the guards around her, grab her, and be off into the woods faster than the soldiers guarding her can react."

"What about Kassandra and me?"

"Without question the elves will pursue us anywhere we go. So I think it would be best for you and Kassandra to leave town shortly after Phyra leaves and eliminate our pursuers one by one until you catch up with us."

"And about the wraiths? I think they are different than the ones we encountered at Sternz or at the village a few days ago."

"Why would they be any different?"

"Well, not *they*; just one of them. There was one wraith that was different from the others. I know this wraith is a woman, but instead of a single dagger she had two, and I bet they are still coated in cobra venom. She also had a small cape covering her right shoulder, and I'm fairly certain she had hair."

Puzzled at Liam's description, Vernon tried to remember anything about such a wraith but couldn't seem to do so. Frustrated at the news, he frowned and whispered, "Hopefully we can avoid any trouble with her and the rest of the wraiths."

As light from the dawning sun began to push the darkness of the alleyway aside, Vernon motioned for Liam to leave. "We should part ways before too many people wake up. We don't want to cause any unneeded attention. Go and try to get a little rest and let Kassandra know what the plan is for now."

Liam began to walk out of the alley but then stopped and whispered back to Vernon, "I might have found someone who might be able to help us. It's a long shot, but you would be the best one to convince him."

"Who?" Vernon asked.

Liam stepped back toward Vernon and whispered, "His name is Clark. I don't know much about him. Kassandra and I only met him yesterday. All I know is that he used to be an officer in the Crixarian army, and that for some reason he left seven years ago. Maybe you could somehow get him to help us."

Vernon considered the idea but then asked, "Why did you say it was a longshot?"

"He has a family now. He lives with one of the elven soldiers and together they adopted a young half-elf girl. If you think you can convince him he runs his own whittling stand in the center of town in the mornings. He is slightly overweight and has short black hair like yours."

Liam walked out of the alley and back toward The Elven Whisper. Vernon stayed hidden in the alley for several minutes before heading out. Too awake to be able to go back to sleep he decided to talk a walk toward the center of Bakea and maybe talk to Clark.

The cold streets of an early morning Bakea were peaceful to Vernon, a vast difference from the bustling streets the past two nights. As more and more people began their day the streets gradually become more active. Looking ahead Vernon spotted Quintus Soelous and his patrol extorting another human. Not wanting to have to deal with him again, Vernon darted into the nearest alleyway. While looking behind to make sure Quintus didn't see him, Vernon bumped into a figure in front of him. When he turned his head, what he saw sent chills down his spine—a wraith, but unlike the others. She had two cobra-hilted daggers strapped to her thighs, a small black cape covering her right arm, and small strands of dark, raven hair covering her face and mask.

Struggling to find something to say, Vernon stared blinking at the wraith whose dark eyes seemed to pierce into his very soul. From under her mask, the wraith spoke, "Can I help you?"

Vernon still could not think of what to say. The wraith reached for one of her daggers and began to draw it. Vernon eyes widened now as the wraith stepped toward him with cobra venom dripping off her dagger.

"Sorry for bothering you," Vernon finally managed to say.

The wraith stopped advancing but kept her dagger out as she questioned him, "Who are you and why did you come in here?"

"My name is Jake, and I am a mercenary looking for work. I was walking in the street and saw someone ahead of me that I would have rather not dealt with, so I was going to cut through here. I am terribly sorry for bumping into you."

Now sheathing her dagger, the wraith motioned for Vernon to leave. "Go, but know that if you ever *bump* into me again, I will not hesitate to kill you."

Vernon hurried out of the alley back into the streets of Bakea.

As soon as Vernon disappeared, Isila snapped her fingers. Two wraiths that had been hiding in the shadows stepped forward. Isila said, "I want both of you to follow him. He didn't seem too surprised to see me, as if he already knew I was here. Find out if he really is who he said he is, and if anything about him seems suspicious report back to me, and I'll handle him personally."

Vernon finally slowed down enough to catch his breath and regain his composure, all the while thinking to himself, "I just can't catch a break in this city."

Vernon had made his way to the center of town—the central market place. Even in the early morning the market was packed, with lines to the stands backing up and making the entire area crowded. Scanning the stands around the massive market Vernon finally spotted Clark, whittling away for a small group of elven children. Vernon watched as Clark finished turning the small slab of wood into a beautiful horse. The children clapped, and Clark gave the small, wooden horse to one of the children and sent them on their way.

As he approached Clark's stand Vernon said, "Good morning friend. Besides the cold it seems as if will be a lovely day."

"That it does," Clark replied with cheer. Dusting wood chips off his fur jacket, he added, "I haven't seen you in town before. You must be here for the festival."

Glad that he finally found someone pleasant to talk to in Bakea Vernon replied, "You could say that. My name is Jake, and I am a mercenary. I figured this would be a good place to find work."

"A mercenary huh? You must have been on a few interesting journeys."

Looking around them at the crowed market Vernon replied, "Well I don't have much to do today. If you'd like I could stay and tell you a few tales."

Clark grabbed a small wooden stool and set it beside him for Vernon to sit on. "Sounds good to me. People normally order my goods in advance so whittling can get quite boring sometimes. My name is Clark," and he extended his hand to Vernon.

Vernon shook Clark's hand and sat on the stool, a little eager and a little nervous. Eager because he hoped to gain an ally, but nervous because he must come up with several stories to tell Clark.

"What would you like to hear first? I once had to single hand-edly retrieve a necklace that belonged to a lord of Vetin from a group of 20 bandits. Or the time I was hired to escort a priest's wife across Tarium, who was trying the whole journey to get me to sleep with her?"

The day passed, and several hours flew by. Clark and Vernon laughed as Clark asked, "So even with the priest in the hallway she still took off her dress?"

"That she did," Vernon said with a grin. "The priest only paid me half of what he promised because to this day I bet he still thinks I slept with his wife, which I did not."

Clark finished whittling a wooden soldier and Vernon asked, "So what about you Clark? I assume you haven't been a whittler all your life. Do you have any interesting stories?"

Shaking his head Clark replied, "My life hasn't been the most interesting. I've been here in Bakea for seven years, found a woman I love and that loves me back, and we adopted a beautiful little girl together," smiling as he said the last part.

Vernon prodded, "What about before that? No interesting stories about then?"

Now with a blank expression Clark replied, "I used to be an officer in the Crixarian army, but nothing good came of that."

Surprised Clark admitted his past so quickly, Vernon asked, "Are you not afraid they will retake Xanica and find you?"

"No," Clark said. "If they take Xanica back I will go wherever my family goes, which will inevitably take me to Azara."

Vernon's hopefulness turned to curiosity and he asked, "Did you fight in any battles?"

"A few."

Seeing the sorrow on Clark's face, Vernon said, "You know, I've been to Crixaria a few times. Such a beautiful country and surprisingly friendly people."

As if reminded of home Clark replied with a hint of a grin, "Yes it is. Sometimes I honestly miss it, but I am happy here. What parts of Crixaria have you been to?"

Instinctively replying, Vernon named his hometown, "Redoak is undoubtedly my favorite. And the Regnier family were such gracious hosts."

Clark dropped his knife and broke out in a sudden sweat. His face pale, Clark jumped to his feet. "It is time for me to head home. It was a pleasure talking with you Jake, and I hope you have a wonderful stay in Bakea." Then Clark hurried off into the streets without cleaning up his whittling stand or giving Vernon a second look.

Vernon was baffled, but then a dark, horrific thought popped into his head. Thinking back over their conversation, Vernon tried to decipher why Clark became so horrified at the sound of Vernon's last name. He shook his head and his blood began to boil. All thought of capturing Phyra and even the war with the elves, faded to insignificance. The only thing now on Vernon's mind was, "Is this the man? Is this the man who raped my sister?"

20

B ethany's muffled screams echoed through the camp, while the Crixarian and Tarian forces waited for the order to once again march toward Xanica. Wrapped up in a large blanket in their temporary tent, Kaia and Alyssa snuggled together reading a children's book. When they finished Alyssa turned her sad face to Kaia and asked, "Kaia, when is Bethany going to get better? I miss her."

"I wish I knew, but I hope very soon."

"Me too," Alyssa said. "Will she turn mean like Momma did?"

"I don't know. But I do know one thing," Kaia said.

"What's that?" Alyssa asked.

With a wide smile, Kaia leaned in and answered, "Even if Bethany gets worse, I'll never stop playing with you."

Alyssa's baby blue eyes lit up with excitement, and she hugged her sister as hard as she could. "I love you," Alyssa whispered.

Kaia hugged Alyssa back, "I love you too. I won't ever leave you, I promise."

Bethany's agonizing screams interrupted them, but they were no longer muffled. They were as loud as painful screams could be. A few moments passed before the screams become muffled once again.

Alyssa pleaded, "Can you please go check on Bethany?"

"Don't you want to come with me?"

Alyssa looked down at the ground and muttered, "Seeing her like that makes me sad."

Kaia stood. "It's alright. I'll go check on her, and I'll be right back."

"Promise?"

"I promise."

Exiting the tent, Kaia found Tori sitting exactly where she said she would stay—by a fire with Gregory and some other Crixarian soldiers. The clear sky and bright sun overhead provided some warmth from the cold but not much. Tori heard Kaia approaching and stood. Kaia reached out and took hold of Tori's hands. "Where are we off to now?" Tori asked.

"Alyssa asked me to check on Bethany but... But I already know how she is. She is the same as she was yesterday, and the day before that, and the day before that. Constantly in pain with nothing anyone can do to help her."

With every step they took, the screams got louder and louder. Trying to take Kaia's mind of off it, Tori said, "Let's talk about your magic."

Surprised, Kaia replied, "My magic? Why would you want to know about that? No one has ever asked me to talk about it."

"For one," Tori said, "The elves hate that you have it, and I hate the elves, so there is a good reason. And secondly, it's interesting to me."

"Well... I don't know how to explain it."

"Surely there must be something interesting you can tell me. Ever since I was little, I loved reading the stories about famous mages and all the many things they could do with their powers. I've always wondered about how it all worked for them."

Seeing the curiosity on Tori's face, Kaia smiled and tried to think of something to tell her. After failing to pick a subject, Kaia simply said, "You can ask whatever you wish, and I will try to answer it the best I can."

Without even having to think about it, Tori asked, "How does it work?"

Chuckling at Tori's enthusiasm, Kaia took a deep breath and tried to answer. "To be honest I don't really know how it works. It's just something I can do. When I want there to be fire in my hand, I concentrate about that, then tighten my arm, and then I have a ball of fire in my hand."

"Does it ever hurt?" Tori asked.

Even though Tori couldn't see her, Kaia shook her head, then answered, "Not unless I do too much. The best way I can explain it is that using my magic would be the same as someone else exercising. The more I practice the better I get, but if I do too much it drains me, and I could die."

Nodding her head, Tori pondered Kaia's words before asking another question. "Is that why at Sternz it took two elven mages to bring a meteor down from the sky?"

"Yes," Kaia answered. "If either one of them had tried to do that by themselves they would have drained their bodies of energy and probably died."

"Too bad that didn't happen," Tori chuckled. "That would've made things a lot easier. Has there ever been a time when you couldn't use your magic?"

"Unfortunately, yes. It was uncomfortable and even a little stressful when I couldn't use it."

"What happened?"

Kaia rubbed her hands together. "When I was little, Bethany and I were playing in the gardens one summer day when I tripped and fell. I tried to catch myself on the ground but ended up spraining both of my hands. As long as my hands were hurt, I couldn't use my magic, and even though I've always felt it was a curse to have it, it was stressful to think I might never get to use magic again."

Bethany's agonizing screams grew too loud to ignore even from several tents away. Kaia led Tori toward Bethany's tent.

"When will it be over?" Tori asked.

With sorrow in her voice Kaia replied, "When mother had Cormorden two years ago, Benjamin said that one of two things will happen. If you survive, you fall into a deep sleep to make up for being constantly awake and screaming, or your bones snap and you have only a few moments of peace before you die."

As they reached the tent, Bethany's screams were almost too much for Kaia's soul to handle. Her hands trembling, she took one step, but then fear of what she might see made her hesitate. She had not been allowed to see her mother when she contracted Cormorden. All the horrible stories she had ever heard about Cormorden rushed into her thoughts.

Tori felt Kaia's fear and hesitation and reached for Kaia's hands and whispered, "If you do not wish to go in, you do not have to. I will find out how she is and be right back."

"No, this is something I must do. She is my sister, and I need to see her."

Taking several deep breaths Kaia readied herself for what she might see. With Tori beside her, Kaia walked toward the entrance of the tent. Two Vicar's Chosen stood motionless guarding the entrance, unfazed by the screams. Pushing aside the flaps, Kaia saw Bethany strapped to the table with a rag stuffed in her mouth. Her eyes were wide open, bloodshot, and swollen as her entire body thrashed under the straps, her skin a pale grey that showed most of her veins that almost looked black. Bethany's bloody fingernails had clawed grooves into the table. Kaia spotted several rags drenched in blood on the floor. Benjamin and Alezzia sat on each side of her, watching her.

Alezzia looked up and saw Kaia, then stood and walked toward her. "This is no place for you. You should be with Alyssa."

Not able to take her tear-filled eyes away from her sister, Kaia was barely able to reply. "She wanted to know how Bethany was. So I said I would come check on her."

Alezzia sighed, laid her hands on Kaia's shoulders, and looked directly into her eyes. "Go back to Alyssa. You don't want to be here if Bethany doesn't survive."

Suddenly Bethany's screams stopped. The shaking and thudding against the table stopped, and Bethany lay motionless on the table.

Rushing forward to her sister's side Kaia begged, "Please, please be alright. Don't die, please don't die."

Alezzia smiled with relief as Benjamin replied, "Your sister will live. We all would have heard her bones snap if she was going to die. Now Bethany will sleep. Could be for a few hours—or days—but Cormorden has run its course. She will survive."

Alezzia hugged Kaia and said, "I'll will take you back to Alyssa. There are things that we need discuss."

Kaia wiped the tears from her eyes and walked back out of the tent followed by Alezzia and Tori. As they exit, they saw that both Crixarian soldiers as well as Tarians had gathered around to hear of Bethany's fate.

Alezzia spotted General Izak and Captain Harrison and addressed them. "Your Princess has survived Cormorden. She lives to see another day." Cheers and clapping began to echo through the camp at the sound of the good news. Raising her hand for silence, Alezzia continued, "At first light we will break camp and once again resume our course for Xanica."

As the relieved crowd dispersed, Alezzia turned to her shaken daughter and said, "Now, there are some things we need to talk about—things you should have been told about long ago."

Confused and slightly worried, Kaia nodded and walked beside her mother with Tori and the two Vicar's chosen following them. Alezzia stopped and turned around to Tori. "I wish to speak to my daughter alone."

Tori's motionless eyes stared forward as she spoke to the Vicar's Chosen next to her, "I don't suppose one of you could escort me back to my quarters?"

Before either could reply, Alezzia addressed both of the Vicar's Chosen, "You two will continue to follow Kaia and me, but at a distance."

With everyone now walking away from her, a baffled Tori said to herself, "Well, I guess I will just stay right here then."

"Mother," Kaia asked. "Why are you acting this way? What is it that you wish to tell me?"

Alezzia sighed, "Now that the stress of Bethany getting Cormorden has passed, a new issue has arrived."

Kaia could see her mother's gaze scan those around them, "What might that be."

"Have you ever heard of someone with Cormorden ever having children after contracting it?"

Kaia searched her memory, "No, I don't think I have."

"Benjamin says that is because one of side effects of Cormorden is making the survivor unable to bare children. No matter if they are a man or woman, no children have ever been born from a person with Cormorden."

Realizing what her mother was about to say Kaia started to sweat as her nerves began to take hold. All she could do was shake her head in disbelief.

Alezzia nodded, "Without a son, your father's lineage, and title as king, would pass to whomever married Bethany, but now that she cannot produce children, the next King of Crixaria, will be whoever marries you. And you will be Queen."

Kaia struggled to find words. She had never once thought that she would be Queen. She had always been told that Bethany would be Queen, and that she would become the wife of a noble in Crixaria. This? This was too much.

Alezzia led them in silence through the camp and past both Crixarian soldiers as well as Tarian paladins. Once they arrived in an area of the camp with fewer people around, Alezzia turned to Kaia and whispered, "I know why you were born with magic."

Stunned at her mother's words, Kaia immediately stopped walking. Her heart raced. Sweat burst onto her palms. She turned to her mother and asked, "Why are you telling me this now? Why not any of the times I asked you before? If you have always known, why did you lie to me for 23 years?"

As Kaia's voice grew louder and louder, Alezzia shushed her daughter and whispered back, "Because your father wanted you to have as happy and as normal a life as you could. He wanted to make sure that you felt that you fit in as much as you could."

Growing more confused and agitated, Kaia paced back and forth trying to make sense of this new revelation. She finally looked her mother square in the eyes and demanded, "Tell me. Tell me right now, and please do not leave anything out."

Alezzia motioned for them to continue walking. Kaia complied and Alezzia quietly explained, "As you know, I was not born a noble. I was born to a small and very poor family that lived alone in the woods close to the city Ashton. For generations my family had stayed isolated from the rest of the world, only going into the village for supplies. One day I traveled with my mother to Sternz for flour, and tomatoes, and seeds. That's when your father saw me. He used to say that from the first time he saw me he knew that he would marry me. Even to this day many of the nobles in Crixaria despise me for not being of noble birth, but they all loved and respected your father, so they went along with it. No matter how much I tried to push him away back in those days, he persisted in trying to win me over. And even though I tried to hide my feelings, I fell for him almost instantly.

"But there was one thing that terrified me—one thing that I believed would turn him away from me, so I hid it for several years until the day he asked me to be his queen. To my surprise he did not care. He said that he loved me for me, and that nothing would ever change that."

Kaia asked, "What were you afraid of telling him? What were you trying to hide? What is wrong with me?"

"Nothing is *wrong* with you. Don't ever say that again. When Bethany was born the idea of her having magic wasn't even a thought, and at first we didn't think you did either, but as you know that changed."

Kaia begged, "Mother you are not making any sense. Please just tell me. I deserve to know the truth."

Barely nodding her head, Alezzia looked around to make sure no one was within earshot before leaning in close to Kaia and whispering, "Kaia, you have elven blood in your veins."

Horrified, Kaia struggled to remain standing. In disbelief she whispered back, "No! That's not possible. All the elves have ever wanted to do is kill me. The elves hate everyone that isn't one of them. I can't be part elf."

Continuing to explain, Alezzia gently pulled Kaia close to her and said, "I know it's hard to believe, but it's the truth. Your great-great-grandfather was a full-blooded elven mage who traveled here and fell in love with a human woman. Your great-grandfather was born a half-elf and did not have any magic. He lived to the age of 507 and only had one child, your grandmother. She also found love, and she and your grandfather, may they rest in peace, had me. I could live to be around 125.

"You and your sisters will age the same as any human. I am only one-eighth elf so my ears are shaped normally for a human. With you only being one-sixteenth elf, I never thought that your great-great-grandfather's magic could be in you, but I was wrong. Your father knew you would feel like an outsider your entire life because of your magic, and he didn't want you to feel even more alone as part-elf."

Struggling to hold back tears and standing motionless with a blank stare, Kaia whispered, "Why are you telling me this now?"

Still holding her daughter close, Alezzia answered, "Because now that your father is gone, my enemies will use all they can to prove me a false queen. If that happens, they will try to dethrone me, possibly kill me as well as you and your sisters for not being of a noble family in addition to being part elf. I wanted you to know so that in case it is discovered you will be ready for whatever happens. Please, do not tell your sisters. I will tell them when the time is right, but for now this stays between us."

Still struggling to cope with what she was just told, Kaia replied to the only thing that made sense to her right now, "If you think some of the nobles are going to try to dethrone you, why leave Sternz? Why let the nobles run Crixaria while you are gone?"

Alezzia's normal, serious demeanor of returned. "Because not all of the nobles are against me. For 500 years the Allister family has ruled Crixaria, and many nobles want to continue that legacy. With my absence from Sternz, our enemies there will be revealed—and dealt with."

21

Kassandra and Liam strolled through the hectic streets of Bakea. Keeping their ruse going, Kassandra had her arms wrapped around one of Liam's, and she had a bright smile on her face. She looked upon Liam's face and became agitated with his normal brooding expression. Once again, she pinched his side, and he flinched. She whispered, "How many times do I have to remind you to look happy?"

Grunting because his side hurt, Liam bit his tongue as he replied, "Well maybe if you didn't pinch my side every ten steps, I might be a little happier."

Pleased that she annoyed him, Kassandra giggled, "You need to enjoy yourself today. The third day of the festival is an all-day feast. We will get to eat all the food we can get our hands on. There is no reason you can't be excited for it."

As if ignoring her on purpose, Liam didn't answer. He scanned the crowd, looking for any signs of trouble. Irritated, Kassandra decided to tickle his ribs. Instantly Liam snickered and jolted to the side, bumping into an elderly elven woman. Kassandra could barely contain her laughter as Liam apologized, "I am so sorry ma'am."

As the elven woman sneered at Liam, he turned back to see Kassandra about to burst into laughter. "I never knew you were so ticklish."

Before Liam had a chance to say anything, Kassandra smiled and lowered herself and positioned her hands in front of her, ready to tickle Liam again.

As Kassandra stepped toward Liam, he pointed a finger at her and insisted, "Don't you dare!"

"Oh I'm going to, and you can't stop me."

Inching closer and closer to Liam, Kassandra's smile widened, but before she could pounce, a little girl yelled with joy, "Liam! Kassandra!"

At first horrified to hear their real names, they both soon relaxed when they saw little Lyla running toward them. She ran to Liam first, and he knelt down just in time for her to hug him tighter than he expected. As soon as Kassandra approached, Lyla ran and hugged her too.

Happy, but confused, Kassandra smiled at Lyla, "It's good to see you too. Are you all by yourself?"

"No, Mommy is right behind me."

They looked up and saw Numeri, franticly searching for Lyla. Numeri wasn't in her elven uniform but rather in heavy leather clothes topped with a warm fur cloak. "Lyla? Lyla where are you sweetie?"

Seeing Numeri's worried face, Kassandra let go of Lyla, raised her hand in the air drawing attention to herself, and shouted, "Lyla is here with us Numeri."

Upon seeing Kassandra wave at her, Numeri rushed toward them. Lyla turned to Numeri, "I had to come say hi, Mommy. You told me it's rude not to say hi to friends."

The upset expression faded from Numeri's face. With a gentle and caring smile she replied, "I guess I have, haven't I. But please don't run off on your own like that again without letting me know where you are going."

As Numeri lifted Lyla up into her arms, she looked around at all the people passing by and said, "You know, you were lucky that Kassandra and Liam were here. You wouldn't want to accidentally run into Tantabus next time would you?"

Gasping at the name Lyla shook her head and replied, "Oh no."

Remembering the name, Tantabus, from somewhere before,

Kassandra turned to Liam and said, "I know that name. Didn't you tell me about that?"

Barely giving any effort in reply Liam stated, "No."

"Oh, I remember now," Kassandra said with cheer. "Gregory, I think, said something about a Tantabus one time. But I can't remember what."

Gently swaying Lyla in her arms, Numeri explained, "Tantabus is no more than a bedtime story we elves tell our children to scare them. The *Elven Nightmare* we call him."

"Can I hear the story again mommy?" Lyla asked.

Numeri chuckled, "Sweetie you know it'll scare you again. And I'm sure Kassandra and Liam don't want to be bothered by it."

Kassandra, knowing that Liam would agree with Numeri, decided to reply first, "Oh it won't bother us at all. I'd like to hear about this Tantabus."

As she stroked Lyla's hair, Numeri began to tell the story, "Tantabus, the Elven Nightmare, once struck fear into the entire Elven Empire. This beast ravaged the heart of Azara for absolutely no reason. Going from village to village, town to town with only one thing on its mind—blood. The men, women, children, even the old and infirm all were slaughtered by Tantabus. For months Tantabus's blood trail grew thicker, until one night Prince Domatin caught up to the monster. A furious battle ensued that cost the lives of many fierce elven warriors, but in the end the Prince Domatin prevailed and is even here in Xanica to protect us now."

Intrigued by this Tantabus character, Kassandra nodded her head and said, "An interesting story. Sounds like Tantabus was quiet a menace. No wonder you use it to frighten the children."

"Mommy," Lyla interrupts. "Why didn't daddy want to come today?"

"He said he was feeling sick and was going to take a nap."

Lyla pouted, "But he didn't look sleepy or sick. Can I go get him? I think that would make him happier."

Numeri smiled. She knew Lyla would not let this go. "Oh alright," she said. "We will go get him together."

Lyla jumped out of Numeri's arms and Lyla bolted off in the direction of her home. Numeri turned to Kassandra and Liam, "Well, I guess we are going to get Clark. Will you two be at the feast tonight?"

Kassandra again replied before Liam could say anything, "Of course we will be."

Numeri hurried off after Lyla. Kassandra wrapped her arms around Liam and asked, "Well what would you like to do now? Should we go to the feast or walk around for a bit more?"

Liam looked bothered more than usual as he grumbled, "I don't care."

Frustrated at Liam's tone, she led them forward while fussing, "Seriously? Now you listen to me. We are supposed to be madly in love and about to be married. Do you know exactly how hard it has been for me not to go run off to the tavern for a little bit of fun? No, I don't think you do. All you have done these past few days is stay grumpy, when that is not what you are supposed to be doing. All I ask is that you smile every now and then, especially when we are out in public."

Kassandra noticed Liam trying to hide his sadness behind his normal demeanor, but a little bit poked through as he replied, "It's difficult to break out of my role."

"Your what?" Kassandra asked. "What do you mean, your role?"

Continuing to survey everyone around them Liam responded, "Vernon is our leader. He comes up with the plans and knows the best way for us to accomplish what we need to. Konar is our support, both physically and mentally. If anything needs to be lifted or pushed out of the way he is one to do it, as well as providing some sort of small life lesson when we need it. You provide us with excitement. You are always doing whatever you can to make sure we are always positive, and as friendly as you are, everyone likes you. Me... well when things get too bad or if someone is too difficult, it's my job to kill whoever or whatever is in our way. I'm just a killer. That is all I will ever be."

Seeing past his brooding façade, Kassandra noticed the depression in his voice, but she refused to agree with him. With a sincere smile, she nudged him to look at her. Once their eyes met, Kassandra replied, "That's not true."

"No?"

Kassandra took a moment to make sure Liam didn't look away before she answered. "No. You're not our *killer*. You are our *protector*."

A confused look appeared on Liam's face, "What do you mean, *protector*?"

"I know that anytime I get in a bad situation, as long as I have you beside me everything will be fine." For the first time, Kassandra saw Liam smile. Not just any smile, but one that a person cannot hide. Then she added, "Now don't make me start singing the Now and Forever song. Because I'll do it, right here in front of everyone, and draw as much attention to us as I can."

Before either of them could say anything else, a shout pulled their attention away. "All hail Phyra! All hail the Governess!"

Phyra, dressed in her long blue and white gown and accompanied by only one guard, walked through the streets greeting the people of Bakea.

"Oh crap," Liam muttered.

Confused, Kassandra questioned, "What? What's the matter?"

Casting his eyes toward Phyra, Liam replied, "Do you see the woman guarding Phyra? That's Tauriel."

"Who?"

Liam looked around for somewhere to hide as he explained, "She was the elven officer at Sternz I saved from Zafrinia's men. The only time you two met was in the warehouse when it was on fire, so I doubt she will remember your face, but if she sees me our cover will be blown."

As Phyra and Tauriel got closer, Liam spotted a merchant's stand and turned to walk behind it . Kassandra stood with the crowd gathering to greet Phyra. She noticed how the citizens, both human and elves, all praised and loved Phyra. So much so that Phyra felt comfortable with only one person guarding her. Through the crowd, Phyra saw Kassandra, stopped, and made her way toward her. Kassandra was taken aback by this turn of events.

Halting directly in front of Kassandra, Phyra looked her over head to foot and said, "Hello beautiful. I don't think I have seen you in my city before."

Dumbfounded, Kassandra finally managed to reply, "It is a pleasure to meet you, Governess. I have heard so much about you."

"Please," Phyra responded with a smirk. "A woman as beautiful as you can call me Phyra."

Nervously chuckling Kassandra bowed and replied, "And you may call me Mary."

"I like that name," Phyra said. Then Phyra took Kassandra's hand, raised it to her lips, and gently kissed it. Smiling sensually, Phyra whispered, "I hope to see you again soon."

As quickly as they appeared, Phyra and Tauriel disappeared back into the crowd. Liam walked back to Kassandra and asked, "What was that all about?"

"I think the Governess has taken a fondness to me."

22

Once again, Vicar Matthew addressed the ambassadors from Vetin along with Ovkon the dwarf. "So, gentlemen, are we in agreement?"

Ovkon and Edek nodded their heads, but Johnathan and Francisco paused. Mathew gave both of them a quick stern look and repeated, "Are we in agreement?"

"We agree," they reluctantly mumbled.

With a contented smile, Matthew looked at everyone and said, "Good. Now let us review each of our parts in this matter. I will go first." Clearing his throat and grabbing a parchment of paper off the table, he read aloud, "Tarium will aide in this war both financially and militarily. The bulk of the infantry will be made up of my paladins numbering in total of 300,000, while the rest of the paladins will protect the supply lines feeding our armies as they march toward Azara. I will send 100 Vicar's Chosen along as well to provide security to our leaders on the field and to take care of any sensitive matters. Tarium will also provide both Crixaria and Vetin with any financial support in matters relating to the war at an interest of 10 percent to be paid within 20 years."

Setting his parchment back on the table, Matthew motioned toward the ambassadors from Vetin to read theirs. Francisco and Johnathan looked at Edek and glared at him to read it. Grabbing the parchment, Edek read, "Vetin and her people will be the primary source of food and livestock for the armies. Vetin will not weaken its southern border with the Dwarves but will provide an additional 100,000 soldiers to the human army, including Rangers as well as light cavalry. We will send 100 of the 200 light cavalry we brought as an escort to this meeting to rendezvous with the advance force moving into Xanica. They will inform them of what happened here as well as support them in any way they can."

Now everyone looked at Ovkon who already has his parchment in his hands. Looking mischievously at both Johnathan and Francisco, he read, "The Dwarven Alliance of Schelmar will continue its assault on the Elven Empire. We agree to put as much pressure as we can on them to distract them from the humans. Upon the arrival of the humans in elven lands, both humans and dwarves will simultaneously push further into Azara and finally meet up at the city of Serpent's Pass, before pushing together towards the capitol."

As Ovkon finished, Johnathan scoffed in reply, "How are we going to know for certain if Crowned Lord Gothvar accepts these terms?"

Ovkon took a deep breath and replied, "Because all he will be agreeing to do is to continue what we have been doing for years. Nothing extra will be required from us."

Feeling as if everyone was finally content with their roles, Matthew stood. "Now let us part ways and see to it that we keep our promises."

They all rose and one by one walked through the door and into the halls of Sternz's Citadel and went their separate ways. Matthew remained at the Citadel. As he watched the others depart he thought, "Now we might actually have a chance."

23

Konar sat by a small, crackling fire with Blaster across from him staring off into the woods toward Bakea.

"Only a few more days," Konar assured Blaster.

Blaster released a small puff of air through his nose but didn't move from the position where he had been sitting the past few days.

Glancing at the three horses tied up next to a tree, Konar reached for the last remaining jug of wine, but to his utter disappointment, the jug was empty. "Out of wine," he said. "I hope they are done soon too."

Konar tried to relax by the fire, but soon restlessness overtook him as he pondered what might happen tonight. "I don't suppose you want to do anything do you?" he asked Blaster.

Moving only his eyes, Blaster looked at Konar then looked toward the sounds of the festival. "That's alright," Konar yawned. "Maybe I'll fall asleep before it happens this time."

Minutes pass. Konar's eyes become heavy and he began to lower his head. A barely audible whisper jolted him awake. He scanned his surrounding area, but nothing had changed. Blaster was still looking out toward Bakea, and the horses still stood calmly tied up to a tree. Hopping up to his feet, Konar walked over to the horses and began to pillage through the travel packs.

"I must have packed more," he mumbled to himself. "I can't possibly be out of alcohol."

Another inaudible whisper put him on edge even more and he

started begging to himself, "No, no, no, no, no. Come on please, I need something!"

Another whisper, this time audible, in the voice of a small child, said, "You let us die."

Konar froze, petrified at what was happening around him. For the first time in years, Konar had not had a drink of alcohol before he fell asleep, he knew this would be the worst night in years, and he was terrified.

Now another whisper from behind him, but a man's voice—one he recognized, "You let me die."

The hair all over his body stood up and he felt sick in his stomach. Shaking, he turned around, inch by inch, second by second, until he spotted it. Several feet away in the woods stood Sal, Konar's first human friend, staring emotionless back at him. Sal stood with skin as pale as the moon, and his armor, similar to the Tarium volunteers, bloodied around the gaping hole where an elven spear skewered him.

"I'm sorry," Konar cried. "I tried, but there were too many."

"You let me die," Sal whispered.

Closing his eyes, Konar repeated, "I'm sorry." When he opened his eyes, Sal was gone.

Relieved, Konar took several deep breaths to try to regain his composure, but the child's whispers returned, "You let us die."

Now recognizing the sweet voice, Konar fell to his knees, staring off into the woods doing his best to hold back the tears threatening to flood his eyes. Again, the child's whisper echoed, "You let us die."

Konar hunched over, clasped his hands over his ears, and shook his entire body trying to block the whispers. But even with his ears covered the child's whisper continued, "You let us die," over and over again, growing louder each time. "You let us die!" Becoming more agitated, "You let us die!" Repeating itself without stopping "You let us die! You let us die! You let us die!"

With so much pain in his heart, Konar reared back on his knees and stretched toward the night sky. He screamed as loud and as long as he could. As his scream faded, he looked down, but his eyes locked onto two more figures in the woods. Standing side by side were Tamar, his wife, and Quanet, his daughter, standing mere feet away. Their skin was grey and many bloody wounds covered their bodies. Unable to hold out any longer, streams of tears poured down his face.

"I'm so sorry," he wailed. "I should've known it was trap. I should've known to stay behind and make sure you were safe."

"You let us die," whispered the child.

Staring back into Quanet's lifeless eyes, Konar whimpered back, "I tried to save you, to save you both, but I wasn't fast enough, wasn't strong enough."

Konar raised his hands and tried to grab theirs but his hands passed through thin air. Overcome with grief and sorrow, he lowered his head and whispered, "Not a day goes by that I don't think of you both. Not a day goes by I don't I feel the hole left in my heart after you two were taken from me. And not a day goes by that I don't think about your smiles and your laughter."

When he looked back up, Tamara and Quanet were no longer staring at Konar but pointing toward the camp where he and Blaster were staying. All at once the sounds of the night came back to him, one in particular, Blaster's deep menacing growl. Konar glanced at Blaster and then back to Tamara and Quanet but they were gone. Konar snapped back into reality and rushed to Blaster to see what was wrong.

Blaster stood firm, focused on something in the woods. At first Konar didn't see anything, then a slight sliver of movement caught his eyes. His eyes widened as he made out the outline of a Wraith of Colubra watching them.

Looking back down at Blaster he noticed that Blaster was about to take off toward the wraith but Konar petted Blaster's head and whispered, "Stay. It could be a trap."

The wraith turned and ran back toward Bakea. Blaster's growl stopped and Konar said, "Whatever happens next is not going to be pretty. They now know you and I are here."

24

At the center of Bakea near the large stage and forum, countless humans and elves danced around bonfires as minstrels and dancers performed on the stage. Kassandra sat beside Liam enjoying a plate full of food next to a warm fire. Liam finished his cup of water and Kassandra turned around and smiled at everyone gathered, people of all ages, both humans and elves, dancing and cherishing each other's company. The cold night air didn't seem to bother anyone as they all smiled and laughed with each other.

Seeing Kassandra's happy but curious face, Liam asked, "What are you thinking about?"

Continuing to gaze at the festivities, Kassandra replied, "Do you ever wonder if maybe one day the whole world could be like this? Where no one cares what race you are and just be happy?"

Without even a moment of thought, Liam responded, "No."

Kassandra fussed, "Not even a little bit of optimism from you tonight?"

"You asked me a question," Liam answered. "And I told you what I thought."

Laughing to herself and shaking her head, Kassandra continued, "Alright then grumpy, care to elaborate on why you think that?"

"Because all of this is a lie. Look around us. None of this will last. This façade of a festival and town are just here to distract from the real world. The real world where men like Domatin can act however they want without any thought of consequences. Bakea does nothing more than make people forget about their problems. Since we have been here have you thought about any of the villages we passed through on our way here? The villages where even innocent children were slaughtered?"

Guilt rushed over Kassandra as she realized that she *had* forgotten about the villages, and that maybe Liam had a point. After a moment of thought she said, "Well what about the Governess? From what we have heard, Phyra Ophidian seems like she actually wants to help Xanica and everyone living here."

Again without a second thought Liam answered, "I doubt it. She is an Ophidian, just like Domatin. She may seem innocent and caring, but she is only here for as long as it suits her. If the resistance had ever gained a strong foothold here, she would have fled back to Azara. If she truly cared for the humans living under her reign, why did the elves start massacring entire villages again? All Xanica and Bakea are to her are places where she can indulge herself in whatever fixations she wants to without repercussions."

Even though Liam's words seem to make sense, Kassandra refused to let her spirits sour. She jumped up out of her seat, turned to Liam, and smiled. "Sometimes you need to just let go and forget about the bigger picture. Now come on—dance with me?"

Caught off guard by Kassandra's request, Liam struggled to focus, "I uh, I don't dance."

"I promise it'll be fun," Kassandra pleaded.

"I'll be fine here, but you go ahead."

"Suit yourself, "Kassandra said and then walked to a nearby group of people dancing. Liam marveled at how Kassandra could walk up to strangers and blend in so easily. Then he wondered why he becomes so nervous when she asked him to do things with her, or why he couldn't find the time or the words to tell her how he felt. *Even if I did tell her, why would she have any feelings for me? She is a noblewoman from Vetin while I'm just a dirty ex-slave.*

"Liam!" He heard Lyla yell.

Liam looked up just in time to open his arms to catch her. She leapt into his embrace as Numeri approached.

"Where is Miss Kassandra?" Lyla asked.

"Dancing," Liam pointed to Kassandra.

"I'm going to go dance with Miss Kassandra," Lyla informed her mother.

"Have fun, but don't go out of my sight."

Numeri turned to Liam, "Too tired to dance?"

"I'm not a good dancer. Where's Clark? I thought you two went to get him?"

"We did," Numeri replied. "But he must have caught a bug today at his stand. He even left early and has been pale all day, refusing to come to the festival tonight because he said he was sick."

"Mommy," Lyla shouted. "I'm hungry. Can we go get food?"

Smiling, Numeri walked toward Lyla and Kassandra, and then stopped to look back at Liam, "You don't have to be good at something to have fun. Having fun is not about what your are doing, but about who you are doing it with." Liam simply smiled and nodded his head and watched Kassandra continue to dance to the upbeat music as Numeri and Lyla left to go find food.

Liam's attention was drawn to the Wraiths of Colubra who appeared on the rooftops and to the sudden influx of elven guards patrolling the area. He knew that meant Phyra Ophidian was about to arrive.

Cheers erupted from the center of town. While the music continued, Liam noticed that people were trying to make their way to the Governess. Kassandra walked over to him, sat on his lap sideways, wrapped her arms around his neck, and whispered, "I've got an idea."

"Why are you sitting on my lap?"

"We are soon to be married, remember? We have to keep up our cover, especially now that there is more security watching everyone."

"So what's your idea?"

"Well," Kassandra whispered. "I think we both can agree that

Vernon's plan is terrible. Ambushing a large column of heavily armed elves with only the five of us isn't going to work, but I have a new idea. You saw earlier how the Governess seemed to be attracted to me? I believe I'm going to take her up on her offer."

"You're joking?" Liam blurted.

Kassandra continued, "It's a great idea! She will more than likely take me to a private room in her manor where it'll just be the two of us. Then I'll say that the room is stuffy and crack the window, so you know which room I am in. After I knock her out, you'll be waiting below to catch her, and we can sneak out of Bakea before anyone can figure out what is happening."

Still pondering her words, all Liam could think to ask was, "Then if you plan on trying to seduce Phyra, why are you sitting in my lap where the guards and wraiths can see you?"

"I plan on losing whatever eyes are on me in the crowd, silly. And we can't look like we are scheming here, now can we?"

As the crowd became louder and Phyra got closer to them, Kassandra gave Liam a long hug. "I'll be fine," she whispered. "And even if this goes sour, I know you'll be right outside waiting to come help me."

Kassandra stood up and Liam asked, "What am I supposed to do in the mean time?"

Kassandra said, "Go find Vernon and let him know what is happening."

Kassandra hurried off into the crowd to make her way to Phyra. Not letting her nerves get to her, she focused and took a deep breath. She could see Phyra greeting and dancing with people. Squeezing her way through the final row, Kassandra came face to face with Phyra and the two exchanged bright smiles.

"Mary!" Phyra cried out. "You have no idea how excited I am to see you!"

Kassandra matched Phyra's enthusiasm, "Not as excited as I am to see you. Honestly, I haven't been able to keep my mind off of you since this morning."

Pleasantly surprised, Phyra addressed the crowd surrounding her, "Come now everyone. Do not stop the festivities just because I have arrived. Please go enjoy yourselves!"

The crowd returned to their dancing and socializing. Phyra whispered to Kassandra, "Sorry about that, Beautiful. Now we have some privacy to talk."

Phyra rested her hand on Kassandra's hip as she led them down the street. "So Mary," Phyra began, "What do you think about Bakea and the festival?"

Deciding to be honest, Kassandra replied, "I've honestly never seen anything like it before. It doesn't seem like anyone cares whether you're an elf or a human."

"Excellent!" Phyra exclaimed. "I'm glad you are having a wonderful time. Have you tried any Bakea wine yet? It's the tastiest thing Bakea has to offer." Then Phyra then leaned toward Kassandra and whispered, "Well, maybe second tastiest."

Kassandra laughed and moved Phyra's hand lower. Kassandra smiled, "You get right to the point don't you?"

"No time like the present," Phyra replied. "And besides, your beauty and this cold are making my thighs a bit frosty."

Knowing what Phyra meant by that, Kassandra replied, "Then perhaps we should go warm them up?"

Delighted to hear Kassandra's suggestion, Phyra smiled, "How does it sound if we go to my manor for the night? We can see which tastes better, the wine or..."

"I'd be thrilled," Kassandra said, even though she couldn't help but think of all the ways that this could go wrong.

25

A clouded moon rested in the sky as Vernon stared at the door to a house. Leaning with his back against a building several houses away and in his full armor, he stared long and hard at the door, oblivious to anything and everyone around him. He forgot about the war with the elves and his mission in Bakea. One thought consumed him—Clark.

Knowing the woman and young girl who left the house earlier could return at any moment, Vernon decided he could wait no longer. He strode across the street, and made his way to the door. He noticed candlelight coming from inside the small house. Reaching for the door, he realized his hands were trembling. He clinched them into fists and embraced the anger boiling inside him.

Without a thought of being polite, Vernon pushed against the door and was surprised to discover it was unlocked. Staring into the open area he surveyed the room closely, looking for any sign of movement. The flickering candle caused the shadows in the room jump around, making it difficult to detect movement. Knowing that Clark had probably deduced Vernon's real identity, he decided to try and draw him out. Clearing his throat, Vernon said, "I just want to ask you a few questions."

Nothing moved. Nothing made a sound. Desperate to know the truth, Vernon took one step inside, followed by another, and another until Vernon heard the shuffling of footsteps to his left.

Clark rushed forward at Vernon swinging wildly at him. Vernon stepped back, allowing Clark's clenched fist to catch only air. A quick blow caught the whittler off-guard and sent him sprawling on the floor.

"Why are you here?" Clark demanded as he regained his feet. "What do you want?"

In a seething tone, Vernon replied, "Earlier, when I brought up the Regnier family, you panicked and ran away. Tell me why."

Clark clamped his mouth closed to prevent the words on the tip of his tongue from spilling out.

"Why?!" Vernon shouted again.

"You already know why. Why else would the Regnier family hire a mercenary to track me down?"

"I'm not a mercenary."

"Then why were you looking for me, and how did you even find me?" he asked, glancing to the door leading outside.

"I didn't come to Bakea to find you, but I'm glad I did. The only reason I even spoke to you earlier was because we thought you might be of some help to us."

"We?" Clark questioned. "What is going on? Who are you?"

Anger dripped from Vernon's voice, "I am Vernon Regnier."

All the color drained from Clark's face. Vernon seized the opportunity and hurled himself at Clark, punching him in the jaw and sending him thudding against the wall.

Clark regained his focus in time to avoid Vernon's next punch. As Vernon's fist crashed into the wall, Clark managed to land a punch of his own into Vernon's side. Shaking the pain off, Vernon lunged at Clark and tackled him to floor, smashing the dinner table. Each tried to gain an advantage, but Vernon's superior training earned him the upper hand. Pinning Clark beneath him, Vernon grabbed a leg from the shattered table and held the splintered tip against Clark's neck.

Clark froze. Now almost berserk with rage Vernon shouted, "It was you, wasn't it? You're the monster that forced himself upon my sister!"

Clark's eyes glazed over, and regret crept across his face. If Vernon saw it, he ignored it.

"Wasn't it?" he yelled again.

"It was an accident! I was drunk and chewing on Eacru root. I didn't know what I was doing until after it was over."

"And you just ran away like a coward. You didn't even have the honor to face judgment like a man—like a soldier."

Panic-stricken, Clark shouted back through his tears, "Not all of us were privileged like you. You, so high and mighty, being a nobleman's son and all. You didn't have to work your way up the ranks to become an officer. I did! If a nobleman like yourself had done what I did, he might have stood trial, but the result would be nothing more serious than a slap on the wrist, a small fine, a payment of some sort to the girl's family for the loss of her honor. But I'm a commoner. I would have been executed. I would have been made an example of; paraded as a reason why commoners shouldn't be allowed to become officers."

"And if it was your child, your little girl, who was brutalized by a commoner, what would your response be then? What justice would you demand? How can you live with yourself? You're a monster *and* a coward. I feel sorry for the woman and child who have to live with you and see you every day."

Vernon pressed the splinted table leg deeper into Clark's neck. But the door burst open and Liam walked inside.

"Vernon don't do this."

In disbelief Clark asked, "Liam, you know this man?"

"Don't say a word if you know what's good for you," Liam said without taking his eyes off Vernon. He took a step forward. "Vernon this isn't you. The Vernon I know wouldn't murder even a guilty man without first letting him stand trial."

Vernon fixed his gaze at Clark and said, "He admitted to it. The entire reason I joined the army was to find him, and now that I have him, you want me to let him go?"

Liam squatted down and put his hand on Vernon's shoulder. "If

I were in your position, what would you tell me? You and I both know you'd tell me that the right thing to do would be to make him stand trial. What would your sister want? Doesn't she get the right to have justice, rather than vengeance?"

Vernon's hand trembled as he muttered, "Liam, we both know you wouldn't follow your own advice right now."

"You're right," Liam replied. "If I had a sister and he had done to her what he did to yours, I would kill him. But you are *not* me. Out of all the officers in Crixaria you were selected to lead us, and this *isn't* you. Right now, Kassandra and I need you."

With his eyes filling with tears, Vernon said, "If I let him go, he will run again, and I may never have this chance again."

"He might," Liam answered. "But if he does, then after this war I will help you find him."

"Why?"

A small smile formed on Liam's face. "Because you are my friend."

Slowly Vernon released his hold on the club, and it fell to the floor with a dull thud. Clark let out a long sigh of relief as Vernon stood.

Liam and Vernon walked together out of the house without saying a word, leaving Clark on the floor. Vernon, still shaken and upset, rubbed his side as he asked, "So why do you two need me right now? The plan is to wait until the end of the festival and then strike on the road. How did you even know that I was at that house?"

Making sure no one was around them Liam quietly answered, "The plan has changed, and you're not going to like it. Kassandra has decided the best way to capture Phyra is to seduce her and then knock her out so we can sneak her out of town. I went to Harper's Hall and the owner said you had been asking about Clark. So, I hurried here to check and see."

Taking a deep breath Vernon replied, "Do you two have a way out of the city?"

"No," Liam admitted.

"What about weapons if we run into trouble?"

"No."

"So, let me get this straight," Vernon said. "Kassandra may or may not be alone with Phyra, and she may or may not get a chance to knock her out. Then if she does knock her out the plan is to simply walk out the main gate with Phyra, without weapons and without horses?"

"Pretty much," Liam shrugged.

Vernon pondered their options. After some thought he looked at Liam and answered, "Alright then. But if we are going to make this work, you need to be ready to help Kassandra. I'll make my way to the main gate and find some way to get my sword and shield. Hopefully it won't be too heavily guarded. And I will try to get the gate open and ready for us."

Liam nodded, and walked off toward Phyra's manor. Vernon took a final look at the open door of Clark's house, then turned and walked in the direction of the main gate. That odd feeling washed over him—the same feeling had been ignoring since he bumped into that cloaked wraith in the alley. Vernon scanned his surroundings, and saw a shadowy figure perched on a rooftop above him. The wraith disappeared.

"There's no turning back now," he muttered to himself as he ran toward the main gate.

26

In their full ethereal, scale armor, Domatin and Leontina road their horses along a small dirt road under a moonlit sky. But even with 36 praetorians walking around them and 100 elven soldiers in front and behind them, the silence was maddening. Only the marching of footsteps filled their ears. Side by side on their horses they continued toward their destination—Bakea.

Finally Domatin turned a sarcastic smile to Leontina, "Have you had a good day, Imperator?"

"Why do you care?"

"Because we are friends, are we not? We have spent so much time together these past few months, and I feel like I've known you my whole life."

"I doubt that," she muttered back.

Unflinching, Domatin continued, "You've been rather harsh with me the past few weeks. Any particular reason why?"

Taking a long, deep breath of the cold night air Leontina bitterly replied, "Why are you still here? When Empress Juliana told me that you were to accompany my army to Sternz she said it was because you needed to redeem yourself and grow, but I think the reason you haven't left is not because you needed to grow, but because you are looking for something—or someone."

Agitated, Domatin replied, "Careful with your next words, Imperator."

Now, feeling as she has the upper hand, Leontina continued, "Because if you were only supposed to redeem yourself at Sternz then you should have returned to Azara by now. Which means you must have failed at Sternz. And now we have another problem with your demeanor. You continually boast that you are the greatest fighter we have. Then why is it you did not fight at Sternz? Surely if you are as good as you say you are, you shouldn't have anything to fear if you ran across a certain—someone."

Domatin replied, "I wasn't the one who lost the siege."

Leontina muttered, "Only because of your incessant meddling and your cowardice. If you had simply told me about the Vicar's army, I may have been able to come up with a plan or a trap, rather than be embarrassed and defeated. I have been leading troops for centuries, and it just so happened that my first defeat was the first time you were present. Perhaps *you* were the reason we lost the siege."

Domatin rolled his head around before looking at Leontina with an uneasy smile. "You are so arrogant that you can't see the bigger picture. If I had not been there, the walls would not have fallen, and your defeat would be even more of an embarrassment. Leaving when I did was the only way you had a slight chance of victory. Maybe if you had taken the walls of Sternz faster you could have moved your army inside the walls to fight the Vicar. *Not* telling you about the Vicar's impending arrival was the best thing I could do. If I had told you, both you and your officers would have been distracted from taking the walls. But, let's just say I *did* stay. I would surely have been killed, I can promise you that, and that would have made your defeat not only an embarrassment, but a catastrophe. The famous Imperator Leontina would not only have lost the most important siege for our god Colubra's sake, but you also would have been responsible for the death of a member of the royal family."

Scoffing at Domatin's words, Leontina retorted, "You are just a prince. Ever since Ucidere and the age of the Nezdra, our people have been led by women. The Empress is the absolute ruler, every leader of the Wraith's of Colubra has been a female, and in 15,000 years there have only been three male imperators. Whatever powerplay you are trying to accomplish here, I guarantee it won't work, for you are just a man. You wouldn't even be alive if I hadn't helped your brother find you. The only reason I even tolerate you is because of the respect I have for your mother and brother."

"What? No respect for my sister?" Domatin carefully inquired.

Leontina stared blankly for a moment, caught her breath, and replied, "Heiress Seneca is not empress yet. Perhaps when she ascends to the throne she will earn my respect, but until then..."

"I honestly do wish you saw the bigger picture. You are so blind. Perhaps it is arrogance or blind loyalty, but it changes nothing."

Leontina chuckled, "Is this the part where you threaten that you will be the death of me? You've said that before. I think we both know that it is an idle threat, but if you are going to do it, you had better hurry. We should arrive at Bakea within the hour."

Turning to face forward once more, Leontine sat with a smug smile on her face as they marched toward Bakea. Domatin did the same but he whispered to himself, "Just you wait Imperator. Just you wait."

Sitting in a stiff, wooden chair in the common room of Phyra's Manor, Tauriel struggled to get comfortable as she considered the day's events. The palisade didn't have any breaches, all guards were at their posts, and she had stationed eight guards outside of the room Phyra and the human girl went into. The lateness of the night resulted in a heavy yawn escaping her mouth. She stretched as far back in the stiff chair as she could and started to relax, but jumped to her feet when Isila appeared right in front of her.

Tauriel muttered, "Do you always have to sneak up on me?"

Isila, still wearing her tight, black, leather armor and cowl, quietly stated, "We need to talk."

"What's the matter?" Tauriel asked as she rubbed the back of her neck. "You seem more uptight than normal, if that's possible."

Glancing around the room to make sure no one was listening, Isila answered, "We are both the heads of security during Phyra's stay at this festival. So before I make a decision I respect you enough to get your opinion on the matter."

"What is it? What is going on?"

"I have many wraiths inside the city. I also ordered a few to patrol the woods outside the walls, and one of them has come back with an interesting report. The wraith was patrolling the area near the statue of the Hero of Aclia when she spotted something strange; an orc accompanied by a large black wolf. The orc seemed overtaken with some form of madness, crying and screaming at nothing."

"An insane orc and a wolf. That does seem odd," Tauriel replied. "But why do you want my opinion on this matter? If you feel the need to send some wraiths to take care of it, you don't need my approval."

Gazing deep into Tauriel's eyes, Isila added, "Because the orc had three horses."

Tauriel nodded. "Better be safe rather than sorry."

Just as Isila turned to go give the order, a wraith ran into the room and handed her a scrap of parchment. Tauriel stood in stunned amazement as Isila furiously ripped the parchment into pieces.

"What is it?" Tauriel asked.

"Two men were overheard talking about kidnapping Phyra, with the help of a woman they named as Kassandra."

The pieces of the puzzle clicked into place for Tauriel. An orc, a large, black wolf, two men, and a woman named Kassandra. "They're here!" she shouted as she turned and ran up the stairs toward Phyra's room. "Sound the alarm! Intruders are attempting to kidnap Madam Phyra!"

Isila turned to the wraith who brought the message. "Take care of the orc and wolf. I will go to the main gate. When they hear the alarm whistle, they will panic and try to rush to the gate before we can send more soldiers there, but I will be there to intercept them."

27

With every passing moment Liam grew more anxious. Standing concealed in an alley, he gazed up at a window on the second floor of Phyra's manor. The longer he waited the more troubled his thoughts became. He wondered if this was even the right window, or if Kassandra was in danger. With cheerful festival-goers and occasional patrols of elven soldiers passing by, Liam contemplated whether he should storm the manor and find Kassandra, even without any weapons. After what seemed an eternity, he finally spotted Kassandra peeking out the window.

She stuck her head out, looking side to side for Liam, who quickly stepped out of the shadows. Kassandra smiled and loudly whispered, "I hope I didn't keep you waiting for too long."

Making sure no one was around, Liam walked across the street and under the window, "Hurry up! We need to get going as soon as we can."

"Where's Vernon?" she asked.

"He is at the gate making sure we have a way out."

Kassandra retreated back into the room out of sight, but seconds later she whispered, "Get ready."

Liam looked up as Kassandra dropped Phyra, wrapped in sheets, out the window and down to Liam. He was barely able to stretch his hands out before Phyra came crashing down on him. Kassandra suppressed a quiet giggle as Liam got the breath knocked out of him when he and Phyra fell to the ground.

Kassandra hopped out of the window and landed on her feet next to Liam, "The mighty Liam, brought to his knees by the Governess."

Groaning, Liam shoved Phyra's unconscious body off him. "You could have given me a bit more warning. I wasn't ready."

"Uh huh," Kassandra laughed, "Quit stalling we need to get going."

Liam picked Phyra up, then stopped and asked, "Am I going to carry her by myself?"

Still smiling Kassandra replied, "Of course. I can't be expected to do all the work."

Liam hid his grin and slung Phyra over his shoulder. "She isn't dead is she?"

"Of course not," Kassandra said. "She just hit her head against the wall. Really, really hard."

They turned a corner where dozens of festival-goers were talking with each other under the night sky. Kassandra pondered aloud, "Perhaps we should try the alleys?"

Considering their options, Liam replied, "Some of the alleyways probably have wraiths in them, but out here we just have to calmly walk by without anyone asking questions."

But sounds begin to echo behind them that forced their course of action. Distress arrows screeched in the night air and people began to shout. They both looked back at the window and saw Tauriel pointing at them.

Liam said, "Run!"

More distress arrows screamed above them as they ran toward the gate, street by street, corner by corner. Crowds of human and elven families rushing to get back to their homes provided extra chaos to cover their retreat. When the finally reached the main gate, they saw Vernon fighting two elven soldiers. The corpses of five dead elven soldiers littered the ground around them.

With his sword and shield in his hands, Vernon focused on the elf in front of him, while the second was trying to move behind him. Vernon pivoted and swung his sword sideways, slashing the soldier across the chest. As the elf dropped his sword and shield Vernon turned and faced the final elf, who upon seeing Kassandra and Liam running toward the gate, dropped his sword and ran into the chaos of Bakea.

With the elves out of the way, Vernon turned his attention to the gate. Sheathing his sword and dropping his shield he summoned all his strength and began to push against one of the large, wooden doors. Grunting and straining, the heavy door creaked open. As Kassandra and Liam drew close he gave one final shove, and the gate opened wide enough for them to exit Bakea.

"It's good to see you both," Vernon panted as they all paused to catch their breath. The respite lasted only a moment as Vernon spotted a Wraith of Colubra—not just any wraith, but one with strands of raven black hair, and a small black cape on her right shoulder.

Vernon snatched his shield from the ground. "You two get out first," he ordered. "Phyra is the reason we are here. Get out, find Konar, get your weapons, and get out of here."

Liam nodded and began to maneuver himself and Phyra's body through the gate, but Kassandra protested. "No! We are not going to just leave you here to die."

"I'll be right behind you," Vernon promised. "Just as soon as I deal with this wraith."

With a frustrated growl Kassandra turned and followed Liam out of the gate. Vernon planted his feet and raised the top of his shield to the bottom of his eyes as he readied his sword. The nervous sweat on his forehead chilled him as the wraith drew closer. Vernon could see her eyes, filled with determination and focus.

The wraith did not appear to be in a hurry, sure of her kill. But from an alleyway someone charged, catching her entirely off guard. At a dead run the man grabbed her around her waist, and picked her up, and hoisted her above his head. He ran with the flailing wraith straight toward a large stone building. The wraith managed to draw one of the daggers at her side and plunged it deep into the man's back just as he hurled her head-first into the stone building. The man fell to his knees in pain, but turned to Vernon and cried out, "Go!"

Though the man was shadowed by the night, his features began to take shape. The man struggled to stand up and Vernon finally saw the face of Clark.

"Go," Clark insisted. "I'll buy you as much time as I can."

Vernon started toward him, but arrows whizzed past him, and dozens of elven soldiers, led by Legatus Tauriel, were running toward him.

"You're dead if I leave you here," Vernon said through clinched teeth. They both watched as the fallen wraith regained her feet, and wobbled unsteadily. She was stunned, but still alive.

"I'm dead no matter what," Clark replied. "I ran like a coward once. At least this way I die like a man, like a soldier of Crixaria. Now go!"

Vernon nodded and sheathed his sword. He snatched one of the elven swords on his way through the gate, and once outside he shoved the door closed and pushed sword diagonally into both gates, pinning them shut. Vernon turned and ran as fast as he could up the hill and into the woods toward where Konar and the others should be. He paused for a moment to see if the gate remained, but his eyes were drawn to a wraith jumping down from the wooden palisade. Vernon was sure it was the same wraith that Clark had attacked.

The wraith locked eyes with Vernon and she began to shamble toward him with both of her daggers drawn. The effects of the blow to her head appeared to be wearing off, and she moved faster than Vernon thought possible.

If he could reach the rest of The Unbroken Vernon thought he might stand a chance, but after reaching the top of the hill, he saw no one. He had no choice but to turn and ready himself for a fight. He didn't have long to wait. The wraith cleared the top of the hill and walked inexorably toward him. She was close enough that Vernon could make out fresh blood dripping from one dagger. He knew the substance dripping from the other dagger was cobra venom.

The wraith spoke, "Vernon Regnier. A Crixarian noble who leads The Unbroken, the saviors of Sternz. I wonder how true your reputation is without the rest of your little group."

Vernon replied, "It'll be the death of you. I've killed many of your fellow wraiths before. I'll have no problem killing another."

Even with a mask covering the lower half of her face, Vernon could tell the wraith was smiling. "Do you want the honest truth, human? All of our best wraiths are dealing with matters concerning the dwarves. There has not been a single wraith engaged in human lands during this entire war who was beyond middle rank in my order. Until now."

Vernon eyed her curiously. "*Your* order? So, you are the leader of the Wraiths of Colubra?"

The wraith stopped walking and with her dagger still in her left hand she reached up to her right shoulder and cut off the cape, revealing large, white, scale armor, enough to cover her arm, overlapped from her wrist to her elbow and from her elbow to her shoulder.

Isila stared at him, like a snake waiting to strike. She raised her daggers and pointed them at Vernon. "Your journey ends here human."

Isila darted toward him, faster than Vernon imagined possible and attempted to stab his neck and chest. Barely able to lift his shield and dodge out of the way, Vernon didn't have time to recover before Isila launched her second attack. She brought both daggers down hard and swift at Vernon's head, but he rolled backwards out of the way.

Breathing heavily, Vernon decided to go on the offensive. Swinging left and right, high and low, he attempted to land a blow on Isila, but she easily deflected all of them. Even with his strength Isila parried his attacks. He swung his sword at Isila's right side, but she lowered her body and raised her arm, deflecting his sword into the air. Isila thrust the blood-covered dagger up toward Vernon's face, slicing his cheek.

Isila muttered, "You are lucky I didn't sheath my dagger after I killed your friend. I won't make that mistake again." She wiped the blood off on the leather covering her thigh, then dipped it back in its sheath, recoating it in cobra venom.

Straining for an advantage, Vernon feigned an attack on her left while bashing her with his shield, but Isila saw past his ruse. She sidestepped away from the shield and slashed down at Vernon's wrist. He dropped his shield in time to avoid the venom-laced daggers, but realized he was now on the defensive.

Holding his sword with both hands Vernon parried Isila's rapid attacks, but for each blow he managed to deflect Isila was able to scratch his armor—not deep enough to touch his skin, but deep enough to leave marks.

Being driven backward, Vernon struggled to maintain his footing on the uneven terrain. His foot caught on a tree root and he fell to the ground hard, losing grip of his sword.

Isila shoved her foot onto Vernon's throat. Raising her daggers high in the air she muttered, "From the rumors I heard, I expected far better."

Before Isila could deliver the final blow, a familiar yell grabbed Vernon's attention. Liam leapt toward Isila with a sword in each hand.

Now it was Isila's turn to be on the defensive. Vernon watched in amazement as Liam forced Isila back even quicker than she pushed him back. Left, right, up, down, Liam's blades slit the night air. Isila was barely able to deflect the blades from her body. Reaching the top of the hill, Liam could see a garrison of elves exiting Bakea and rushing toward them.

Knowing he didn't have time for a drawn out fight, Liam dropped the sword in his left hand and punched Isila in the face. Before she could recover, he kicked her in the abdomen, sending her tumbling back down the moonlit hill.

Vernon regained his feet as Liam recovered his sword. They

exchanged nods as Konar, Kassandra, and Blaster appeared from the backside of the hill. Liam said, "They are sending soldiers. We need to go. Now."

"Agreed," Vernon replied. "But where are our horses?"

They looked at Konar, who was carrying Phyra's wrapped up body, but who also sported a heavily bloodied left arm.

"The horses are gone," Konar said. "But that is a story for another time. I will tell you once we get moving."

"Where do we go?" Kassandra asked.

Vernon pointed to his right and began to lead the way deeper into the frigid forest. "First of all we need to lose the elves that are following us," Vernon said. "After that we can worry about where we need to go. Konar what happened to your arm?"

"Wraiths," Konar replied. "Two of them. Blaster killed one, but the second managed to cut me with his dagger and scared the horses away. Not to worry. Not enough venom got in me to do any serious damage. I might throw up. A lot. But I'll be able to keep whatever pace you set."

A distress arrow flew overhead. The elves had crested the hill and spotted them. Vernon could see only around 30 elves chasing them. But that arrow would alert all the others from Bakea to their location. They needed to leave before things got overcrowded.

28

The morning sun peeked over the Crixarian and Tarian encampment as everyone began to gather their things and pack their tents. Kaia groaned as she pulled the last tent stake out of the ground, still groggy from lack of sleep and annoyed at the cold weather. After yesterday's hard march they arrived near Black Marsh, and the stench of the marsh made it difficult for them to sleep. But the encampment was awake with movement as everyone hurried to get ready to leave. Kaia saw Bethany walking nearby and started toward her, eager to talk to her sister and ask her how she was feeling, but as soon as Bethany saw her, her face soured, and she turned to walk off in another direction.

Kaia was upset as she realized, *This is how Bethany will act from now on, just as Mother did when she recovered from Cormorden, incessantly scornful and disappointed at everything.* Kaia's sadness grew as she remembered all the times she and Bethany had laughed and played together growing up, and she knew that they would never share those kinds of moments again. She prayed they would at least have some happy times in the future.

Her reverie was broken by the sound of soft footsteps and she turned to see Benjamin smiling at her. He tried to offer comfort. "She will get better in time. If I remember correctly it took your mother a week before she even spoke to anyone other than myself."

"Benjamin, why are you so different than my mother and Bethany?"

"What do you mean?" Benjamin replied with his eyebrow raised.

"I know you had Cormorden. It changes those who survive it, yet you appear unchanged. If anything you seem more hopeful, and not as hateful."

Benjamin paused for a moment before he explained. "To be sure, when I first recovered, I let the memory of pain consume me. I did many hurtful things, particularly to those I felt had harmed me. But then I met someone who had survived Cormorden long before me, and that encounter set me on the path I'm on to this day—to help restore order to this world, and to help other survivors as well."

Even though she always felt uneasy around him, Kaia smiled at Benjamin. Before she could say anything else Alyssa ran up from behind, jumped onto her back, and gave her a big hug.

"I found you!" Alyssa shouted.

Laughing as she pulled her sister around, Kaia replied, "Yes you did. Are you having fun this morning?"

"Yes," Alyssa nodded. Then Alyssa saw Benjamin and skipped over to him, "Mister Benjamin, will you please tell me another story?"

"Another one?" Benjamin questioned. "Which one would you like to hear about this time?"

"Can I hear about The Hero and the Nezdra again?"

Benjamin laughed and leaned down to pick her up, "Didn't I tell you about them yesterday? And the day before that?"

Alyssa smiled ear to ear, "But those are the best stories. I'm going to grow up and be just like the Hero of Aclia."

"She wasn't the nicest of ladies, but alright, I'll tell you," Benjamin said. With a gentle smile he began the story once again.

Kaia returned to packing her tent but paused when Gregory and several other Crixarian soldiers began pointing and laughing at a nearby spot on the ground. Kaia followed the pointing fingers toward someone's tent and supplies, but noticed that it wasn't set up from the night before. Then she looked back at Gregory and the soldiers to see them pointing up at the ridge behind her, toward Black Marsh. Off in the distance Kaia could see a figure slouching over and sulking at the peak of the ridge. It didn't take long for her to figure out who was up there and remembered the story Tori and Gregory told her about Zafrinia.

Kaia grabbed a fur blanket and walked toward the ridge.

"Whoever you are go away," Zafrinia sniffled.

Kaia stopped and observed the grass beside Zafrinia all ripped out of the ground. She knew that even if she didn't admit it, Zafrinia was feeling completely alone and needed someone to talk to.

Kaia tried to gently place her hand on Zafrinia's shoulder to comfort her. "Don't touch me," Zafrinia ordered. Kaia could see how red and swollen her eyes were.

Kaia looked past Zafrinia toward Black Marsh. Though it had been almost three years since the battle, there were still remnants on both sides—pieces of elven scale armor twinkled in the morning sun, and swords and spears stuck out of the murky wetland.

Looking helplessly out over the marsh Zafrinia quietly sobbed, "He died out there, all alone and confused." She tried to grab more grass, but it had all been torn out, adding to her frustration. Instead she grabbed a handful of dirt and squeezed it with all her might. "I know what you're thinking—that I deserve this; that I had it coming. Well, you're wrong. I deserve so much worse. I know you've heard the story. Who hasn't? I left the man who loved me more than life itself, a man that just wanted to make me happy and smile and laugh—for someone else. But how was I supposed to know his family would turn on him? I thought that if I hid the truth from him it would soften the blow. How could I know that his own mother would call him a failure, just because he didn't have an answer for her?"

Zafrinia's head fell forward. She released her grip on the dirt and covered her tear-stained face. "No one told me how much I would miss him. No one said how painful it would be to forget the sound of his laugh, or the way he looked at me with that stupid grin on his face. I tried to make things right. I went to find him. But all I found was his ashes as his family wept. They all screamed at me. They blamed me for his death. But I know the truth. Sal didn't die here at Black Marsh. Sal died the day he found out why I had left him."

Zafrinia's hands moved from her face to her hair and she yanked at it. "And everyone down at that camp just laughs at me for it. None of them understands how much I wish I could change what happened. None of them understand the worst part of it all."

Though Zafrinia said to not touch her, Kaia couldn't help but feel as if that was what she needed right now. Kaia knelt behind Zafrinia and gently placed a hand on her back. Tears rolled down Zafrinia's face as she explained, "Four days before I left him, his mother almost died. He never knew his father, so she was all he had. After hunting in the woods, he came home to find her on the floor, with hand marks imprinted on her neck. Thieves had broken in and when she resisted, they tried to kill her. I can't imagine what it must've felt like for him to hold his mother's body, thinking she was dead. I left him alone during his time of need, and she turned on him so quickly, just because I lied."

Zafrinia let go of her hair and placed her hands back on the ground as she continued to cry. "It wasn't the elven spear that killed him. It was me. Princess, if you ever find someone that loves you, don't ever let it go. Love isn't always about some mystical spark or about material things. It's about how that person can make you feel, comfortable, that you can trust them beyond even yourself."

Zafrinia's sobbing finally stopped and Kaia felt her grow tense. "I swear to you, Sal, I'll make things right. You always supported me and told me that I was the best warrior you knew. I promise one day that'll be so, and I swear that I'll kill every last elf I get my hands on for taking you away from me, taking you away before I could make things right."

Kaia looked back at the camp and saw that everyone was about ready for the day's march. Tenderly rubbing Zafrinia's back, she whispered, "The army is about to leave. If you want, I will help you get your things ready."

Zafrinia stood up and sniffled, "Thank you, Princess."

Kaia smiled and wrapped the fur blanket around Zafrinia's shivering body, and they walked back down the hill to the encampment.

29

The Unbroken continued to run across the frosted ground through the thick woods of Xanica with distress arrows screeching above them. Kassandra saw that Konar, whose normally dark green skin had paled from the cobra venom in his veins, was struggling to keep up with the rest of them as he carried Phyra.

"Vernon!" she shouted. "Konar needs to rest. We've been running all night. If we keep this up we will all be too tried, cold, and hungry to keep going."

Through winded breaths Konar mumbled, "I'm fine, I promise. I can keep going as long as you need."

Vernon glanced back and was startled by how bad Konar looked. He didn't think the cobra venom could kill Konar, but it was clearly taking its toll on him. But Vernon could also see the elves, though distant, were slowly but steadily gaining ground.

"How much longer can you keep going?" Vernon asked.

"As long as I need to," Konar replied, but none of them believed he could continue this pace much longer.

Phyra, who had awaken in the night sarcastically muttered, "If it'll make things easier, feel free to drop me off anytime."

"Quiet," Liam coldly said.

Phyra began to respond but for the first time she got a good look at Liam's face and instantly fell silent. She whispered, "You. How are—You can't be here."

Vernon struggled to reach a decision. If they slowed their pace, the elves would soon overtake them. Yet Konar was fighting the effects of cobra venom, and all of them were nearing exhaustion. They needed rest, food, and water.

"Vernon," Kassandra insisted. We can't keep this up."

"I know I'm…" Vernon's voice trailed off when he saw their escape route. "Quickly, this way!"

The thick Xanican forest faded as they approached the spot Vernon was looking for—the top of a hill overlooking a large valley where thick fog covered the ground and only the tips of the trees were visible.

After taking a moment to catch his breath, Vernon began to walk down the hill and motioned the others to follow him. "We are going to lose them in the fog."

Liam, Blaster, and Konar quickly followed, but Kassandra hesitated. This forest was bigger and darker than the one they just ran out of. "We'll lose them alright," she mumbled to herself, "if we don't lose each other in the fog first."

They all stuck close to one another as the fog grew thicker. They were only able to see a few feet in front of them. Vernon motioned for them to gather around him at the stump of a broken tree. As they gathered close, he whispered, "We already lost the other two parties that were chasing us, so this has to be the last one. I estimate no more than 30 of them behind us, so here is what we are going to do. Konar will stay here with Phyra and gather his strength while the rest of us go take out the elves."

From behind them they heard the shouts of the elves urging each other to stay close and not get separated.

Vernon continued, "Keep moving at all times. Pick your targets when they are alone. One by one. Run in, kill. Run back into the fog. Confuse them. Strike from different areas at different times."

Liam nodded. He and Blaster disappeared into the fog. Konar plopped Phyra onto the cold ground, then dropped down beside her, resting on the stump. Vernon walked into the fog, leaving

Kassandra who balked while studying the trees and grey fog. "I don't like this idea. I don't like it one bit. *Go into the foggy woods Kassandra,* they say. *It will fine,* they say." But she put one foot in front of the other until she too disappeared from sight.

The elves, no more than three feet apart from each other, walked slowly in the fog with weapons at the ready and shields raised.

"Argh!" cried out an elf. Those nearest found a bloodied body lying on the ground.

Then another cry, and an elf fell, pierced through the heart by a silent arrow. Seconds later another terror-filled scream cut through the fog, accompanied by a wolf's fearsome growl. The search party discovered the third body with his neck ripped apart.

"Form up," an elf ordered. Another elf yelled back, "Quiet you fool, they will hear us."

The first elf called back, "But if we group together then they won't…" Her words stopped, and they knew she had fallen.

A clash of steel to their left followed by a growl created a sense of panic among the elven soldiers, who were now shaking not just from the cold but from fear—fear of what they cannot see. One by one they fell, until only a handful were left.

Kassandra drew another arrow and readied it on her bow, prepared for when the fog revealed another elven soldier. Hunched over and slowly walking on the frosted ground that crunched under her feet, she stopped and listened for any sounds, but heard nothing. No voices. No clashing of steel. Nothing but the silence of the fog. Her grip tightened on her bow, and her eyes moved franticly back and forth trying to find any signs of movement. It was no use. All she could see was the fog shrouding everything. Her breathing quickened, and she wanted to call out to the other members of The Unbroken, but she too feared what she could not see. Memories of how her sister was lost in the woods clawed at her mind.

Her grip on the bow loosened, and it fell from her fingertips. Stumbling backwards she hit a tree and slunk down. Sitting at the base with her back against the tree and her head ducked between her knees, she rocked side to side staring at the frosted grass. The trees began to close in on her, and her eyes filled with tears. Hopelessness was about to overtake her, but then she felt familiar breathing on the back on her neck, breathing that she immediately recognized as belonging to Blaster. All her fear melted away as Blaster moved around in front of her, wagging his tail, and looking at her with his piecing, yellow eyes.

Kassandra laughed with relief and hugged Blaster as tight as she could. Blaster let out several low barks, and in moments Vernon and Liam arrived, their weapons covered in blood. Wiping her nose as she picked up her bow, Kassandra smiled and said, "Can we please leave now?"

Liam and Vernon had a pretty good idea what had just happened, and silently agreed to not bring it up. Liam knelt and scratched Blaster behind the ears. "Find Konar," he whispered.

Blaster let out one bark and began to sniff the air. After picking up the scent, they all followed the large wolf until they arrived where Konar and Phyra were still sitting by the tree.

Even in his weakened state Konar smiled when he saw Kassandra. "You got lost in there, didn't you?" he laughed.

"Not a word," Kassandra snapped.

Liam helped the orc to his feet, then asked Vernon, "What now? Do you even know where we are?"

Vernon shook his head. "Right now we are going to eat and rest. Tomorrow we will worry about finding our way back to the resistance."

30

Standing atop a hill overlooking Bakea with the morning sun hidden behind a cloudy sky, Domatin and Leontina stared disapprovingly at Isila and Tauriel.

Tauriel lowered her head and spoke first, "I am sorry Imperator."

Leontina sighed and replied, "It's alright Legatus. We will get Madam Ophidian back. Hopefully sooner rather than later."

Hiding a smirk on his face, Domatin turned to Leontina and said, "This must be embarrassing for you Imperator. First you lose the siege of Sternz and now a member of the royal family has been abducted from your soldiers. Perhaps your reputation was exaggerated."

Grinding her teeth Leontina cringed as she coldly replied, "If you hadn't made things difficult with the orcs, we could have been here sooner."

"Oh, I'm sorry," Domatin answered cynically. "I apologize for getting more orc mercenaries to fight for us. Next time I'll just leave everything to you and your incompetence."

As Leontina was about to yell back at Domatin, several elven soldiers walked up the hill along with a female elf in chains. The soldiers forced the woman down on her knees in front of them. Leontina took several steps toward her.

"State your name," Leontina demanded.

Looking Leontina in the eyes the woman responded, "My name is Numeri Haya."

Leontina squatted down in front of Numeri and asked, "You have been accused of sheltering our enemies and aiding in the kidnapping of Governess Ophidian. How do you respond?"

Numeri's head lowered, "Not guilty. I did not know who they were. I was just being polite and friendly to people who helped my daughter."

Domatin stepped forward and added, "That doesn't explain why the human you shared a bed with allowed them to escape."

Her face blank with defeat, Numeri muttered, "Clark was a simple, kind, and loving man for years. He wouldn't do something like that without a reason. They must have forced him somehow, or else he wouldn't do something like that."

Domatin leaned close to Numeri and said, "But you did know he used to be a Crixarian officer, didn't you? I guess it's a good thing he is dead, one less human to fight later."

Numeri stayed silent out of heartbreak, anger, and confusion. Domatin stood up straight and proclaimed, "Even if she didn't aid them, she is without a doubt guilty by association. Everyone needs to be on their guard in these trying times. You will be made an example of, to make sure others do not repeat your mistake."

"You have no authority to do that. She is a soldier under my command," Leontina protested.

"Tell me, Imperator, who has the most authority in Xanica?"

Leontina slowly answered, "That would be Madam Ophidian."

Domatin continued. "Since my cousin is no longer in a position to be Governess, doesn't that mean the next immediate royal family member gains the Governor's spot?"

Leontina's fists clinched. "Only until a new Governess is appointed or the previous one is returned."

A single victorious laugh came from Domatin. "But for right now, I am the Governor of Xanica, which means that I *do* have the authority."

Domatin turned back to Isila and Tauriel and said, "We cannot allow the humans in Xanica to believe we are weak. They have to know that any town or village that aids the resistance will be punished. All elves living in Bakea will be allowed to pack up their possessions and move elsewhere. You will confiscate all the wealth any humans have and send them on their way. Any half-breed mongrels are to be rounded up to be sent back to Azara as slaves, and then I want you to burn Bakea down to the ground."

Numeri raised her head and pleaded, "No, you can't do that! Please!"

Domatin backhanded Numeri across the face, then knelt down in front of her, grabbed her chin, and said, "As for you, you will accompany the next convoy to Azara and be left exiled in the Eacru Wastes. Maybe you'll die in the desert, or maybe the orcs will kill you—either way is fine with me. As for your half-elf daughter, she will come back to Azara and be one of my slaves. Perhaps she will scrub my floors, or maybe I'll use her to entertain guests when she is older."

Numeri screamed as she lunged at Domatin, but the soldiers held her down. Domatin looked back at Tauriel and Isila and motioned for them to make their way down to Bakea. Isila started down the hill immediately, but Tauriel hesitated and looked at Leontina, who nodded, sending Tauriel down the hill as well.

Satisfied with his decision, Domatin turned to Leontina and said, "Now Imperator, tell me about any spies we have in the resistance."

31

Malum grunted as he stood in his tent looking over reports spread across a small wooden table, growing more upset by the moment. "Jenna! Get in here now!" he shouted.

Jenna, a young resistance fighter with dark skin and thick black hair, quickly entered the small tent, "Yes sir?"

Slamming his fists on the table, Malum shouted, "Are you sure these reports are accurate?"

"They are, sir," Jenna replied with confidence.

Malum crumpled a handful of the reports in his hands before tossing them angrily around the tent. "Two weeks!" he yelled. "It's been two weeks since Phyra was abducted, and you're telling me no one has seen her or The Unbroken since?"

Jenna moved to the table and replied, "Sir, we have scouts out looking for them day and night. We will find them."

Still frustrated, Malum slammed his hands on the table, "We have to find them before the elves do, or else..."

His words trailed off as Makay stuck his head through the tent opening. Makay, with dirt and grime all over his face, had the widest of smiles as he said, "I found them."

Malum bolted around the table and exited the tent. Looking around he saw no one, just the fur tents of the resistance. He turned to Makay and scolded, "Makay, this is not the time for one of your jokes."

"It's no joke," Makay continued to smile. "They were half-frozen and starved when I found them. They are resting at the camp center, getting warm by the fires, and eating some fresh food."

Malum stomped toward the center of the camp. A crowd of resistance fighters had gathered around The Unbroken, but when Malum appeared, they quickly parted. Cheers and clapping echoed throughout the camp as Malum approached the fire where Vernon, Konar, Liam, Kassandra, and Blaster all sat shivering and sipping steaming soup. Phyra was still rolled up in her dirty sheets.

Makay came running up and patted Malum hard on the back, "I told you they could do it."

Malum glared at the gathered men and woman and shouted, "Alright everyone, the show is over, get back to your posts! Jenna, escort the Governess to a guard tent. Put her in chains, and post sentries. I want 20 of our best guarding her at all times. And keep eyes on her at all times."

"Yes sir," Jenna replied before leading Phyra away.

Malum exchanged appraising looks with The Unbroken, then nodded and said, "Rest up. We will talk once you are warmed and fed." Without another word he turned and stomped back to his tent.

Makay grabbed a small log and plopped down on it. He smiled as he said, "It's a good thing I found you when I did. Another day or two and your beautiful faces may have been covered in frost."

"Thank you Makay," a shivering Vernon replied.

Kassandra finished a sip of her steaming soup and griped, "Malum didn't even say thank you. I'm not sure he was happy to see us with Phyra."

Makay explained, "Oh, he was quite impressed to see you. In all the years he's been here, I've never once seen him nod his head that much. Trust me, he is impressed. Not that he would ever admit it. You five managed to achieve something that we have been trying to do for years. For the first time we finally have an advantage in taking back our home."

Konar, already on his third bowl of soup, looked around at the hundreds of resistance fighters and asked, "Why are so many of you gathered in one spot? I thought the resistance was supposed to be spread throughout Xanica. Where, exactly, are we?"

"We are in Clearwater Forest, about 50 miles from the Crixarian border. And, yes, normally we are spread out, but Malum has ordered all resistance members to meet here," Makay answered.

"Why would he do that?" Kassandra interrupted.

"A few days ago," Makay continued, "We received news that a large army is approaching Xanica, made up of Crixarian and Tarian soldiers."

Vernon immediately interjected, "That's surprising that they are coming here so soon. How many are in the army?"

Makay shrugged his shoulders. "We have no idea. But we have sent people to rendezvous with them, and hopefully a week from now they will be here."

"That's good news," Konar added while swallowing the last bit of soup.

Makay nodded in agreement, then a sorrowful expression crossed his face. "There is something else."

As they all listened closely, Makay continued, "After you captured Phyra, her cousin Domatin became the new acting governor. And his first order was to burn Bakea down as an example to any who would help us. We don't know the details yet, just the rumors of death."

Silence fell over the group as they remembered all the burnt villages and charring corpses they witnessed when they first entered Xanica. Vernon thought about Mr. Harper and his daughters. Kassandra remembered the inn keepers, Clara and Titus. Liam thought about Lyla, then he dropped his bowl of soup and let it spill on the ground while he just sat and stared into the raging fire.

Konar saw the concern and despair on his friends' faces. He asked, "What happened to those who lived there?"

"All elves who lived in Bakea were allowed to pack up their belongings and leave. All humans were stripped of their wealth and personal items before supposedly being allowed to leave. But we have reports that the elven army actually may have slaughtered many of them. And those of mixed blood have been taken back to Azara as slaves."

Liam stood up and kicked his bowl into the fire, then turned and walked away. Blaster followed him.

"Is he going to be okay?" Makay softly asked.

Kassandra answered, "I honestly have no idea. He has been acting strange ever since we came to Xanica. I'm going to go check on him."

As Kassandra walked off after Liam, Vernon took a long breath, looked at Makay and inquired, "Once the army arrives, what is the plan?"

"Malum is figuring that out right now, but there will be much to do once they arrive, so you all should rest and regain your strength while we wait."

Kassandra walked around the camp hoping to catch sight of Liam. After several fruitless minutes she at last saw him striding up a hill outside of camp toward the forest, with Blaster walking beside him. Rushing to try and catch up, she shouted, "Liam stop!"

Either he did not hear her or he chose to ignore her, but he kept walking without turning back.

Kassandra stopped at the last tent at the edge of camp and watched as Liam and Blaster disappeared into the darkness of the forest. Part of her said to go after him, but another reminded her of her sister and what could be waiting in the woods. She took one step forward before fear overtook her, and she turned around and walked back into the camp, reassuring herself as she walked, "He'll be fine. Blaster is with him."

32

"Are we there yet?" Alyssa asked Kaia for the 13th time.

Riding horseback together with the army surrounding them, Kaia smiled back at her sister, "Almost." Pointing to a ridge less than a mile away Kaia continued, "You see that ridge? The scout said that once we pass that, we will be at the new campsite."

Kaia looked around them at the army marching forward under the morning sun. Crixarian soldiers were leading the way while the paladins from Tarium brought up the rear. In the center near them, the new soldiers from Vetin numbered only 100, but Kaia could tell they were some of Vetin's elite cavalry. Their horses were smaller and less heavily armored than Crixaria's cavalry, but Kaia knew that these horses were much faster and more mobile. The soldiers wore thin, smooth, white, steel armor with padded, white leather underneath.

Tori rode beside Kaia and Alyssa. "I'll be glad once we are finally there. I'm tired of being on this horse all day every day."

Zafrinia rode slightly behind them. "If you'd like, I can take you to the woods, and we can find out how far you can get without any eyes."

Tori's grip tightened on her reigns, but before she could say anything, Kaia said, "We are almost there, so there is no point in starting another argument." Tori and Zafrinia both sulked in their saddles but remained quiet.

Alyssa began clapping her hands, "We are here!"

A thick forested pass led through the ridge, and they could see resistance fighters guarding the way as the Crixarian soldiers passed through. Ahead of them they could hear the sounds of cheering, and once in sight of the camp itself they saw resistance fighters hugging and shaking hands with the Crixarian soldiers. Then Kaia caught a glimpse of a familiar face—Kassandra, who was walking into a tent with a young man from the resistance. Kassandra caught sight of Kaia, smiled, and waved. Kaia smiled and waved back, happy to finally reach the camp.

Zafrinia sarcastically muttered, "Who would have thought she would be doing that?"

"Hush," Tori snapped.

Once they reached the center of the camp, Kaia spotted Vernon standing alongside Makay and a man she did not know, a man dressed in slightly rusted Vicar's Chosen armor. Blushing as she locked eyes with Vernon, her heart raced with excitement. But then a stray thought drove all her happiness away. *What would he say if he knew I am part elf?*

That negative thought disappeared as Vernon walked toward her with a smile and said, "It's so good to see you again, Kaia."

Before she could reply, Alyssa stretched her arms out at Vernon and reached around his neck. Laughing, Vernon lifted Alyssa off the horse and hugged her. "It's good to see you too, princess."

Alyssa turned to Kaia and with a sly grin said, "He hugged me first."

Behind them they heard horses' hooves as Queen Alezzia, Benjamin, Bethany, and General Izak reached the center of the camp, followed by six Vicar's Chosen. Alezzia wasted no time addressing Vernon, "Who is in charge here?"

With Alyssa still in his arms, Vernon replied, "My Queen, may I introduce Malum. He is the leader of the resistance." Vernon motioned to the man standing beside Makay.

As Malum took a single step forward, the six Vicar's Chosen immediately stepped in front of Queen Alezzia with their heavy maces and steel shields ready for combat. "Is there some sort of problem here?" Queen Alezzia demanded.

In a monotoned response, one of the Chosen answered, "That man is the coward, Malum. A former member of our order. Disgraced as a man of low faith to the One."

Unflinching Malum took one step forward and pointed a finger at the Vicar's Chosen who spoke. "You are the cowards. While you hid behind the riches of Tarium and that corrupt ruler, Vicar John, I was helping those who believed in the One. I'm glad Vicar John is dead. He was an old, corrupt, lying, pathetic excuse of a man who only cared for his own self-interests rather than those of the faith."

Before the situation could get out of hand, Queen Alezzia nudged her way past the Vicar's Chosen and cleared her throat. "Malum is it? I'm sure we have much to discuss, and I hope without any further disagreements."

With a scowl on his face and still eyeing down the Vicar's Chosen, Malum muttered through his teeth, "Follow me. And if your officers would care to accompany us, I will explain the situation."

Alezzia nodded and followed Malum up a small hill and into the larger command tent, followed by Izak, Benjamin, and several resistance fighters including Makay. Vernon turned to Kaia and said, "I'm sorry, but Malum insisted that I be in there with them."

"I would expect you to," she answered with a smile.

Izak leaned out of the tent and yelled, "Captain Harrison, Lady Sophia, Zafrinia, Gregory. I need you four in here."

Vernon gently touched Kaia's hand before making his way into the tent. The space inside the tent was clearly divided—those from Xanica stood on one side of the table while everyone else stood on the other side. Vernon crossed to stand beside Makay, who was staring open-mouthed at something on the other side of the table.

Vernon turned to see a young woman walk into the tent behind Gregory—a young girl with long golden hair and a soft, angelic face. Her armor was that of the Vetin cavalry, but upon her breast plate was a small golden dove.

Vernon grinned and discreetly elbowed Makay's ribs. Makay startled and asked, "What did you do that for?"

Vernon whispered, "Because you were standing there with your mouth open, like a fool."

Makay closed his mouth, then whispered back, "She is an angel, nothing less. And I am going to marry her one day."

"Just like that?" Vernon asked with one eyebrow raised.

With an innocent grin Makay replied, "I doubt even you could resist my charms if I turned them on you."

Once everyone was in place, silence filled the tent. Each person appeared to be waiting for someone else to start. Izak took the initiative. "I am General Izak of the Crixarian army and I—"

Malum interrupted, "How many soldiers did you bring?"

Izak paused, unaccustomed to being interrupted. At last he replied, "Fifteen thousand."

The morale of the resistance fighters in the tent quickly faded. Even Makay let a slight frown show. "That's it?" Malum asked.

A cynical smile crossed Alezzia's. "I see. Our help is unwelcome. Perhaps I should just turn my army around and go back home."

Sensing the situation about to get out of control, Benjamin added, "We apologize for such few numbers. The decision to come here was made rather rapidly and this was the best we could do in such short time."

Malum, not even glancing at Benjamin, continued to stare at Alezzia while harshly replying, "I was not talking to you, whoever you are. I was talking to your Queen. If I wish to speak to you I will let you know."

"Benjamin is my head advisor and you will treat him with dignity and respect," Alezzia informed him.

"Respect?" Malum questioned, "How am I supposed to respect *him*, let alone *you*, a mother who would drag her three children to a war torn country?"

Trying to ease the tensions in the tent, Makay spoke up, "Thank you for allowing The Unbroken to come here. They managed to capture Phyra Ophidian, the elven Governess."

Everyone looked at Vernon who nodded, but said nothing. Izak looked back to Malum and said, "Well that's good news. Have you tried to ransom her back for any kind of leverage?"

"No," Malum coldly answered. "Neither have the elves offered us anything for her, and if they were going to offer anything, they would have already sent an emissary to find us." Malum looked to Jenna and nodded for her to speak.

Jenna stepped forward. "It took two weeks after The Unbroken abducted the Governess for us to locate them. That was just over a week ago. Once we received word that your army was approaching, we assumed it was with a force large enough to push the elves out of Xanica once and for all. So, we sent word to all of our agents and gathered all of our fighters, hoping to defeat the elves in a single, decisive battle."

Malum interrupted, "But now the elves know exactly where we are. They have gathered all their forces, reportedly more than 35,000 foot soldiers, and are marching toward us as we speak. We have 7,000 able men and women ready to fight, combined with your 15,000 that makes our strength up to 22,000. Most of my soldiers are either veterans of the old Xanican army or experienced fighters, but even with the advantage of fighting for their homeland it won't be enough. The only reason you were able to hold out as long as you did at Sternz was because of your walls. We don't have that luxury here. So, if anyone has any ideas, let's hear it, for I have none, and I would rather not have to face the fact that I may have gathered everyone here just to die."

Izak answered, "First things first. We need intelligence. I suggest we send out scouts to determine the exact location of the elven army. Once we know their location and strength, we can make a more effective plan. In my experience worrying about what you don't know or can't control doesn't help anyone."

Silently nodding, they all agreed. But Malum fixed on Alezzia with a dead stare. "If we fail, just know that all here in Xanica will blame you—and you alone."

33

Kaia walked through the camp at night with a hood over her head. After five days of waiting, and of being followed by Vicar's Chosen wherever she went in the camp, Kaia strolled through the shadows, watching people. This was the first time in her life she had been away from Sternz. Her entire life, she had felt caged up and guarded behind the walls of Sternz. Now she wondered, why shouldn't she be allowed to see how people behave and act when they are not around her, not forced to be polite because of her royalty?

Shifting through the shadows, Kaia moved from tent to tent, hiding and watching the people. Some were full of joy, sitting and drinking with old and new friends. Others sat in silence, fearful of what might happen in the next few days. After turning another corner Kaia thudded against someone, and fell backward onto her bottom. She looked up and saw Benjamin looking down at her.

"What are you doing by yourself at this hour of the night?"

Kaia regained her feet, and began dusting off her backside. "I just wanted to see what the people are really like. This is my first time away from Sternz, and mother still refuses to let me be free."

Benjamin gently placed his hands on her shoulders, smiled, and said, "Your mother is just trying to keep you safe."

Sighing as she continued to watch the soldiers, Kaia looked down at her feet and muttered, "You are going to tell mother about this, aren't you?"

When she chanced a look at Benjamin's face she was surprised to see him shaking his head. "Don't worry. Your secret is safe with me."

"Really?"

Benjamin nodded, "Just because your mother and I both have Cormorden, do not think that I don't like to have a bit of fun every now and then. Follow me, I think I know where you might find some interesting people to watch."

Kaia, surprised but also excited, walked side by side with him through the shadows of the camp. Watching every group of people she could, Kaia noticed how young and frightened the Crixarian soldiers seemed compared to the paladins and the resistance fighters. "Why do all of our soldiers look scared?" she asked.

Benjamin paused for a moment to let some soldiers pass, then he answered, "Most of the soldiers from Crixaria are new recruits. Most of Crixaria's veterans are either too wounded to fight or have been given leave to go see their families before we march to Azara. If I had to guess, only one out of every 15 soldiers we brought from Crixaria have ever been in a battle before."

Kaia watched closely how Benjamin moved, and she noticed how well he could blend in with the shadows. She whispered, "You've done this before haven't you?"

"Oh, many times," he answered. "Like you, I sometimes venture alone to observe people. Of course, I have different reasons than you but still, it is something we have in common."

"What are your reasons?"

"I wasn't always a doctor. I used to be a soldier, and I like to try to measure how well a person can fight and survive during war. You may consider it an odd thing, but it is what I do."

Intrigued, Kaia probed further. "What do you mean by that?"

"As dismal as it sounds, most of the men and women you see here will not survive this war. Not just from battle, but from hunger, disease, and even wild animals. Of those who do make it back home, most will be changed for the worse, scarred by what they have seen. Only true warriors will be the ones who make it back home. I try to figure out who will survive and who won't."

Struggling with his answer and all that it implied, Kaia decided to change the subject. "You were a soldier? Did you fight against the elves at the start of the war?"

"I was a soldier long before that—I'm quite a bit older than I look." He stopped and faced Kaia. He deliberately pulled his shirt open revealing a long, grotesque scar across his chest. "This was given to me by a very vengeful woman."

"Who was she?"

Benjamin closed his robe and forced a rueful smile. "Another story for another time. Perhaps I'll tell you once the war is over."

They continued to walk through the camp until finally Benjamin stopped by a tent overlooking a large group of people below. "Here we are," he whispered.

Kaia looked down the hill and saw familiar faces. Vernon sat in the center with dozens of soldiers from all countries around him. Konar sat beside him drinking from a large jug of mead. She then saw Kassandra laughing with Sophia Lati, the leader of the Vetin light cavalry, and lastly, she managed to find Liam sulking in the shadows behind them petting Blaster.

Kaia watched Vernon and heard everyone congratulating him on capturing Phyra Ophidian. Benjamin knelt beside her. "Tell me, Princess Allister, are you a wolf or a sheep?"

Kaia raised an eyebrow. "I don't know what you mean."

"Take everyone down there, for example. Out of the dozens of them, only a handful of them are willing to do what it takes to end this war. You see, most people like to consider themselves wolves, but when push comes to shove, they will mindlessly do what everyone else around them does—just like sheep. Look at her," he said, pointed at a young resistance fighter. "Watch her closely, and you will see what I am talking about. Her posture and expression are those of a leader, but if you watch her eyes you'll see that she is constantly searching for approval—like a sheep. If you are ever watching someone without their knowledge, their eyes will always tell you who they truly are.

"Now consider Vernon and Unbroken. You know first-hand how effective they were in the defense of Sternz. Each one is a wolf in their own right—dangerous, to be sure. But when you put wolves together in a pack, they become something more, something—extraordinary; a force to be reckoned with. So I'll ask you again. Are you a wolf, or a sheep?"

Kaia pondered for a moment before answering. "Perhaps after I've had time to figure out who I am, and what I can do, then we will know. For now, I believe I'm more of a bird just released from her cage."

Benjamin's lips hinted at a smile.

Kaia watched as Kassandra walked away from the fire with a good looking young paladin, and she noted by looking at Liam that this made him both agitated and sad. Benjamin, saw it too and said, "Now you see what I'm talking about. If you had been down there with them you would have been distracted, and you would never have seen that. But from up here you can truly tell who a person is and what goes on in their heads. That is why getting the high ground in a fight is advantageous. It allows you to see all that is happening."

Kaia's eyes landed on Sophia Lati. She realized from the first moment she had seen her, Sophia wore a soft, sad smile most of the time. "What do you know about her?"

"A great deal," Benjamin answered. "She and Kassandra are both noblemen's daughters who grew up together in Vetin, becoming quite close. A few years ago Sophia contracted Cormorden. It affects a person, as you well know. After that their friendship began to fade. They say that she is the best horse warrior that has ever lived. I'm sure that claim will be put to the test shortly. Her fellow soldiers have begun to call her the Maiden of Vetin."

"The Maiden of Vetin? Why do they call her that?"

"After she recovered from Cormorden, Sophia Lati gathered a small band of light cavalry and for three years, scoured Vetin for bandits. They say she never lost a single soldier in that time, and practically rid Vetin of bandits. Someone of her skill will be valuable to our fight."

"You are different than most people with Cormorden. Rather than growing scornful and hateful, you seem more understanding. Sophia also seems different—sad, rather than angry or condescending. What makes her so different?"

"We are who we are," Benjamin answered. "For most, Cormorden makes them hate everything they once loved. I found a higher purpose. For Sophia—I cannot say. Perhaps she misses her old life, before Cormorden."

Screams from the far side of camp shot through the chilly night air. Chills run down Kaia's spine as she recognized the scream of her little sister. She took off running toward to the sound, then the screaming stopped which made Kaia run even faster than she thought possible.

Making it back to the tent she shared with her sister, Kaia shoved her way past the gathered crowd and saw the corpses of the four Vicar's Chosen that were guarding their tent. She pushed into the tent where Izak and her mother were comforting a sobbing Alyssa. In the center of the tent, Bethany stood. Blood covered her night dress as she hovered over the body of a man with his head bashed in.

In Izak's hands Kaia saw the same mask as the figures in the woods were wearing weeks ago—a black painted sack with white paint outlining and crying from the eye-holes. Kaia took a closer look at the man's face, and was shocked to see human ears.

Izak explained, "From what Bethany has said, he wasn't trying to kill Alyssa, he was trying to take her. Alyssa's screams awakened Bethany, and—well—you can see what happened."

"But he isn't an elf," Kaia said.

Izak sighed, "I know. And he isn't from Xanica either."

"How do you know?" Kaia asked.

After another long pause Izak finally replied, "Because his name is Eric Tobin and he was an officer in our army. He was with us at Sternz."

34

Kassandra rose early the next morning and stood up, yawned, and stretched. An icy breeze from outside urged her back under her blankets, and after several moments of silence she began to fall back asleep. Just as she closed her eyes, the shuffling of feet outside woke her back up. Wrapping herself in her blanket she groggily made her way outside and saw Liam sitting by the fire. She looked around at the other tents and realized it might be very early since the sentries were the only other people awake. Liam noticed Kassandra and muttered, "I'm sorry if I woke you."

Kassandra yawned, "I was already up. Last night was pretty disappointing, so I came back here and feel asleep early."

As another icy breeze brushed against her face, Kassandra groaned but then walked out to the fire with Liam and sat down beside him. Looking at his tired face she asked, "Are you still having nightmares?"

"Are they that noticeable?"

"That depends," Kassandra joked. "If you consider that sometimes while we were at Bakea you woke me up with your thrashing on the floor, then yes."

Liam continued staring into the fire, then softly said, "I'm sorry."

Kassandra placed her hand on top of his and said, "I know you don't like to talk—ever, let alone about anything that is bothering you—but you know you can talk to me."

Liam looked Kassandra in the eyes for but a moment and smiled at her. Kassandra smiled back, knowing that it was genuine.

They continued to sit by the fire peacefully for several minutes until Liam broke the silence. "Why are you really here?"

"What do you mean?"

"Back at Sternz we all told each other why we were here—Vernon wanting to find the man who hurt his sister; Konar seeking redemption. All you said was that you thought it was the right thing to do. But I think there is something more to it."

Hoping that sharing her story might encourage Liam to tell his, Kassandra said, "You're right. I left to get away from my father. After my mother died and my sister disappeared, I was all he had left. He paid a retired Vetin ranger to teach me how to use a bow and how to take care of myself, but that wasn't good enough for him. In everything I did he had to have a say on the matter, and I felt like I was a prisoner in my own home. Always forcing me to go to balls and banquets to meet other noblemen's sons; but that kind of life wasn't for me. I know he did what he did because he wanted to keep me safe, but I just needed to be free. I needed to be able to make my own decisions without his overbearing presence. So, one day I decided to leave and volunteer for the Crixarian army. Three years later... here I am."

Kassandra smiled at Liam and watched him closely, hoping he would finally open up. To her dismay, he did not. She grunted under her breath to keep from snapping at him, since she knew that wouldn't do any good. Instead she patted his hand and said, "I'm here stuck with the best family I could hope for."

Blaster's head jolted up and his tail began to wage furiously as he sniffed the air. They both looked in the direction Blaster indicated and saw Makay running shirtless toward them as fast as he could. As he reached them he stopped to catch his breath. "Is Vernon awake yet?" he panted.

"No," they both answered.

Makay grinned as he ran into Vernon's tent. Moments later

Makay ran out of the tent back the way he came, followed by Vernon who was running as well.

Kassandra stood up and yelled, "What is going on?"

Vernon shouted over his shoulder, "Our scouts are back, and have news of the elven army!"

Upon entering the command tent, Vernon saw many familiar faces. Dozens of officers from every army had gathered to hear the news.

Malum, who was standing at the center of the tent, cleared his throat and addressed them. "Now that we are all here, I have some news from our scouts. The elves have gathered all of their forces and are marching here to try and rescue Phyra Ophidian. Our scouts estimate that they have around 35,000 soldiers along with 3,000 orc mercenaries."

Captain Harrison let out a disheartened grunt. "Our 22,000 against a much more experienced and better equipped army of 35,000—and now there are orcs. Not great odds."

"Don't be so depressed," Makay tried to lighten the mood. "You forget that we have been fighting our own war here for almost 16 years, and never once have the odds been on our side. Malum might have come up with a plan that could work."

Malum slapped a map of Xanica down on the table in the center of the room. Stretching it out he pointed to their location at Clearwater Forest. "We are here. The elven army is approximately four days march away from us. I suggest that instead of fortifying our position here, we move to the village of Cedartown and meet them head on."

Most of the Crixarians and paladins in the tent looked at each other in confusion. With her arms crossed a grumpy Zafrinia fussed, "Head on? That's suicide and we all know it. The elves would prefer to fight us in an open battle."

A confident grin appeared on Jenna's face, "But that's why we are doing it. The elves are known for their overconfidence, and if we give them what they want, they will make a mistake."

General Izak leaned over the table and studied the map carefully before asking, "Why Cedartown?"

Malum pointed to a river on the map close to the village. "This is the Tarmount River. This time of year, it should be too frozen for boats to navigate through, but not frozen enough for soldiers to walk across it. I suggest we march our armies there and use it to our advantage. If we use the river to protect one of our flanks, and the rough terrain on the other side to guard our other flank, the only way we can be attacked is where we choose to be. We can lure the elves into a trap and crush them. With the resistance's knowledge of fighting in this terrain along with your experience fighting the elves in open battles, we just might have a chance."

Izak stood up straight and nodded. "Then I suppose we should awaken the troops and prepare to march to Cedartown."

35

The sharp crackle of fire echoed from hundreds of campfires through the human camp as many settled in for the night. While most decided it best to rest as much as they could before the coming battle, a few sought comfort in talking with friends, or making new ones. Makay sat around one such fire, his fellow resistance members smiling and laughing as they discussed recent events.

Makay leaned in close and said, "I kid you not, this girl is the prettiest I've ever seen."

"A girl from Vetin?" jeered one of them. "How could one from *there* have caught your eye?"

"You just don't understand, "Makay replied with a grin. "This girl—I could feel it the moment I laid eyes on her—she will be my wife one day."

"Wife? You will scared her away as much as The Elven Nightmare Tantabus scared the elves."

"That's not true! My charms will guarantee she will fall madly in love with me on the first date."

A familiar voice from behind him dripped with mockery. "And when have your charms ever gotten you *past* a first date?"

They all turned to see Jenna, her long black hair blending in with the night as she joined them around the fire.

"Not even the elven Empress herself could resist me if I tried."

"Ha! And how exactly would that go?"

Makay looked around the campfire, a grin growing large on his face as he answered, "Well, we all know the elves love their snakes, so I figure the best way one could seduce ole Empress Juliana, would be through an elaborate, interpretive dance."

Those around started to chuckle as they could see Makay doing his best to run away with the story. His face like a child trying to out-boast to his friends.

Jenna chuckled as she palmed her face. "An elaborate dance? Care to demonstrate for us?"

"If you insist," Makay jested as he hopped to his feet, but a familiar shadow in the night caught his attention, "Liam! Come over here. Join us. What are you still doing up?"

Liam answered, "Trouble sleeping," and appeared with Blaster from the darkness within camp.

Liam hesitated as he drew closer. The look on the resistance members faces was not one he was used to. Instead of the normal disapproving looks from Crixarians or Tarians, these resistance fighters gazed at him with a sort of awe.

Makay, noticing his hesitation, walked over to him, wrapped an arm around him, and walked him to the campfire. With a friendly push Makay sat Liam down by the fire.

Liam surveyed those around the fire. While they were of all ages, and he could tell they had all seen their fair share of fighting. None seemed the least bothered that they would be fighting again in the next couple of days.

Jenna gazed at Blaster, who had nestled close to Liam's feet. While Blaster may have looked relaxed and ready to fall asleep, she knew that if anything happened that wolf would be ready to fight faster than anyone here. *Like Liam*, she thought, *always on edge, always ready to fight.*

"You really should relax," Jenna said. "No one here wants to hurt you. None of us would even dream of being able to hold our own against you."

Makay saw that this did little to ease Liam. "Think of it this way, Liam. If you hadn't been taken to Azara, you would have been right beside us, fighting against those elven invaders this entire time. Just imagine all the trouble you and I could have gotten into. I'd be super stealthy in stealing documents or assassinations, and if I did get into any trouble, Liam would mop up any enemies we come across."

Jenna chimed in, "What you mean is, when you messed up Liam would be their to save you?"

Makay clapped his hands and proclaimed, "Exactly!"

While the resistance members chucked, Liam asked, "How do you know that I would have joined the resistance? And if I hadn't been taken to Azara, then I wouldn't fight like I do now."

"Because you are a true son of Xanica," Jenna said. "Just like us. We can tell when we've found one of our own."

The resistance members around the fire nodded and echoed her. Makay smiled. "She's not lying. Why, I bet if the Knights of Xanica were still around, you'd probably be one of their most skilled members!"

"I doubt it," Liam answered, "I hardly know anything about them."

"Then you're in no better place," Makay said. "Ask any of us here, and we will tell you all you need to know."

Each took turns telling tales of Knights of Xanica; each smiling as they talked about their personal heroes.

"Remember Bertrand Charny, the Hotspur? They say his temper had no equal, leading the charge against the orc horde of the Kahnz Tribe 400 years ago. They say he single-handily slew five dozen orcs before the rest of the army caught up to him."

"Or what about Jean Coutelle, the Scarred Beauty? She once was engaged to be queen, but after a nasty ambush by bandits left her face deeply scarred. Instead of marrying and becoming queen, she chose to spend the rest of her days hunting all bandits who escaped justice.

"You can't forget about Gareth of Evalon. A Knight said to have been so pure of heart and kindness that even those he fought often laid down their weapons, and some even repented and joined the Knights themselves."

Makay butted in. "Now, all of them are honorable mentions, but you can't beat the last Grandmaster of the Knights, Hugh Molar. The youngest ever Grandmaster, he defeated the False Knight and helped guide Xanica to its most stable and peaceful time ever."

They all kept bickering, trying to remember the best of the Knights, but Liam looked to the one who had remained silent and kept a firm, saddened gaze into the fire. "Jenna, what about you? Who is your favorite Knight?"

Her gaze held firm, she did not move as a small tear rolled down her cheek. In a hushed and lonely tone, she answered, "Gerald Villiers."

While almost everyone else was still bickering, Makay had overheard Jenna. For the first time Makay wasn't smiling, rather a look of concern crossed his face. He said to her, "Want to show everyone the tunic again to help morale? I'm sure Liam would like to see it."

Liam could tell it was just to get Jenna away from everyone. That name, Gerald Villiers, she must have known him before the Elven Crusade. Liam leaned close to Makay and whispered, "Will she be alright?"

"Jenna? She'll be fine. She just knew that Knight from her childhood is all. Jenna may only be 26, but she was here before anyone else. Somewhat of Xanican Resistance Royalty. I joke all the time that she must have been quite the terrifying ten-year-old, holding a sword too big for her. But she was here before Malum, or even myself."

Liam nodded before the next question entered his head, one he had been wondering about even before the Siege of Sternz, "What was Xanica like before the invasion? I don't really remember."

Makay's bright smile returned. "It was, and still is, the best kingdom ever. It is the oldest in all of Aclia, established way back in, I think, the year 17 After Liberation."

He turned to one of the members behind him who nodded in

confirmation. Makay turned back to Liam, "And still here all the way in 15,107 After Liberation."

Makay again turned to the resistance member behind him, who this time held up nine fingers. Makay once more returned to Liam, "Make that 15,109 After Liberation. The other human kingdoms would be lucky to even be here if it wasn't for us. For thousands of years we held the line against the ravenous orc raiding parties. We may not have had the wealth of the Tarians, or the cavalry of Crixaria, but we had our Knights."

Liam could see the wonder in Makay's eyes as he continued his tale. "Cities like Sternz or Tarium are newer, but they don't have the history ours do. The history of the old capitol, Evalon, or even Bamberg, or Bayeux have volumes on them. Sprawling and towering cities made of white stone and topped with green shingles. Why, I'd be there right now if the Elven Guard didn't know my face. And despite the elves trying to hide our past from the children—"

Jenna returned and finished Makay's sentence, "We won't let that happen. We won't let them get away with killing our Knights at Chinon."

"Or massacring the entire Valois Royal Family," shouted another.

"Or killing our nobles and taking the land for themselves," hollered another.

Jenna walked over to Liam with an old satchel in her hands. She sat beside him and placed his hand on the satchel. "What is in here are the two most valuable things we have. To most of us it is more valuable even than our Governess prisoner."

Liam cast a quick glance to the others around the fire—each had their eyes glued to the satchel. Jenna undid the straps and pulled out the first item—an old, battered flag of Xanica, its dark green background trimmed in a strong white. The emblem—a majestic stag with twelve antlers, reared up on its back legs , a crown resting on one of the front legs.

An odd sense of warmth overtook Liam as he tentatively reached out and placed his hand on the flag. Jenna reached into the satchel and took out the second item—an old tunic, one from a Knight of Xanica. Made of the same dark green, in its center was the symbol of the Knights—a flaming sword in white with three white stars above the sword.

Makay smiled as he watched everyone look at the flag and tunic, each with a sense on longing in their eyes, a longing to go back to a time before the elves had torn their country apart. He looked to Liam. "This is what we are all fighting for. We are fighting for our home."

Jenna neatly tucked the flag and tunic back into the satchel, "And we will do whatever it takes to get our home back."

36

Two days later they arrived at Cedartown. The combined human armies marched through the small town and made their way close to the river. Their scouts reported that the elven army had assembled just a few miles to the east, so they began to assemble their forces in preparation.

Overlooking the hilly terrain in front of them, The Unbroken stood in their armors, surveying the frosty ground ahead of them as everyone scrambled to get ready.

"Vernon!" Izak shouted from behind. "Bring The Unbroken and come with me."

They followed him to a gathered party of all the officers and leaders from every army. As the last few remaining officers gathered around and the Queen and Benjamin stood behind them all, Malum and Izak stood side by side to address them.

"Listen up!" Malum yelled, "Ahead of us we have a difficult task. We are outnumbered two to one by a well trained and experienced elven army, led by Imperator Leontina herself. However, together, General Izak and I have come up with what we believe is a plan that will grant us victory this day."

Malum respectfully nodded to Izak who continued. "Due to the experience the Crixarian army has in dealing with elven armies in an open battle we shall be leading the way in the center, along with the paladins and volunteers from Tarium. Thanks to the frozen river of Tarmount we do not need to worry about our left flank. But in the event the unexpected happens, and due to the uneven terrain ahead of us, the cavalry will remain here to protect the Queen and the royal family. An additional 2,000 of our troops will remain as well to act as a reserve."

Izak nodded to Malum who again stepped forward to address the resistance fighters. "As we all know, Imperator Leontina favors ambush from her opponents' right flanks. The Siege of Sternz was an exception to that strategy, and we all know how that turned out for her. That, combined with the river being frozen I believe we can expect her to return to her old habits and send a large force to our right in an effort to surprise us or perhaps even attack our camp. That is where the resistance and I will be. There is only one path that will allow a large force to our right flank—a path that leads to the top of Cedar Hill, about half a mile away. I will lead my resistance fighters up to that hill, and we will ambush the ambushers. After that we will proceed down the hill to flank the elves and put enough pressure on them to force them retreat."

Enthusiasm and confidence in the plan replaced the dreary attitude of the past few days. As the assembled forces quickly dispersed, Izak waved Vernon to him. He placed his hands on Vernon's shoulders and said, "I have a favor to ask of you. I know that you all work better as a group, but Malum suggested and I agree that it would be best if you split up for this battle."

"How so?" Konar stepped in.

Shifting his attention to all of The Unbroken Izak continued, "Konar, while you and Vernon are in the center with me, Liam, Kassandra, and Blaster all have skills which are better suited for ambush—Liam with his quickness, Kassandra with her bow, and Blaster with his nose."

Each member of The Unbroken exchanged long looks with each other, then nodded in agreement. As they were about to part ways, Alezzia and Benjamin walked toward them.

"Just a moment please," Benjamin said.

Izak quietly groaned as he turned to them, "What is it we can do for you?"

Alezzia walked past him and stood in front of Kassandra, looking at her closely. "Miss Verbeck," Alezzia said, "I would feel much better if you were to stay behind and protect Kaia during the battle."

Caught off-guard by the queen's request, Kassandra took a step back, not knowing what to say. All she could mutter was, 'Sure?'

A relieved smile crossed Alezzia's face. She said, "Good. Ever since that Crixarian officer attacked my family, we don't know who we can trust. Your skills as an archer will be quite useful in the event of another incident like that. And Benjamin assures me that you are a trustworthy person." Alezzia turned and walked back toward the camp, followed by Benjamin. Izak harrumphed, then made his way toward the front line.

Everyone else stared at Kassandra, who shrugged her shoulders and said, "What else was I supposed to say?"

Konar looked past them and began to laugh.

"What's so funny?" Vernon asked.

Barely able to breathe Konar said, "Makay just got slapped by a little girl."

They turned to where Konar was looking and saw Makay walking toward them, with a bright red palm print on his left cheek. Even with the obvious pain Makay still had his normal wide smile as he strutted forward. Vernon asked him, "What did you do to get slapped that hard?"

Makay rubbed his cheek and smiled. "I walked up to Sophia Lati, and told her how radiant she looked and that I would marry her someday. I suppose this was her answer."

Kassandra started to bellow into a chuckle, "That was a horrible idea! Sophia and I are friends but she is without a doubt the most independent girl I know. And besides that, she has stated many times, both before and after she got Cormorden, that she will never marry."

"I don't care," Makay grinned. "Cormorden or no Cormorden, I will wear her down eventually. Just you watch."

Toward the front line Malum called out, "Makay! Get your soldiers ready to go. We are leaving now!"

Liam knelt and scratched behind Blaster's ears. "I guess that means it's time for us to leave."

Liam nodded at everyone as he and Makay hurried off to join up with the resistance forces.

Vernon noticed that many of the resistance fighters, perhaps one in six, had blue bands tied around their arms. *Some sort of internal identification symbol,* he supposed.

Konar playfully wagged his finger at Kassandra, "Now, promise not to get yourself lost in any woods while we are away."

Kassandra returned his sarcasm, "Only if you promise not to get wounded for once."

"I'll do my best, but no promises," the orc grinned.

Kassandra looked behind her at the command area and mumbled, "I suppose I better get to the princess. We wouldn't want anything bad to happen to Vernon's future wife."

"Take care of yourself, Kassandra. And the princess," Vernon smiled.

Kassandra turned and walked toward the command area. Konar and Vernon could tell how annoyed she was at the situation. Taking a deep breath, Konar looked ahead of them at the army and asked, "Do you think we can win today?"

Vernon surveyed the scene before him. "Look at them," he said nodding toward the soldiers, many of whom he knew would not live to see another sunrise. "They are saying goodbye to friends, writing last minute letters to loved ones. Some, like that poor fellow, are throwing up from their nerves building up. Can we win? Yes If everything goes according to plan—but it's going to cost us dearly."

37

Standing on a hill by a barren oak tree, Imperator Leontina looked with confidence at her army below gathering into their formations. Eight female elven officers stood behind her, including Tauriel, waiting for their orders. After waiting for almost an hour, one of the officers, a young elven woman with short golden hair, stepped forward and politely asked, "Apologies Imperator, but what are your orders?"

"Be patient just a few more moments Legatus Conra, our information should arrive here shortly."

Stepping back into line, Legatus Conra and the others remained quiet as they continued to wait for their orders. After some time, Domatin approached. The Legati glanced at him for a brief moment then something behind him caught their eyes. Quickly all eight unsheathed their thin curved swords from their waists and began to walk toward the woods where a Crixarian officer with a full steel helmet stepped out of the woods behind Domatin.

Hearing the commotion behind her Leontina, without even turning around, shouted, "Stop! She is no danger to the Prince or myself."

They stopped, but kept their swords ready.

Finally turning to meet them, Leontina motioned for the Legati to sheath their swords. Then she turned to the Crixarian officer and asked, "What have you learned?"

The Crixarian officer raised her hands to remove the helmet to reveal Isila's face underneath. Tossing the helmet aside, Isila ran her fingers through her hair and reported, "The soldiers from Crixaria and Tarium will be making up the bulk of their central force. They intend to use the frozen Tarmount River as protection on their left flank, but have kept 2,000 in reserve as well as approximately 100 light cavalry from Vetin, lead by The Maiden of Vetin herself. The resistance however will be moving on their right flank to Cedar Hill, waiting to ambush the force they predict you will send there and eventually move to flank us and force us back."

Worried looks crossed the Legati faces, but Leontina smiled. She turned to look at her officers. "You see, being predictable has its advantages. In their haste and desperation for victory, the humans assumed that I would continue my normal strategy, and they were right. But now, in their haste, we have the advantage."

Turning to Isila, Leontina rubbed her hands and asked, "Were you able to deliver my message to our spies in the resistance?"

"I was Imperator."

The smile on Leontina's face grew as she turned back to all of the Legati and said, "Well, if the humans want a surprise, I'll give them one."

Turning to gaze upon the elven army below, Leontina gave the orders, "For the main battle we will position our troops into the Triple Acies formation. Legatus Divia, you will take command of our auxiliary forces from the humans loyal to us. Legatus Alypia, you will lead our least experienced elven soldiers in the second line, engage only after the first has made contact with the enemy. Legatus Vestus, I need you to lead our most experienced elven soldiers in the third line, but unlike line two, I want you to wait to engage the enemy. Wait until it seems like both our forces are tired and then charge in to give a morale boost as well as to dishearten the humans. Legati Miseli and Helvii, you two will gather 500 soldiers of your choosing and I want you to wear as little armor as you can and try to cross the river to taunt the enemy camp. We know the

Crixarian Queen and her family, including the abomination, are there, so if you can draw away the humans' reserve forces, do so, but do not engage with them. If they move to engage you, break away and cross back over the river. Legatus Conra, I need you to stay with our trebuchets, but it doesn't seem as if the humans know we have them, so only use them if we get in trouble. That leaves just you two, Legatus Dezipie and Legatus Tauriel. Both of you will be in charge of the force we are sending to Cedar Hill, if the humans want a fight there, then they will have it."

All the Legati bowed their heads in compliance and as Tauriel raised her head back up, she saw Isila whisper something into Domatin's ear, perhaps more information. Grinning as he nodded his head, Domatin then faked a cough to draw attention, "And where will you be Imperator? Cowering in the back with the reserves as you normally do?"

Leontina's calm demeanor vanished. "You really think I'm cowering with the reserves?"

"Oh, I didn't mean it like that, it just seems unfair for all of our brave and loyal soldiers out fighting on the frontline for their commander to remain safe, while the human commanders fight beside their troops. If I remember correctly even the King of Crixaria fought beside his army at Sternz. I mean if I was ordered to fight in this cold while my commander stayed warm and safe in the rear, I might have second thoughts about it."

Visibly agitated Leontina's grip on her sword handle tightened, and with a stern look she replied, "Alright then Prince. How about this, since you boast all the time about how great of a warrior you are, why don't you and I go out there together, side by side, and show everyone how much we care about them."

Expecting his grin to fade, Tauriel was surprised when it grew. Without hesitation Domatin answered, "Believe me I would like nothing more than to fight against the humans in an open battle, but alas I cannot. For right now I am acting Governor of Xanica, and since you've already lost one member of the royal family, I think everyone here can agree that it would be better for you not to take the chance of losing another one."

Glaring at Domatin, Leontina took a step forward and questioned him, "Do you even want us to rescue Phyra? Perhaps this sudden rush of power has clouded your mind and made you power hungry. Why shouldn't I think you are trying to kill me just to gain control of the army?"

Domatin slouched down and feigned a pout. "Imperator you wound me. I would never think of such a thing. Why, I have ordered Isila to take ten of her best wraiths and go rescue Phyra. And yes, in the past I questioned your leadership at the army, but I know that is not my place. If it makes you feel safer I will even lend you 15 of my Praetorians to keep you safe."

Growling under her breath, Leontina continued. "I know what you're doing. You are trying to discredit me in front of my officers to replace me. Well it won't work. I will not only lead our forces into battle, but I will take command of line one."

Tauriel watched closely at Domatin, who seemed satisfied. "It's a start."

Leontina flinched and snapped back at Domatin, "A start? Do you want me to charge the humans by myself? Or perhaps I'll just draw my sword and fall on it, since that is clearly what you want."

"Now, now, Imperator," Domatin replied, "It is true that we have had our differences in the past, but I only said that to try and make you reconsider."

Growing confused at Domatin's response, Leontina's eyebrows raised as she said, "What do you mean reconsider?"

Pointing to the gathered Legati, Domatin explained, "While you had your back turned to them and told them where they were going to be during the battle, I watched their faces and Legatus Dezipie as well as Legatus Tauriel both grew worrisome at the news that they were going to Cedar Hill."

Tauriel's heart sank because she knew what Domatin said was true. As Leontina turned to them with a shocked expression,

Tauriel and Dezipie lowered their heads. Slowly walking up to them Leontina asked, "Is this true?"

Neither of them lifted their heads as Tauriel whispered, "Yes Imperator."

Lightly touching their chins and lifting them up Leontina asked, "Why?"

Unable to bring herself to answer out of shame, Tauriel remained silent but Dezipie spoke, "You are sending us to Cedar Hill where the humans plan on ambushing us. We don't know where the ambush is, and I know that I and the troops we send up there will feel as if we have been sent to die."

Leontina answered, "Then I will go. I promise that Cedar Hill will be the safest place to be in the battle. Now which of you are going to switch spots with me and handle our reserve forces?"

Before either of them could muster a response Domatin chimed in once more, "I have a suggestion, Imperator."

"What now?"

He smirked as he said, "Tauriel was in charge of protecting Phyra, and she failed at that. Perhaps being rescued by the human Liam at Sternz has made her soft to their cause. Maybe it would be best if she stayed here where plenty of us can keep an eye on her."

The other Legati started whispering about her, for they did not know about what had happened.

With the situation now out of her hands, Leontina nodded and said, "Very well, it is decided."

Leontina walked back to the edge of the hill and looked upon her forces. In a strict tone she said, "You all know what you have to do. Let us win this battle and achieve Colubra's will! You are all dismissed. Oh, and Conra, go find the orc chieftain Gurza Ran, I know where I am going to send his warriors."

As Domatin and the other Legati made their way off the hill and to their posts, Tauriel stayed. After making sure Domatin was out of earshot, Tauriel began to tell Leontina that Domatin may be holding information from them once again, but Isila intercepted her. Grabbing Tauriel's arm in a death grip, Isila forced her in another direction and down the hill.

"What are you doing?" Tauriel said as Isila's grip tightened.

"Be quiet," Isila brought them to a halt.

Rubbing the cloth on her arm where Isila's grip was, Tauriel tried to explain herself, "I know Domatin is up to something and Imperator Leontina needs to know."

Tauriel began to walk back up the hill, but Isila firmly planted her feet and placed a hand on Tauriel's chest, stopping her from walking.

"Just listen to me to a moment," Isila insisted. "There are much bigger things going on that you do not know about, and the Imperator *can't* know about them."

"What is it?"

Isila looked around them before whispering, "I can't tell you now, but if things go the way that they probably will, just know that you will be very scared and confused. When that happens don't do anything rash or impulsive, and I promise that once the battle is over, I will find you and explain everything."

38

"How nervous are you?" Konar asked Vernon as they walked toward the human army gathered in front of them.

"Very. I've fought in a dozen battles against the elves, and I am still just as nervous as I was the first time."

"I am too. The last pitched battle I was in was the battle of Black Marsh, and for all our sakes I hope what happened there doesn't repeat itself here."

Vernon took a moment to remember the battle before saying, "I hope so too, because that was a disaster. We had 80,000 well-trained soldiers and the elves butchered us with only 40,000."

As Vernon finished his words, a somber expression overtook Konar. "I wish I didn't remember it as well as I do, but Black Marsh isn't something one forgets. You were lucky that you weren't as far in the front as Sal and I were. I remember we were all so excited at how quickly we broke the elven center that we charged deeper into the marsh without thinking. The next thing we knew we had fallen into their snare, and they had us trapped on both sides. I can still smell the mud and blood as we were surrounded and forced back."

Attempting to cheer Konar up, Vernon placed his hand on his shoulder and said, "I doubt anything like that will happen today. If we can hold the center long enough for Liam and the resistance to ambush the elves on Cedar Hill and then flank their lines, we have nothing to worry about. We know what the elves are planning and by the end of next week Xanica could finally be free of elven occupation."

"Let us hope so," Konar replied. "Too many people have died in this war. The sooner it can end the better."

A noise drew their attention as they spotted a young Crixarian soldier, no older than 16, hunched over and hurling out his guts. "Are you alright?" Vernon asked.

Upon recognizing Vernon, the young man wiped his mouth and stood up straight, stuttering as he answered, "Ye-, ye-, yes sir. Today will be the first time I've ever fought—just a little nervous is all."

Konar smiled at the young man, nodded his head, and stepped forward. "It's a good thing to be nervous. The worst part will be before the fighting. Once you're in the middle of battle just remember, don't be afraid and focus on your training."

The young man was still shaking, but he picked up his small sword and his beat-up shield and went to rejoin his troop. Making their way to the front line, Vernon and Konar passed through the first few lines of soldiers. In the center of the human army were the heavily-armored paladins from Tarium, with their steel maces and heavy plate armor, as well as the Crixarian soldiers, armed with their standard swords and wooden shields with only heavy layers of wool and cotton for protection. On each side of the army the volunteers for Tarium stood ready, but Vernon and Konar saw Zafrinia in the center directly in front of them, standing beside General Izak and other Crixarian officers.

Spotting them Gregory turned and yelled, "Look at you Vernon! I leave you alone for a few months and you go and hog all the glory!"

Vernon embraced Gregory and said, "It's good to see you old friend."

Gregory replied, "I would have come and said hello in the camp but General Izak has had me quite busy lately. Between us, he has put me in charge of finding out anything about the man who attacked the Princesses. But fear not, I'll make sure nothing bad happens to your little fiery-haired lady."

"Izak couldn't have picked a better man for the job," Vernon confirmed.

Gregory turned and looked to where the elves would come from. His tone turned serious. "If I run toward them first, will you be right beside me? Or will you leave me to die—like at Sternz."

Startled by Gregory's question, Vernon staggered for a moment before answering, "We both know that I didn't have a choice. When you charged out we didn't know that there were two more breaches in the wall. You know that I'll be with you in all things my friend."

"I hope so," Gregory quietly said.

Before they could continue talking, their attention turned to an argument heating up between Zafrinia and Konar.

"I should be the one guarding Princess Kaia, not that whore," Zafrinia shouted. "I've been the one protecting her for the entire trip here. Oh, you think you're so mighty don't you? Walking around like you know more than anyone else here. But how could you? You're just a smelly, dimwitted orc."

Towering over her, Konar leaned forward and yelled back, "So I'm an orc, who cares? An orc's reputation may be one of untrust-worthiness, but at least that's better than being a heartless cheat. Your cold-blooded actions got Sal killed!"

Zafrinia threw her spear to the muddy ground and pushed Konar with all her might as she shouted, "I lost a part of myself when he died, and I will never be whole again, but I am not the one who is to blame for his death. Tell me, who was beside him when he died? Who was supposed to protect him from the elves on that day? You may blame me for his death, but know that I blame you just as much, because I know that if I had been beside him then, he would be standing here with me right now."

Konar leaned in to where his and Zafrinia's noses were practically touching as he heatedly whispered, "But you weren't there, were you? You were far away being a little—"

Konar's words were quickly cut off as Zafrinia head-butted him. But before things get out of hand any further, General Izak stepped between them and shouted, "Enough! Save it for the elves. You can settle this later, but for right now everyone here needs to be focused on fighting the elves and nothing else."

Konar shook his head and spit blood out of his mouth. Zafrinia groaned, picked up her muddied spear, and strutted off to the right of the army. Vernon walked up to Konar and asked, "Are you alright?"

Konar tenderly rubbed his jaw as he answered, "I'm fine. I'll be a little sore tomorrow but—"

Once again Konar's words were cut off, but this time not from being hit, but by rumbling. All the human soldiers stood in silence as the rumbling grew louder. They looked to where the elven camp was to see the first rows of elven soldiers marching over a small hill. In perfect unison, the elves marched in tightly-packed lines, with their white, ethereal, scale armor gleaming in the morning sun.

"Into positions!" Izak shouted. "Paladins to the front! Archers and Crixarians to the rear!"

As the human army began to form up, the elves marched closer and closer, now to within half a mile away. Vernon turned to Izak and asked, "What's our plan, General?"

"The elves look as if they are in formation for their triplex acies. And by the look of it they have around 10,000 in the first line, 10,000 in the second, and 5,000 in the third." Seemingly ignoring Vernon, Izak turned and yelled behind him, "Archers! When they are in range unleash your arrows upon them."

Turning back to Vernon, Izak replied, "Our archers will take out as many as they can before the fighting begins. When the first elven line charges, the paladins will charge right back at them. Then our force will move forward and allow the archers to rain arrows on their second line. Only when the second elven line charges will we join the battle."

"And what about the third line?" Konar questioned.

"The third elven line will have their best troops. Let's hope by then the resistance forces will be done on the hill and out-flank them. And if not—well, it's best not to think about *if not*."

From across the field they heard the elves chant, "Glory to Colubra!" followed by the first row marching toward the humans.

Now within 300 yards, Izak yelled out, "Archers, release!"

Arrows soared through the air above them as the elven soldiers quickly raised up their shields. In the tightly packed lines few arrows made it through the shields. "Again!" Izak shouted and another volley launched. Again, the arrows thudded and shattered against the elven shields with only a few managing to kill. Izak cursed under his breath as fewer elves fell than he had hoped.

With the first line of elven soldiers now a mere 50 yards away, Captain Harrison stepped out in front of the paladins and put on his great winged helm. Raising up his mace he fearlessly shouted the Tarium war cry, "Death to pagans!"

All the paladins raised their maces and cried out, "Death to pagans!" Harrison pointed his mace toward the elven line and cried out as he began to run, followed immediately by the rest of the paladins. Vernon watched closely as the paladins slammed into the elven line. The screams of the wounded and dying rang through their ears as the clashing of steel echoed across the field.

"Everyone move forward!" Izak shouted. The Crixarians and Tarium volunteers marched 20 yards forward and stopped as the human archers raised their bows and released their arrows at the second elven line. The elves did not expect the volley, and hundreds of arrows dug deep into the Elves. "Again!" he yelled but this time the elves had their shields raised and only a few elves fell.

Seeing what was about to happen Konar muttered, "That's not good."

The second elven line rushed forward, yelling as they crashed into the fighting.

Izak stomped the ground in anger. Drawing his sword, he yelled, "Fight today not just to survive but to live for tomorrow! Fight for the memory of King Dylenn, and fight for humanity! To victory or death! Charge!"

Storming forward Vernon, Konar, the rest of the Crixarians,

and the volunteers from Tarium rushed into the battle. Running as fast as he could, Vernon led the charge. Getting closer Vernon made eye contact with an elven soldier who had just killed a paladin. As the elven soldier readied himself for a fight, Vernon had another idea. Raising his shield at the last moment, Vernon used all his momentum and plowed into the elf, instantly knocking the soldier on his back into the mud. Now in the thick of the chaotic fighting Vernon battled side by side with Konar as mud and blood splattered everywhere. Even though the battle had just started both knew that if Liam and the resistance fighters didn't win on Cedar Hill, they would fail here.

39

Standing on a hill overlooking the battle, Kaia watched the raging conflict, too far away to be able to make out where any one person was, but close enough to see which side had the current advantage.

Kassandra stood beside Kaia, looked over at her, and chuckled.

"What's so funny?"

"Why do you look so worried Princess?"

Kaia turned back to the battle and watched for a moment as her stomach churned. "War is nothing like I expected. Growing up we always heard the stories about the heroes of old. Going to war sounded like an adventure where nothing ever went wrong. But out here it seems like a nightmare where everything will go wrong. I wanted to be down there this morning. I thought what I did at Sternz readied me—but after seeing this I am glad my mother forced me to stay here."

Kassandra felt compassion for Kaia and decided to try to comfort her. "War sucks. But what I do is, I try to make the best of all the small moments. No matter how this war ends, all that will be recorded in the history books are the battles and strategies that happened. I, however, will remember the friends I made and the memories we shared. This battle will be bloody, no matter who wins, but if I were you, I would think more on the good memories that you have of your sisters and even of Vernon."

Still gazing out to the battle, Kaia asked, "But what if Vernon doesn't come back today?"

Again, Kassandra laughed, "You don't need to worry about that. He has Konar watching his back. I saw that orc get shot by four arrows at Sternz, and just a few weeks ago had cobra venom running through his veins, and he still didn't die. Konar may be a bit of an ass sometimes, always trying to tell me what to do, but he cares about all of us, and I know he'd rather die than lose another friend."

Kaia smiled at Kassandra, "Thank you."

The galloping of horses rumbled behind them, and they turned to see Queen Alezzia, Benjamin, and four Vicar's Chosen, as well as Sophia Lati and her riders all coming toward them.

Alezzia glared at Kaia and asked, "What do you think you are doing here?"

Kaia stood up straight and answered, "I'm watching the battle. But before you go on a tirade and tell me it's too dangerous, let me ask you this. Is it safer for me to be here watching the battle from a distance with Kassandra protecting me, or for me to stay in the camp where anyone could try to hurt me again?"

Much to Alezzia's dismay, she nodded. They all watched the muddy battle below, but Benjamin watched Kassandra and noticed how calm and relaxed she seemed. Curious, he leaned over and asked, "You don't appear to be very concerned. Aren't you worried for anyone down there? Or maybe Liam and the resistance on Cedar Hill?"

Kassandra snickered as she replied, "I would be more worried about us here than for Liam on that hill."

Intrigued, Alezzia questioned, "And why is that?"

"I don't think anyone can kill Liam. At least not until he kills that Prince Domatin, or whatever his name is. You could probably kill Liam, and he still wouldn't die until that Prince is dead."

Benjamin laughed, but then saw Kaia's sad face and said, "It's a lot different here than at Sternz isn't it?"

Kaia frowned, "I thought Sternz was bad, but this is just so much worse."

Looking back to the cold, muddy battle Benjamin said, "At Sternz things were indeed different. The walls gave everyone a sense of safety that isn't here. If you were wounded at Sternz all you had to do was walk down the stairs, and you were safe. Out there if you are wounded things get so much worse. Nowhere to run, nowhere to hide, and no one to turn to for safety. Even the paladins, in all their armor, have to worry about the mud. If they fall down the weight of it all could drown them."

Kaia flinched at the thought, but then from behind them a lone rider raced toward them shouting, "My Queen! My Queen!"

Alezzia turned her horse around, "What is it?"

The Crixarian soldier pointed back toward the human camp and said, "My Queen, a force of a few hundred elves has been spotted on the other side of Tarmount River. They are wearing little armor and they may attempt to cross the river."

Kaia noticed that this didn't bother her mother as she remained silent and looked at Benjamin. Growing more concerned, Kaia asked the rider, "Could they be trying to get Phyra Ophidian back?"

Not giving anyone a chance to answer, Kassandra said, "If I were the elves, I wouldn't send that large of a force to get her back. A small number of skilled warriors would do better."

"I agree," Benjamin said. Benjamin then motioned for Sophia to come closer.

As Sophia's horse came to a halt, Alezzia said, "Lady Sophia, we need you and your riders to go harass the enemy force. I have a hunch that they are trying to draw our reserve forces away and we can't allow that to happen. Don't engage them unless absolutely necessary."

Kaia noticed that even though it took Sophia only a split second to acknowledge her mother's orders, Sophia ever so slightly glanced at Benjamin who gave her an almost unnoticeable nod.

"It will be done Queen Alezzia," Sophia and rode off with

her 100 light cavalry. Turning their attention back toward the battlefield, they watched as the battle raged on. Frigid grey winter clouds begin to darken the sky as an icy breeze whistled around them.

A troubling thought popped into Kaia's head. She turned to her mother and asked, "What will happen if we lose?"

Alezzia kept her gaze on the battle, "We would go back to Crixaria and wait until all of our forces are ready. Then we will try again in the summer."

"But by then won't the elves have sent another army to try and kill me? And since now Vetin and Tarium have joined the war, won't the next elven army be even bigger than the last?"

"Don't worry about all of that just yet," Alezzia assured her. "We will win this war, I promise you."

Alezzia looked at Kassandra, who was plucking at the string of her bow. Scorning Kassandra, Alezzia said, "Perhaps I was wrong to pick you as protection for my daughter. Maybe you should pay more attention to our surroundings for any sign of trouble rather than playing with your bow."

Kassandra lowered her bow, smiled, and replied, "Right you are Queen Allister." Playfully walking around, them Kassandra surveyed every direction around them before sarcastically stating, "Nope. No elves. We are safe."

Kaia hid a small laugh, but Benjamin warned, "Careful, Miss Verbeck."

Turning back to the battlefield Alezzia continued, "I would have thought that maybe Vernon Regnier would teach you all some manners."

"Trust me, your Grace," Kassandra replied. "He tried, but then he realized just how special we are in our own ways. We are who we are, and Vernon chooses to use us in that way. For instance, take Liam. If you were to take away all his anger and rage, I doubt he'd be as good as a fighter as he is. Me, I try to remain happy and relaxed, so I won't be tense and stressed when something goes wrong."

Kaia looked toward Cedar Hill and said, "Do you think they are fighting over there yet?"

Benjamin glanced toward the hill and said, "Let's hope that they are. The sooner they ambush the elves there, the sooner they can out-flank them and help our main forces below."

40

With Blaster beside him, Liam crept alongside Makay as they snuck their way along a small dirt path on Cedar Hill. The 7,000 resistance fighters were all around them, hunched over, and quietly moving throughout the forest with their weapons ready for anything that could happen. As they walked, Makay turned to Liam and asked, "How many elves do you think they will send this way?"

"I don't know."

"Will they send any Praetorians up here?"

"I don't know." Liam repeated his answer.

"I hope not," Makay replied. "I've never had to fight one, and I doubt I could win. You are the only person I have ever heard of that could kill more than one at a time, and I heard that it was four."

Liam grinned as he looked at Blaster's wagging tail and said, "It was only three. Blaster took out the fourth."

Makay looked at Blaster and grinned. "So Blaster, it would seem that you are a greater warrior than even the great Makay! I honestly don't know how to feel about that."

Blaster wagged his tail faster, and Makay could tell that there was a sly grin on the wolf's face.

"For a wolf he sure is smart," Makay said.

"Probably smarter than most people."

Ahead of them the resistance fighters stopped. All 7,000 waited to see what was happening. Malum ran up to them and motioned for everyone to get off the path. Half the troops hid to the right and half to the left. Makay mumbled, "Here we go."

Off the dirt path, they hid behind trees, rocks, bushes, and anything they could find to conceal themselves. Liam took cover behind a tree, as Makay and Malum hid behind a large rock. Whispering loudly Makay asked Malum, "What is going on?"

"Orcs," Malum said with a grim face. "And a bunch of them. At least 3,000."

Liam whispered, "Did we know that the elves had orcs?"

Malum nodded his head, "Yes, but not this many. Seems our spies were wrong."

"This isn't good," one of the resistance fighters mumbled from behind a bush.

Crouching by a log, another resistance member panicked. "We've all seen how Konar fights. These orcs could be much, much worse."

Grimacing, Malum muttered, "The elves must have known somehow that we would be here. This isn't good."

Then voices from the path silenced them all. Loud deep voices echoed through the forest and grew closer and closer.

Malum quietly yelled, "Don't attack until I give the command."

Several moments passed until finally they caught sight of the orcs. In no formation, the orcs marched along the path, talking and joking with each other as if they were not expecting a fight. The orcs all had varying shades of dark green skin, along with tangled hair and two small tusks on their bottom teeth, just as Konar. Some of the orcs were wearing armor similar to Konar's old armor. It looked as if it had been pulled right out a mountain. Others wore armor made of bones, and some with no armor at all. Each carried a crudely made but powerful weapon.

Liam glanced over at Malum who nodded at him. Liam nodded back, and Malum yelled, "Now!"

From both sides of the path, arrows soared into the unsuspecting orcs as resistance fighters charged into them. Yelling and screaming as they charged, the resistance fighters caught the orcs completely by surprise. Liam ran into the thick of the orc forces and began fighting. Leaping into the air and driving his sword deep into the neck of an orc warrior, Liam then rolled and slashed at the shins of another bringing the orc to the ground. Blaster sunk his razor-sharp teeth deep into the calf of a third orc warrior bringing him to his knees just in time for Liam to slice open his neck. Orc after orc charged at Liam, but each fell dead. Using the orcs' own strength against them, Liam deflected their attacks knowing he couldn't block them.

Fighting beside him, Makay bashed his axe into an orc's chest and yelled, "This isn't as bad as I thought it would be!"

After cutting down three more orcs, Liam took a quick glance at the fighting. The resistance fighters were quickly killing the orcs. With the advantage of surprise, they took out half of the orcs before the real fighting began and were working in groups to take out the rest. But Liam also noticed a small area in trouble. A large orc, bigger and stronger than any other the others, was wildly swinging a giant club, killing three resistance fighters with one blow. Liam looked at Blaster, whose fangs and paws were bloodied, and tapped on his hip twice.

Blaster barked in response, and Liam turned to the orc and began running to him. The orc had a small amount of armor made of bones and was wearing what looked to be a crown made of the bones of small feet. Ducking and shoving his way through the fighting, Liam drew closer. The large orc saw Liam and prepared for a fight, but just as Liam closed in, he slid on the dirt and knelt down. The orc reared back his mighty club, but just as he did, Blaster vaulted off Liam's back and onto the orc. Blaster growled as his teeth shredded the flesh from the orc's neck, and the orc bled to death.

Liam quickly stood up, just in time to deflect an orc axe with his right sword and slash up the orc's chest with his left. Liam, ready to continue fighting, looked around to see all the orcs near him dead. Makay hurried over and cheered, "You beautiful bastard!"

Makay opened his arms and embraced him. "I can't believe it. We won!"

As the last orc fell, cheers from the resistance fighters rang through the forest. Liam noticed that even Malum showed a slight smile.

Makay finally released his grip on Liam and turned to Blaster. "You're a beautiful bastard too. I'd hug you as well if I wasn't afraid you'd bite my hand off."

Blaster let out a bark in reply as he wagged his tail. Liam knelt down beside him and gently scratched behind Blaster's ears.

Again Blaster let out another bark just before licking all over Liam's face. Malum approached, and Makay asked him, "So, what's next?"

Catching his breath Malum pointed to the direction the orcs came from, "We need to go as quickly as we can so we can help our forces at the main battle."

Just as Makay nodded, a resistance fighter, with a small blue cloth tied to his arm, walked up to Malum. The young man didn't seem as happy as the others but Malum nodded at him and said, "Jackson, what is it?"

Jackson walked up to Malum's ear and whispered, "Hail Colubra," then stabbed Malum in the side. His sword pierced one of the rusted areas of his armor and dug deep into his flesh. Malum coughed up blood, but wrapped his hands around Jackson's throat, crushing his windpipe.

In the blink of an eye, all around them, resistance fighters started killing their comrades without hesitation. Makay stood horrified and dumbfounded as he watched his friends kill their own brothers and sisters, men and women they had fought beside for years.

Liam pivoted again and again, not knowing who could try to kill him. Then he turned to Makay just as someone swung a sword at Makay's back.

"Watch out!" Liam screamed, but not quick enough.

The sword slashed deep into Makay's back, and the attacker stood ready for another. Liam bolted toward the attacker and shoved Makay to the ground out of the way before punching the attacker in the face with the hilt in his left hand. As he staggered back Liam drove the sword in his right hand deep into the attacker's stomach. Liam looked back at Makay to see him crying out in pain on the cold grass, blood gushing out of his wounded back. To his right Liam saw Malum bringing his mace down on someone's skull before coughing up more blood and staggering backwards.

Hunched over as blood poured from both his mouth and his side, Malum shouted at the top of his lungs, "Someone blow a distress horn now! They need to know we won't be helping after all."

A long, booming horn echoed overhead, and Liam again looked around hoping for something help him discern who was loyal to the humans, and who was loyal to the elves. From behind him Liam heard someone running toward him. Quickly turning around Liam pointed his sword at the woman, and she raised her axe and shield and looking utterly confused said, "Wait, wait, wait! What's going on? Is Malum safe?"

Liam lowered his swords and replied, "No, he isn't, and neither is Makay."

Turning away from her, Liam spotted several resistance members look at him before turning away to engage with others. He knew that they would not fight him unless absolutely necessary, but then he realized that each of them had a small, blue, cloth tied around their arm, the same as Jackson—the same as the girl behind him. Hearing her raise her axe, Liam turned but not in time. The axe came soaring down. At the last second Blaster jumped on the girl.

Blaster yelped out in pain and fell on the ground, with a large gnash on his left shoulder. Liam's rage grew. The woman tried to regain her feet, but Liam kicked her back down and stabbed her in the throat again and again. A bloodied Blaster wobbled back to his feet, and Liam shouted to Malum, "It's the blue cloth on their arms."

Malum nodded, and as blood seeped through his teeth he yelled,

"Anyone who has a blue cloth on their arm is loyal to the elves. Kill them!"

Malum limped over to Makay, who had crawled to the tree, trying to stand up. Liam saw two resistance fighters stop fighting each other as they realized neither of them had small blue cloths tied around them. With their true loyalties now exposed, those who were loyal to the elves quickly fall, though a few undoubtedly managed to take off the blue cloths. As the fighting ceased, Liam hurried over to Blaster to check his bleeding shoulder.

Looking Blaster in the eyes Liam asked, "Are you alright?" Blaster began to lick Liam's face, albeit much slower than before. Knowing that Blaster was going to fine, Liam watched the surviving resistance fighters gather around them, waiting to hear from Malum. Even with his side bleeding, Malum put Makay's arm around his shoulder and stood both them up on their feet. Taking a deep, painful breath Malum turned and glared at his troops. Malum looked around them, trying to find Jenna but could not spot her. "Jenna," he called out, but she didn't answer.

Two older men stepped forward, carrying Jenna between them. "She is badly wounded, sir."

Jenna's face was a bloodied mess, a deep sword wound gushed blood from forehead to chin. Her head swayed as she tried to mumble a few words, all inaudible. Cursing under his breath Malum looked at a dazed and weak Makay before declaring, "I'm not going to put any more of your lives at risk today. We don't have the numbers anymore to threaten the elves."

One of the resistance fighters questioned, "But sir, what about helping the Crixarians and Tarians down below?"

Nodding at the boy Malum answered, "That's nearly a half mile walk, and I can see that most of you are wounded, some too wounded to fight. Those of you that feel the need to continue, I'm sure Liam over there is going to go. Follow him if you wish. There is no shame for those who don't. Perhaps just being there will let the elves know you are about to flank them. It might be enough to compel the elves with retreat. As for the rest of us we will make our way back to the camp and get our wounded to safety."

Resistance members quickly moved to help the wounded pair up with others who could help them down the hill and back to camp. Liam was about to move toward the main fight when he spotted a woman frozen in fear, staring behind them with her mouth hanging open. In a fearful and hushed tone, she pointed and said, "Oh, by the One, please, no."

Liam already knew what was behind him. As he turned, he felt the air around them thicken with grief as thousands of heavily armed elven soldiers approached from a distance.

Liam readied his swords, looked down at Blaster, and commanded, "Get out of here."

Blaster puffed and whined back at Liam.

Undeterred Liam leaned closer, "You have to go now. Go find Kassandra, and she will bring help."

Blaster whined and limped to Liam's side.

"Blaster, "Liam stated, "I need you to go."

After an agonizing moment Blaster lowered his head and limped off to find Kassandra. Liam walked over to Malum and Makay to form some kind of strategy.

The elven force came to halt less than 50 yards away from the human lines. Malum glared at the enemy force, trying to figure out what they could do. He gently lowered Makay to the ground and said, "I'm going to be honest with you all. This is not going to end well. By the looks of us we have maybe just over a thousand left in fighting condition. I looks like the elves have 3,000 or more."

One of the resistance fighters asked, "Have they just been watching the whole time? Just waiting to see if we survived?"

"Forget those thoughts," Malum snapped back. "Do not allow yourself to be distracted."

Another distressed resistance member pointed to the elves and said, "But look at them! They are just standing there, so close, as if they are taunting us."

Malum closed his eyes and sighed, "You all know as well as I do what will happen if we run. If we leave this hill, the elves will flank our allies and massacre them all. We have to stand our ground here and hold them as long as we can."

"But we can't fight against that many for long," a third person said. "We will all die if we stay here."

Malum nodded. "I know. But you are fighting for you homes, for your children, and their future. If we let the Elves past, they will rule over Xanica for generations. But if we stay, and fight, and die, we might be able to buy the main force enough time to defeat the elves on the field and prepare for this force." Malum then turned to a man with a horn and ordered, "Blow more distress signals. I don't expect them to send reinforcements, but it will let them know that we have lost the fight here."

Four more distress signals echoed overhead, then faded into silence. They turned to face the elves. Fifteen praetorians made their way to the front of the elven force. They pointed their dual bladed swords and laughed at the clearly shaken humans. Liam saw Imperator Leontina smiling on her horse toward the rear of the elven army. Liam wondered how they could possibly survive, then one horrid thought popped in his mind.

Dropping his head and closing his eyes, Liam mumbled to Malum, "I know what I have to do."

"What are you talking about?" Malum asked.

Liam began to walk alone toward the elves, mumbling to himself "This is what he wants."

Confused, Malum called out, "Liam what are you doing?"

Liam stopped walking and glanced back. Malum could see tears forming in Liam's eyes as he answered, "You'll know what to do."

With a firm but saddened gaze, Liam focused his eyes in front as he walked toward the elven force alone. Seeing a lone human walk toward them, the elven force erupted into laughter, especially all 15 praetorians in the front, who walked forward as well. All the elves found Liam amusing except for one, Leontina. Her eyes widen as she feared what might happen. Shouting at the top of her lungs she yelled, "Quickly, kill him." But no one heard her over the laughter.

Now between the two armies Liam stood in silence, only 15 yards away from the approaching praetorians. One of them yelled out, "Just who do you think you are? Walking up to us like you own these woods."

Staring at his feet, Liam thought of all the rage he had bottled up—all the torture he had endured, all the humiliation that had been forced upon him, everything he had tried so hard to not think about since arriving in Xanica, all the pain and sorrow he has endured and hidden deep inside.

He raised his eyes and answered the praetorian, "Just a boy. A boy, stolen from his home, from his parents, from his country. Taken to a foreign land full of greed and sin, and forced into slavery. Trained to kill for your entertainment as a gladiator. Just a boy stripped of everything that made him human. You even gave me a new name, one that gives you nightmares."

Suddenly all 15 praetorians stopped in their tracks frozen in fear, some began to shake. They surveyed Liam until one of them dropped his duel bladed swords and asked, "What is your name?"

"My name is Tantabus."

Roaring louder than before, Liam let all his rage and pain overtake him as he rushed toward the praetorians. In shock, they stood motionless, unable to move until Liam reached them. Still screaming, Liam slit the first two praetorians' throats with a single swing of his sword. The others soon recovered and tried to surround and swarm him, but it didn't work. Liam cut them down, one by one.

Sitting on the ground Makay stared in awe, "He's been holding back all this time."

Sensing that now the elves were just as afraid of Liam as the resistance was of the elves, Malum limped to the front of his soldiers and grabbed the satchel from around Jenna's neck. He took the old and battered Xanican flag. Finding a long, broken branch, he tied a corner to it and raised it high. With blood seeping out of his side and mouth he cried, "This is what you are fighting for. Everything they have taken from you. Use it now. Make them pay. Fight like your Knights of Xanica once did, for now, you *are* the Knights of Xanica! If you want your country back, now is time to take it back!"

All the resistance fighters let out a ferocious cry and charged toward the elves. Even those who were too wounded to fight pressed forward, compelled by the sight of the flag. Death would be welcome if it meant Xanica would be free.

The final praetorian lunged at Liam, but without even looking, Liam raised his sword in time for the praetorian to run his chest right into it. Liam glared at the elven force ahead of him, his bloodlust not even close to being slaked. The berserk was upon him. He didn't look back to whether the resistance was behind him. Liam charged all the Elves. He ran with swords in hand, roaring, striking fear into elven hearts. As Malum and the resistance caught up with him, they smashed into the elven lines, shattering spears and shields alike as bloody carnage ensued.

41

"Can't we send someone to go find out what is wrong?" Kaia asked.

"No," Alezzia answered at the same time Benjamin said, "Miss Verbeck, what do you think we should do."

Kassandra didn't answer. She stood motionless staring toward the hill not knowing what to think.

"Miss Verbeck?" Benjamin said.

"Let me go," she said. "I can be there and back before you even know I'm gone."

Once more Alezzia replied, "No. There isn't a point. We can assume that after blowing a distress horn five times it must mean that they have lost the hill and we shouldn't waste our time."

Kassandra continued staring at Cedar Hill, confused and con-flicted by her feelings. *Liam will be fine*, she assured herself. But something felt wrong. On one hand, it was Liam, the best warrior she has even seen. It would take dozens of elves to bring him down. And Blaster was watching his back. Everything should be fine. Barely nodding her head, she took a slow calming breath. *Of course, Liam will be alright, he always gets out of tough situations.* Then a pain shot through her chest crushing her heart, a pain she had never felt before. *But what if he's not. What if he doesn't come back this time?*

She looked to the battle in front of her. She could tell the elves were winning. Konar and Vernon, her comrades, her friends, were down there, and she was concerned for them, but her heart didn't ache for them. Not like it did for Liam when she looked back toward Cedar Hill.

Why am I feeling this way? It's just Liam, and he always comes back. Comes back to annoy me with his brooding and silence. It occurred to her just how much she enjoyed spending time with him. How much fun it was to pester him. Yes, he frustrated her, but—she never realized how much she had grown to care for him. Until now.

Turning back to Alezzia, Kassandra begged, "Please let me go."

After a long pause, Alezzia replied, "Not yet."

Kassandra bit her lip to keep from shouting in anger at the Queen. She turned and once again stared at Cedar Hill.

Benjamin asked, "What's got you so worried Kassandra? I thought earlier you said you didn't let anything get you worked up?"

Kassandra remained silent, and continued surveying the field between her and Cedar Hill. Her heart suddenly dropped as she saw Blaster limping over a ridge coming toward them. Kassandra rushed toward the wounded wolf, examined his damaged shoulder, and asked, "Where's Liam?"

Blaster whined as he looked toward Cedar Hill. Her heart heavy, Kassandra stood and without a second thought said, "I'm going. You have four Vicar's Chosen who can watch Kaia. Liam wouldn't send Blaster back unless he thought he was going to die, and I am not going to let that happen. I am from Vetin, not Crixaria, so sorry in advance, but I don't take orders from you, Your Highness."

Alezzia shouted, "Oh, but you do. You see, you fight under Vernon Regnier, who in turn fights for me. You fight for the Crixarian Army, and therefore you will do what I tell you to do and that is to stay here and protect my daughter from any danger."

"Mother, it's okay," Kaia said, but her mother snapped, "No, it is not. Miss Verbeck needs to learn that her wants and needs are not greater than anyone else's. Liam is a soldier, and good soldiers follow orders, even if it means they will die."

Glancing back at a bloodied Blaster, Kassandra pointed to the camp behind them and said, "Go get stitched up." Blaster hesitated, but eventually limped off back to the camp. Turning her attention back to the hill, she grew more impatient, more frightened. Scared, because the only thought in her head was that she might never see Liam again. Then a stray thought intruded—how she truly enjoyed their time in Bakea together, how happy she was as they talked, how calm she was around him, and how safe he made her feel.

A sound echoing from Cedar Hill interrupted her reverie. But this time it was not from a horn, but rather an elven distress arrow screaming above the trees.

A small glint of hope sparked inside her.

"What is going on?" Kaia asked. "I thought the elves only shot those in only the most distressing of situations."

"They do," Benjamin answered.

"Does that mean the resistance has turned the tide?"

Kaia's question was answered by a sixth distress horn sounding from Cedar Hill.

Kassandra looked back at them and with her arm extended toward Cedar Hill, pleading, "If we don't send the reserves there now, we will lose at both places. You all can see as well as I can that the center can't hold for much longer. If we don't send help to Cedar Hill we will lose."

Alezzia opened her mouth to speak—then stopped, and nodded her head. She simply said, "You are right Kassandra. With my permission, would you like to lead our reserve forces into battle?"

"As soon as possible," Kassandra answered.

Alezzia turned to one of the four Vicar's Chosen and said, "Ride back to our reserves and let them know they will be joining the fight in the center."

Infuriated and crushed at what she just heard, Kassandra demanded, "What? The center? Not Cedar Hill?"

Alezzia replied, "If we lose Cedar Hill, all we lose is a handful of the resistance. If we lose the center, we lose much, much more."

As the 2,000 human reserves quickly approached, Kassandra

stared at Alezzia. With nothing but fear of losing Liam on her mind, her breathing quickened and her stomach was a burning knot. With the reserves ready to join the fight, Alezzia raised her hand and motioned for Kassandra to lead them.

Casting one final look at Cedar Hill, Kassandra fought back tears, then turned and gazed at the muddy battle below. Without a word, she ran down the slope followed by 2,000 fresh troops eager to enter the fray.

Kassandra slung her bow over her shoulder and pulled out her two daggers. The reserves behind her started yelling as they crashed into fight, cutting down elves on the edge of the battlefield. Kassandra slashed her way to the thick of the fighting where she knew Vernon must be. Any elven soldier unlucky enough to get between her and her destination was cut down mere moments later.

Kassandra finally caught a glimpse of Vernon fighting beside Konar and Izak. Vernon was busy driving his sword deep into an elf's chest when Kassandra approached. Kassandra cut him off before he could even offer a greeting. "Let me go to Liam," she demanded.

"Do you know what is happening up there?" he asked.

"No, I don't. And I don't care. Please let me go. I need to go to him."

Vernon nodded. "Go."

Kassandra inched close to Vernon and stated, "Never again are you going to let us be split up."

Without waiting for a reply, Kassandra slipped thought the battle to the direction of Cedar Hill. Reaching the edge of the battlefield she sheathed her daggers and readied her bow. She saw a small dirt path that led in the direction of Cedar Hill. "Hold a little longer, Liam. Just hold on," she whispered.

42

Leontina shifted in her saddle as she panned over the conflict raging in front of her. Frustrated, she shouted, "What do you mean you've lost sight of him?"

Standing beside her, Legatus Dezipie answered, "He just disappeared, Imperator. One moment he was in the thick of the fighting, and then we lost sight of him."

Sweat began to pour from Leontina's head, and her breathing quickened. Dezipie stepped closer and asked, "How is he alive? I thought Prince Domatin killed him years ago."

Leontina glanced at Dezipie but remained silent. She looked away, disheartened. Feeling betrayed, Dezipie suddenly understood Leontina's behavior. Dezipie looked disgusted at Leontina as she asked, "You knew Tantabus was alive, didn't you?"

Leontina sighed as she gathered her thoughts and replied, "I had my suspicions for a while, but after seeing him fight at Sternz I figured out the truth."

Dezipie grew more confused. "Then why did everyone say he was dead? Why did you not tell us the truth?"

Leontina couldn't bring herself to look at Dezipie. "What do you think would happen if our people knew the truth? You know as well as anyone that there are plenty of people who are looking for any reason to dethrone the Ophidians. Yes, they have ruled over Azara for as long as Azara has been, but there are always those who will try and seek to place themselves in power. If it was known that Domatin was the first elf in over 2,000 years to lose a slave, not to mention Heiress Seneca's well-known issue, then those people would make their move. Yes, sometimes I question Empress Juliana's decisions, and sometimes I outright disagree with them, but anything is better than a civil war that could destroy our people."

Dezipie looked back to the battle and said, "Then we must kill that monster here and now. Both for the battle and for our people."

"He's not a monster," Leontina softly replied. "He's just a sacred little boy, tormented by Domatin longer than he should have been."

Scoffing at Leontina's words Dezipie harshly replied, "Scared little boys don't fight like that. And you know that Domatin wanted you up here for a reason."

"Of course, I know that," Leontina snapped. "Only a fool wouldn't have been able to see that he was trying to manipulate me. I knew he wanted me here, but I needed to know why. I'm still unsure of his exact motives. He already knew that I was aware that Tantabus was alive, and unless he knew—" Leontina's words trailed off as fear overtook her.

"Imperator?" Dezipie questioned.

Sweat dripped from Leontina's forehead, and her fear turned to anger. Her jaw tightened, her fists clenched, and in a deep agitated voice she said, "He is trying to kill me, that arrogant bastard. He is actually trying to get me killed."

"What are you talking about?" Dezipie asked. "Everyone knows you two have your differences, but why would he risk that? How did he even know Tantabus would be here?"

Leontina muttered, "Isila knew. She must have told him, and he took it as his chance to get rid of me."

After a slight pause Leontina composed herself and stated, "I'm going to kill him. I don't care about the repercussions of doing so. I'm going to kill him." Then she turned her horse around and looked at Dezipie, "I will keep the army stable. I want you to ride to the camp and return with our reserves. Let Legatus Tauriel know of the situation, but don't give Domatin any indication of what I am planning. We have to win the battle here, and then I will kill him."

Dezipie peered through the trees at the battle before she answered, "Can you hold out that long? Though wounded and outnumbered, the resistance has been rallied by Tantabus."

Leontina smiled, "Don't worry. I've been in worse situations. Now go! Get the reserves and hurry back!"

They nodded to each other as Dezipie slapped the reigns of her horse and rode off toward the elven camp. But before Dezipie covered 100 yards, Liam emerged from the shadow of the woods. He launched himself off of a large rock, straight at Dezipie, knocking her off her mount. He drove both his swords deep into her neck and chest as they tumbled to the ground.

Still enraged, Liam screamed into her face as blood spouted out of her wounds. Liam pulled his swords out and blood gushed into the cold air. The berserk still upon him, Liam roared like a wild animal before running toward Leontina and the rest of the elven command.

Unable to move or even speak, Leontina stared past Liam at Dezipie's twitching body. She knew the legatus would die within seconds.

"What do we do?" cried out one of the elves.

Leontina at last found her voice. "Launch the distress arrows!"

The elf looked stunned. "How many?"

"All of them, dammit!" Leontina yelled back.

Twelve distress arrows screeched into the air, competing with Liam for generating the most fear in those who heard. Shaking with fear, the elves surrounding Leontina readied themselves, even though they knew they could not stop him.

Liam slid beneath the first two elves, slicing their legs out from under them. He regained his feet in time to slit the throat of the third elf.

"Rush him! Overwhelm him with sheer numbers," Leontina commanded.

Instead of waiting for the elves to come to him, Liam darted to his left, planted one foot on the truck of the tree and leapt into the air in a wide arc over the elves. While still airborne, Liam sliced his swords down and elf's back. Swords dripping with blood, Liam tucked and rolled under an elven sword, then backhanded the hapless soldier and thrust his sword through the elf's mouth, pinning him to the tree. With no time to free the embedded sword from the tree, Liam dodged an elven spear and quickly uppercut the elf along the chest with his remaining sword.

Two elves rushed him from either side. Liam threw his sword at the elf on the left, dispatching him instantly, then turned in time to grab the other elf's spear with both hands. He allowed himself to slide backwards from the force of the attack, then pulled the unsuspecting elf toward him, released his grasp on the spear and grabbed the elf's helmet with both hands, twisting it until he heard the elf's neck snap.

Another elf ran at Liam, but a quick sidestep sent the elf crashing facedown on the ground. Liam jump on top of him and dug his thumbs into the elf's eyes. He left the blind soldier wailing in agony and sprinted to the tree where one of his swords was still embedded. He managed to yank if free in time to dispatch four more elven soldiers.

Leontina trembled at the sight of Liam's bloodsoaked exploits on the battle field. There was no doubt in her mind that the tide had turned and the humans would win the day. She made a split second decision. "Retreat!" she commanded. "Save yourselves!"

Without hesitation, the elven soldiers turned and ran. They ran, limped, and even crawled as they scrambled down the hill to get away from the resistance fighters and the madman who led them.

Leontina turned to flee the battlefield but faced Liam instead. He dragged her from her horse and kicked her to the ground. She raised her hands, whether in surrender or in acceptance of the inevitable, Liam didn't know—or care. He ran his sword through her to the hilt, twisted, and retracted it slowly.

Leontina stayed on her knees as her life's blood flowed onto the already blood-soaked ground. The last thing she saw before darkness clouded her vision was her army of elves running, with one man in pursuit.

Liam. Alone.

43

Pacing back and forth, Tauriel eyed the path that led to Cedar Hill. Paying no attention to the icy breeze, she waited for any news as to what was happening on the hill.

Leaning on a tree behind her, Domatin played with a small yellow ribbon in his fingers as he mumbled, "You really should calm down, Legatus. Stress is not good for anyone's health, especially in this cold."

Tauriel ignored him and continued to pace back and forth. The sound of twigs snapping startled her, and she drew her sword, but it was only Isila—Isila, along with five other wraiths surrounding Phyra.

"My sweet Tauriel," Phyra cooed. She ran a finger down her startled face and said, "How I have missed you."

Phyra saw Domatin and rushed toward him with her arms extended. Domatin embraced her, smiled, and said, "It's good to see you, cousin. It doesn't seem as though you've been treated as badly as I thought."

"Not at all," Phyra replied. "A few nasty words here, a few shoves there—nothing I haven't dealt with in the bedroom before."

As the two Ophidians laughed, Tauriel sheathed her sword and turned her gaze back toward Cedar Hill. Isila silently approached her and , "No matter what happens, don't do anything stupid. I'll explain later."

"Why not tell me now?" Tauriel whispered in response.

Isila glared at Tauriel. "Because now is not the time to cloud your mind with thoughts that are not important yet."

Isila patted Tauriel on the back, then made her way to Domatin and Phyra.

Phyra turned and hugged Isila will all her might. "Thank you for coming to get me."

With the air being squeezed out of her Isila muffled, "I was happy to do it Madam Ophidian."

Phyra released her grip and turned to Domatin. "What is the situation?"

Domatin casually leaned back against the tree. "That, dear cousin, depends on who you ask. I believe everything is going according to plan, but Legatus Tauriel might offer a different response. We still have our third line ready to engage with the humans at the center as well as our reserves, but I believe Tauriel is concerned about the battle on Cedar Hill, especially now, after I think 12 distress arrows have been released."

"Thirteen," Tauriel corrected.

Placing his hand on his chest, Domatin mockingly replied, "Forgive me. Thirteen."

Phyra asked, "Where is Imperator Leontina?"

Domatin pointed toward Cedar Hill. "Up there. And yes, before you ask, Tauriel sent a scout to find out what is happening."

At that moment, from the path leading to Cedar Hill ran an elven scout at full speed. Covered in blood, the elf ran toward Tauriel, who grabbed her by the shoulders and demanded, "Took you long enough. What is going on at Cedar Hill?"

Gasping for breath the elven scout hunched over and stuttered, "Tantabus lives. I saw him. I saw him killing everyone. Imperator Leontina, Legatus Dezipie, countless others—all dead by his hands. I've never seen anything like it. Even the resistance seemed afraid of him. Our forces on the hill are in full retreat, but the resistance is also falling back to their own lines."

"What about Tantabus? Do you know where he is now?"

The scout took another breath before replying, "I don't know. I apologize Prince. I was afraid and ran away."

Smiling at her Domatin replied, "Don't worry about it, you did a fantastic job. Now run along back to camp and get some water."

Tauriel scanned the horizon and witnessed the first few elven soldiers hurrying down from Cedar Hill. She knew what needed to be done to win the battle, but she was overcome with fear—fear of Tantabus, but more afraid of Domatin. Her mentor, her friend Leontina lay dead because of Domatin's manipulation. Chills ran up her spine as she realized that Leontina had been the only person to stand up to Domatin—not even Isila questioned him.

"Legatus Tauriel?" Domatin called.

Slowly turning, she locked eyes with Domatin and his chilling smile. While still maintaining eye contact with Tauriel, Domatin said, "Isila, would you be so kind as to take Phyra back to camp?"

Isila shot a surreptitious glance at Tauriel before nodding to Domatin's request. After Phyra, Isila, and the other wraiths had gone, Domatin and Tauriel stood alone. Tauriel's breathing sharpened as Domatin slowly began to walk toward her, smiling and clapping his hands. "I suppose congratulations are in order."

Tauriel remained silent, unsure of his meaning. Domatin stopped his clapping and assumed an air of authority. "I hereby promote you, Legatus Tauriel, to the rank of Imperator. You are now in full command of our army. Might I humbly suggest a course of action?"

Stunned by the unexpected turn of events, Tauriel nodded her head once. Domatin pointed to the battlefield and said, "You and I both know that you could easily send the third line as well as the reserves into battle and win the day, but is that the *correct* course of action? Our goal was to recover the Governess, which we have accomplished. We have lost Imperator Leontina. Tantabus is revealed as still being alive. This is crushing our soldiers' morale. So, let me ask you—is it be better to send the rest of our forces into battle and perhaps lose? Or would our cause be better served by taking pride in the recovery of Governess Phyra? You can salvage the day by saving what troops remain and moving them to Roughstone Pass to fortify it. It is a strategic retreat rather than a defeat, is it not?"

As much as she wanted to avenge Leontina's death, against both the humans and Domatin, she grudgingly had to admit he was right. Even if they won the battle here today, the humans would return with a much larger army. Nodding her head, she answered, "I'll send word to inform our troops to fall back."

"Excellent!" Domatin clapped his hands. As he turned to walk away, Tauriel asked, "Prince Domatin? Why pick me? Before the battle you made sure everyone knew I was a potential liability."

Domatin glanced back at her, a sly smile creasing his face. "Oh, that was all a lie. I said that to save your life. If you had gone up to that hill you would be dead, and that is something I did not wish to happen. You were clearly Leontina's favorite. Whatever I might say against Leontina, she was a keen judge of military talent. She saw great potential in you—as do I. With that in mind I couldn't simply let you die. After our forces have regrouped and set up camp for the night, I will send for you. We have much to discuss."

44

Kassandra sprinted up the dirt path to Cedar Hill, jumping over fallen trees and sliding under low hanging branches, the only thing on her mind was Liam. She could not discern whether the screams she heard were from elves or humans. Neither did she allow it to distract her from her mission. Nothing else mattered. She ran. She ran to Liam.

As the dirt path leveled, she saw hundreds of elves in full retreat. Some ran as fast as they could, others limped, some carried their fellow soldiers away. A spark of hope entered her heart. Taking quick, deep breaths Kassandra focused on an elf that insisted on holding her ground. The elf stood with sword in hand. Kassandra quickly pivoted and cut her down without breaking stride.

Ahead she glimpsed three elves turning toward her and preparing to fight. Knowing she couldn't avoid them, Kassandra grabbed her bow off her shoulder and pulled an arrow out of her quiver. Running full speed, she pulled the string back and released the arrow, missing her target by several inches. Cursing under her breath she drew another arrow, paused for a brief moment, and released again, this time the arrow found its target. Too close to ready another arrow she ran toward the two.

One of the elves charged toward Kassandra, swinging his sword in a wide arc. Kassandra dropped and slid beneath the elf, immediately hopped to her feet, grabbed her bow at the end, and swung it at the second elf, connecting with a loud smack on her check. She ignored the first elf, who stood dumbfounded, watching as she slung her bow back over her shoulder and continued sprinting up the hill.

Nearing the top, she began to see resistance fighters making their way down the other side of the hill. She went from one person to the next, searching for Liam or anyone she recognized. All she saw were strangers with shocked or contemplative expressions on their faces. As with the elves, some ran, others limped, many carried their wounded with them, exhaustion apparent on their faces. Kassandra spotted a pale and stiff Malum, bleeding from his side, being carried by two other resistance fighters, and then she saw Makay limping back down the hill with a resistance member on each side of him. *Finally, someone I recognize,* she thought.

"Makay!" she shouted.

Makay nodded for the two carrying him to stop when he recognized her voice. Once Kassandra stepped in front of him she saw the deep gash on his back. She considered how weak his face looked, but she had only one thing on her mind. "Where's Liam?"

Makay lowered his head. Kassandra felt a cold pain spread through her veins. "No, he can't be."

"He's not dead," Makay assured her. "But I don't know what he is anymore." The soldier dropped to the ground. Kassandra knelt beside him and demanded, "What happened?"

Makay's face turned hollow as he answered. "We came here to ambush elves, but there were no elves. There were orcs. We ambushed them and beat them quickly enough. We congratulated ourselves on our brilliant strategy. And just as we were preparing to go put pressure on the elves at the center, our own turned against us. They stabbed Malum, cut me, hurt Blaster, and killed so many of us. Malum said there were spies in our midst. I didn't believe him. He was right, but I doubt he ever imagined it could be that many."

"Where's Liam?" Kassandra repeated.

Makay glanced at her for just a moment before continuing, "The elven force just watched from the woods—watched us butchering each other. All was lost. We prepared ourselves to die, but then Liam—Liam became something... other. Something out of a nightmare. I watched him cut down 15 praetorians without taking a single blow in return. It was as if he were death personified. The elves were terrified. Some just stood there, waiting to die, not even raising their swords. He turned the tide

Makay turned his gaze toward Kassandra. "He called himself by another name—Tantabus."

Kassandra's mouth dropped open as she recalled the stories she had heard about Tantabus. After a moment's hesitation, she again asked, "Where is he?"

Makay shook his head. "When the elven line broke and ran, he chased after them. Be careful, Kassandra. When you find him, I don't know if what you will find will be the Liam you know—or something else."

Kassandra nodded, then took off running toward the elven lines. All she saw was death. The dead, both human and elvish, littered the barren forest like fallen leaves, but the number of dead bodies thinned and she pressed forward. Nearing the bottom of the hill with still no sight of him, she began to worry that maybe Liam had chased the elves all the way back to the elven camp—but then she saw him, sitting beneath a barren tree with his head in his hands. His swords were yards away from him, as if he had cast them away.

She approached slowly, as if he were a wounded animal, liable to lash out in pain and fear. Once she was within earshot of Liam, she heard him sniff his nose. She stopped, relieved that she had found him, but apprehensive of what might happen next. She allowed some distance to remain between them, then softly announced her presence.

"Liam, it's me. Are you hurt?"

Liam didn't answer. He just sat still with his head in his hands. The sounds of the battle had settled into the background. The winter breeze sighing through the tree branches made the cold seem somehow more intense. Kassandra took a few more tentative steps until she was standing next to him. Though he was covered in blood and gore, Kassandra was amazed to realize he didn't appear to have a single scratch on him. Liam sniffed again, and she slowly rested on her knees down in front of him.

His hands trembled, but not from the cold. Kassandra whispered softly, "I'm here now. Everything is alright."

"No, it's not."

"Yes, it is," Kassandra whispered back. "I don't care who you are or what you have done. I don't care if you are Liam or if you are Tantabus. All care I about is that you're safe."

"I never did any of the things the elves say I did." Kassandra could hear the torment in Liam's voice. "I never massacred any of those villages or killed any of those people. I went from town to town looking for food and shelter. The elves I encountered, they were all nice people and just thought I was a human traveler. But Domatin couldn't take the chance of someone recognizing me, so any village I went through he burned to the ground and blamed it on Tantabus. I didn't burn those villages, but it's still my fault they are dead."

Softly shushing him, Kassandra whispered, "It's alright."

A small tear ran down his face and dripped off his chin as he continued. "I can't remember my parents' faces, but I can remember the feeling of their blood on my face. Domatin held my eyes open and made me watch as my father's throat was slit. My pregnant mother was stabbed in the stomach as my village burned. I can feel their blood on me right now. I can hear their screams when I sleep. He made me fight against the only other survivors of my village, just for his amusement. He has killed anyone who has even tried to help me."

All Kassandra could think of to do was to place her hands on Liam's. She felt his trembling stop as he slowly lifted his face and looked at her through tear-filled eyes. Kassandra pulled him to her, holding him against her as she softly said, "I'm not going anywhere. I'm never leaving you again."

No longer able to hold his anguish in, Liam began to weep as Kassandra softly rocked him back and forth. As Liam wept, Kassandra just held him, with tears welling up in her own eyes as her heart ached for him. She realized no words would help, so she remained silent and let him cry.

Kassandra didn't know how long they remained there, but at last Liam's weeping ceased, and the only sound left was the icy breeze whipping through the barren trees. Kassandra said, "Come on, we should get back."

Liam sniffled and nodded. He retrieved his swords and together they made their way back to the human camp. Kassandra led them the long way around Cedar Hill to avoid the main battlefield which was heavily strewn with the dead and dying. Though they had plenty of time to talk, neither could find much to say.

Kassandra laughed to herself and started singing, "My darling, My dear."

Immediately recognizing the song Liam laughed out loud. He turned to her and said, "Thank you."

Her eyes widened. "Would you like me to finish it?"

Kindly smiling at her Liam answered, "Sure."

Kassandra wrapped her arm around him and continued her song, *"Only death can keep me from thee, Though the enemy may be near, My love for you shall set me free, I will be waiting for you, Now and Forever, We will be together, Now and Forever."*

Reaching the edge of the forest, they saw the human camp. White and purple tents encircled Cedartown, and soldiers from all their forces were crying out in glee. Liam just stared at the camp. Kassandra knew what he was thinking. She stepped in front of him and said, "Don't worry about them. I won't let anyone give you a hard time. You're still the same Liam everybody knows."

Taking a deep breath, Liam walked with her down the hill. As soon as they cleared the tree line, they saw Blaster, with his shoulder wrapped up in white cloth, limping toward them. Whining with excitement Blaster hobbled along as fast as he could, and

Liam squatted down to greet him. He hugged the wolf close and gently rubbed his back. Blaster licked Liam's face in reply. Liam suddenly realized the camp had turned silent. He didn't bother to raise his eyes. Under his breath he muttered to Kassandra, "I guess they know."

He took a deep breath, stood, and walked into the camp with Kassandra on one side and Blaster on the other. Everyone who recognized Liam just stared at him; some in awe others in fear.

Finally someone called out to him, though not someone he wanted to hear from.

"There he is," the familiar voice called out. "The man of the hour."

Liam acknowledged Alex Pry, the man who helped rape Tauriel, smiling deviously at him along with several other Tarium volunteers. Liam turned his back on Pry, determined to ignore him, but Alex pressed on. "I always knew you to be a monster. I heard some of the resistance fighters say that even they feared you. What did your parents do to make you this way, huh? Did they beat you day and night and say they hated you?"

"Liam don't," Kassandra said, but it was too late.

Liam had already dropped his swords and was sprinting toward Alex who couldn't get out of the way fast enough. Liam gripped him by the collar, head-butted him in the nose, breaking it, and tossed him to the ground.

Alex moaned, "Not again," as he gripped his bloody nose.

The other Tarian volunteers rushed toward Liam, but before they could throw a punch, Kassandra, along with several resistance fighters, stepped up to Liam's aide. As a muddy brawl ensued Liam spotted Zafrinia who was shoving her way toward him. She jumped forward and punched Liam in the jaw. Liam recovered and landed one of his own on her side. A loud horn sounded as Vernon quickly stepped between Liam and Zafrinia. Shouting at both, he said, "Enough! We defeated the elves today, so be happy in that."

With mud all over her face, Kassandra pointed at Zafrinia. "They started it, as always."

"And I'm finishing it," Vernon angrily responded. "The elves are the enemy, not each other. Besides, you are wanted." Vernon led Liam, Kassandra, and Blaster away toward a large tent, where Alezzia, Benjamin, Izak, Konar, Captain Harrison, Sophia Lati, and even Malum, shirtless with bloodied bandages around his waist, waited. As they entered, Konar stepped inside to join them.

"What's going on?" Kassandra asked.

Vernon responded, "I don't know. I was only told to bring you all here when you got back."

Clearing his throat Izak stepped forward, "We are here to discuss you, Liam."

Alezzia added, "Malum has told us about what you did on the hill, and I must say, impressive."

Liam remained still, and silent.

Izak continued, "Everyone here knows that it was a stroke of luck that we won the battle today. The elves still had their third line and their reserves to throw into the fight, but they didn't. Why? We don't know. We might assume it had something to do with your—exploits—on the hill. It might also be that since the elves were able to rescue Phyra Ophidian, that perhaps was their primary goal, though it seems an unlikely reason to retreat when they could have gained both the Governess and a battlefield victory."

"What does this have to do with Liam?" Vernon asked. "Why is he here?"

Before Izak could answer, Alezzia interjected, "Because the elves still outnumber us. We are down to 10,000 able bodies while they still have over 20,000. When we fight the elves again, I want Liam to do whatever it is he just did again."

"No, he won't!" Kassandra shouted. "I won't let you make him go through that again."

Alezzia's eyes darted to Kassandra as she scowled in response, "Miss Verbeck. Of course. Never knowing when to stay in your place."

Not backing down Kassandra continued. "Punish me however you see fit. I am not going to let Liam go through that again. He is a man, not some war machine you can wind up and unleash on the enemy."

Benjamin stepped forward and tried to calm Alezzia. "She has a point. Look at them. They are The Unbroken. They are heroes your army can rally behind. The saviors of Sternz, the liberators of Xanica. If one of them were to fall, even against insurmountable odds, it would be devastating to the morale of your troops."

Still staring at Kassandra, Alezzia allowed the hint of a smile to upturn the corners of her mouth. The smile never reached her eyes. "I suppose you are correct Benjamin." Turning to Malum, she asked, "Where will the elves go next?"

Malum, obviously in pain, groaned and tried to clear his throat of blood. "Roughstone Pass would be my guess," he mumbled. "That is the only way for a large army to get in and out of Xanica from the east, and there is a small castle there that could hold out long enough for another elven army to reach them. They must know this is an advance force and that your larger armies will arrive in only a few months. If I were them, that is where I would go."

Satisfied with his answer, Alezzia stated, "It is decided. We will rest here for the night. At dawn we march toward the elves and hopefully catch them before they reach Roughstone Pass."

Stepping into the tent a resistance fighter bowed his head. "Apologies for the interruption, but what should we do about the elven dead? We have begun cremating ours, but it seems that the elves are withdrawing. Should we cremate the elven dead as well?"

"Yes," answered Izak at the same time Alezzia said, "No."

"No?" Izak bellowed. "For thousands of years everyone has burned the dead. Why are we not going to give them the same courtesy they have given us?"

"Because, it's time the elves learn to fear us. They have killed so many and even your King. Now we will inflict as much pain on them as we can."

45

Carrying one of her wounded soldiers into a tent, Tauriel gently put her on a small cot before glancing up and shouting, "I need a doctor here now!" The soldier was bleeding from a leg wound, her life's blood pulsing onto the ground below. Tauriel looked into the woman's pale, stricken face and said, "It's going to be okay."

Tauriel took a long look around her. The rectangular tent held countless wounded and dying, and it was just one of many tents equally packed. The muddy ground was red with blood as more wounded were brought in.

A doctor hurried over and took only one glance at the woman's leg before answering, "I'm sorry, there's nothing I can do. We've got too many wounded to try and save everyone."

The doctor moved to another patient and Tauriel looked back to the woman, whose pale face was now horrified and her breathing had quickened.

"I don't want to die," she stammered. "Please don't let me die.

Looking around them, Tauriel spotted a few bandages and grabbed. "I won't let you die."

"Have you ever done this before?" the woman asked with tears running down her face.

"No, but I've seen it done before."

Grabbing a knife, Tauriel cut away at the blue cloth around the woman's wound, "This is going to hurt."

Taking hold of a belt, Tauriel wrapped it around the woman's thigh and tightened it as tight as she could. Blood squirted out of the wound and onto Tauriel's face. Tauriel lifted the woman's leg and wrapped the wound. "What's your name?" she asked, but received no answer.

Tauriel froze. The woman was laying still, with her eyes and mouth open, staring into oblivion. Letting go of the woman's leg, Tauriel sighed in defeat and bit her tongue.

Isila's cold voice called out from behind her, "You won't do any good in here. You must know that."

"At least I'm trying."

Isila placed a hand on her shoulder. "I know it's hard for you, especially now that you are Imperator, but you are needed elsewhere."

Tauriel answered, "Oh is that so? I guess this is the time when you take me to Domatin so he can have me killed too."

Leaning into Tauriel's face, Isila replied, "Quiet, you fool! You speak of what you do not understand."

Grabbing Tauriel's arm, Isila moved them outside of the tent into the bitter night air. Isila whispered, "Follow me. It's time you understood what is going on."

Hesitant, but curious, Tauriel accompanied Isila though the camp.

Isila asked, "How much do you know about the political situation back home?"

"Not much," Tauriel replied. "What does that have to do with anything?"

Glancing around them Isila made sure no one was around before answering. "Everything."

Shaking her head, Tauriel smirked, "You've gone mad."

"Leontina's death, your promotion, and even Tantabus—they all connect to what is going on back home."

Nearing a tent with six praetorians standing guarding, Tauriel stopped, "Whatever he wants, I won't do it. I will not be his pawn for whatever game he is playing."

"You won't have a choice."

Tauriel demanded, "You said you would explain things to me, so if I am going to go in there without you dragging me, you better give me something."

Isila stared back at Tauriel for several seconds before nodding once. "How much do you know about the Wraiths of Colubra?" she whispered.

"All I know is that you do the will of Empress Juliana. Little more. You guard your secrets well."

Isila nodded. "To become a wraith is to be chosen. If you are worthy, a wraith will seek you out and bring you to us. Our creed is unbreakable. First, we must uphold all of Colubra's commandments to the letter, without hesitation. Second, we are never allowed to leave the wraiths until death. And lastly, we are not allowed to have a family—any emotional attachment of any sort could be dangerous to our mission. If you had a relationship before you join the wraiths, you are to leave them behind and forget they exist. If you bear a child after becoming a wraith, the child is thrown down a mountain as punishment for your weakness. You are expected to find the body and burn it."

Confused, Tauriel asked, "What does that have to do with Domatin?"

Isila leaned even closer to Tauriel and whispered, "I have a son."

As a wide eyed Tauriel stood still, Isila continued, "Ten years ago I was on an assignment with another wraith. Our mission was to scout the eastern border of Crixaria and see where our armies could march to have the most surprise when entering that country. We developed feelings for each other and became intimate. During the mission, we were discovered by a human patrol. He was killed. I fled back to Azara, but when I realized I was with child, I panicked. I did not want to watch my child be thrown off a mountain, or to burn it's body. Since my mouth was sown shut there was no hiding the fact that I was a wraith. I would be turned in if discovered. I hid in a cave, but Prince Domatin found me. I don't know how, but he did. I was certain he would turn me in, but he didn't. Instead, he offered me a deal—if I would serve him above all others, he would take care of my unborn child. He kept my hiding place a secret and made sure I had food, water, and clean clothes while I waited for my child to be born. When my son came into this world, Domatin took him. He told me that my child was going to a good home. I didn't want to give my son up, but I knew it would be better for him to live his life with a normal family, than for me to try and keep him hidden. As soon as I regained my strength, I reported to the wraith headmaster. No one knew what had happened. Over the next few years, Domatin manipulated situations until I had become the headmaster of my order, and here I am."

"What about your son?"

A painful smile crossed Isila's face. "He just turned nine this summer. I've only seen him from a distance, and I don't even know his name. But I know he is safe. That is why I serve Domatin so faithfully. I know that as long as I do, my son will be safe and provided for."

"So, he is holding your son hostage."

"No. He keeps my son safe and I help him achieve what needs to be done. And when he offers you a similar deal it won't be as a threat or blackmail, but as a mutually beneficial arrangement."

Shaking her head, Tauriel asked, "But what does any of this have to do with the politics back home?"

"That's best for Domatin to explain."

Leading them to the tent, Isila held the flap open for Tauriel. Domatin was laying on his back on his bed. He rose and wrapped a silk robe around himself.

Walking over to a table, he grabbed a jug of wine and two cups and said, "Would either of you like a cup?"

Both shook their heads, and Domatin set the jug back down. Swiftly moving to Tauriel, Domatin smiled, "How is life as an Imperator?"

Tauriel responded, "Confusing."

"I'm sure. Hopefully that will change soon. I have faith in you."

Domatin sat back down on his bed and asked, "So Imperator Tauriel, what do you think of my sister?"

Surprised at the question, Tauriel tilted her head as she answered, "I have never met Heiress Seneca, so I don't think it is fair for me to have an opinion about her."

Watching Tauriel closely Domatin asked another question, "Do you know about her—issue?"

"Only in rumor," Tauriel answered honestly. "I have heard that she hears voices."

Domatin glanced at Isila as he replied, "The rumors are true. My sister sometimes has fits where she screams at voices in her head and sometimes she even has conversations with them. Some of our enemies back in Azara say that she is not fit to rule when our mother dies. Seneca is a very smart girl, and I know she will be an excellent empress, but I need your help in making sure her enemies don't try to harm her."

Tauriel shot a quick glance at Isila, who simply nodded back.

"I love my sister," Domatin said. "And I would do anything necessary to keep her safe."

"How do I fit in?" Tauriel asked.

Domatin smiled, "I'm glad you asked. I am sure that Isila has explained her situation already, and I am going to offer to help you just as I did her. You see, I know how sick your mother is."

Tauriel's heart dropped as fear and anger wrestled within her. Tauriel looked Domatin directly in the eyes and said, "Don't you lay a finger on her."

Domatin raised his hands. "She is in no danger from me. What I am offering you, Imperator, is financial support. I know how difficult and expensive it must be to provide for her all on your own. If you promise to serve me, I promise to pay for all your mother's expenses and make sure she has the best care day and night."

Tauriel stood silent, in thought. On one hand, she would be Domatin's pawn, but on the other hand, her mother would be cared for better than she could provide and maybe get the help she needed. Tauriel knew there could be only one answer, "I accept."

Hopping off the bed, Domatin grinned. "I'm so glad. Isila will protect my sister from the shadows and you will protect her in the event of a civil war. Now if you'd be so kind, I would like to suggest our next course of action."

Tauriel followed Domatin to a table in the room where he spread out a map of Xanica. She still felt conflicted. Domatin was an arrogant, sly, and manipulative man, but knowing that he had a reason—his love for sister—for the first time, she felt compassion for him. She asked him, "What do you have in mind?"

"I know you want to move our remaining forces to Roughstone Pass, and I agree. But first I want to go here." Domatin placed his finger on a spot on the map with nothing on it—no village, no natural resource, nothing.

"That will add two days to our march to Roughstone," Tauriel protested.

"I know. But this is where we must go if we are to solve our Tantabus problem."

Tauriel placed her hands on the table and leaned toward him. "Tell me why. You came with us to Sternz to kill him, so why did you look so happy when you heard he had revealed himself to everyone?"

"After Leontina lost the siege of Sternz, I knew it was only a matter of time. So, I decided to use his hatred for me to my advantage. On our travels together, I asked Leontina many times what she thought of my sister, and never once did she give me any inclination that she would protect her in the event of civil war. So, I decided to have her killed and make you Imperator in her place."

Unable to wrap her head around that, Tauriel clawed at the table, "But how did you know that Liam would do that?"

Domatin smiled. "Because, Imperator—I *made* him. I practically raised him. I know what makes him tick. I've been playing a little game with him lately."

"A game? What do you mean?"

"Oh, little things, like reminding him of where he came from. Do you honestly think I started burning villages just to send a message to those who were helping the resistance? Of course, that is what the people assumed, but I did it to get inside Liam's head, to remind him of the night we met. I knew he would show up in Xanica eventually, and I wanted to be prepared to start toying with him."

"But why?" Tauriel questioned.

Domatin poured himself a cup of wine and took a sip before explaining. "You know firsthand how he fights. I created him. I also know how to break him. I could probably beat him in a fight without playing mind games, but this is so much more fun. When he gets into that state of mind, he becomes predictable and leaves himself open to attack."

"You've seen him like that before?"

"Oh, many times," Domatin answered. "And so have you. You see, back when he used to fight in the arena, sometimes I would put him into that state of mind if there was a difficult fight ahead. Take for instance the Harvest games four summers ago. He single-handedly had to fight eight orc warriors. I spent hours before hand reminding him of everything I had done to him, making him hate me, and using that hatred to make him win."

Tauriel shifted and glanced back at Isila. "I thought you said this fit into what is going on politically back home?"

Clearing his throat to draw Tauriel's attention back to him Domatin continued. "Let me finish and you'll understand. When I attacked those first seven human villages 16 years ago, it wasn't just a meaningless massacre. I had plans even then to safeguard my sister. You are her protector with your army, Isila is her protector with her assassins, and Liam was supposed to be a prototype for her personal bodyguard."

Laughing at the idea, Tauriel replied, "I seriously doubt he would volunteer for that position."

Domatin smiled. "You'd be surprised what people will do when properly motivated. Contrary to what many people say, love is not the best motivator. Hate is—by far. People fall in and out of love many times in their lives, and they always tell their current partner that they are the one they love the most, even if it's not true. Hate, however, is something that does not change. No matter how long it's been, you never forget those you hate for doing wrong to you.

I closely watched the seven humans I had brought back from Xanica to see who I could do the most damage to, who I could make hate me the most. Out of all of them I noticed one, the youngest, who was all alone, scared, and shy. He didn't talk to any of the others. I knew that he was the one.

I told five of the seven that he was the weakest of them all, that they would be rewarded for bullying him, making him feel even lonelier. I told the sixth, Maggie I think her name was, to look after him and if she did then she would be rewarded as well. I made Liam look to that girl as a mother-figure, as someone who would look after him and protect him. As you know, I eventually had them all fight each other in the arena. I knew the others wouldn't give Liam a second thought, so as they killed each other, I watched him cower behind Maggie. When it was just Maggie and Liam left, I knew Maggie couldn't bring herself to kill him, so she made him fight her with the intention of dying.

Right there, at that moment, Tantabus was born. In the years that followed I made sure his skills grew with each day and night. Before he escaped, I was slowly introducing him to Seneca. My plan was to start to beat him and for Seneca come to his aide time and time again. If I could make him care for her and love her for protecting him, I knew he would protect her until death. If that worked, I would replace him with an elf, one that would live as long as Seneca.

But it didn't happen. So now I have to kill him before we return to Azara, or else my family's enemies will grow."

Pointing again to the blank spot on the map, Domatin said, "I have one more game to play with him. Then he will come to me unprepared and unfocused. That is when I will kill him."

46

Finishing a gulp of ale, Konar yawned then asked, "When are we going? I'm starving."

Konar stood impatiently waiting for Kassandra and Vernon to meet him by the fireplace. Dressed in warm furs, Vernon answered, "You know you could have left already if you're that hungry."

"I know," Konar said. "But I'm being polite and letting you all get some food before I eat all of it."

Kassandra popped her head out of her tent and joined in, "Oh you'll be passed out drunk before we even get half way there."

Vernon added, "It is nice that Cedartown is throwing a feast for the army tonight."

"You're telling me!" Kassandra said as emerged from her tent wrapped in furs. "It'll be nice to finally have a home-cooked meal again. Warm potatoes, fresh hot bread."

Looking over toward Liam's tent, Kassandra hollered, "Liam! You're coming with us, right?"

Liam replied, "No," from inside the tent.

"Why not?" Kassandra walked to his tent and stuck her head inside to find Liam stretched out on the cold ground. "What are you doing?" she asked.

With Blaster beside him, Liam stared at the top of his small tent, "I'm tired. I think I'll just stay here and try to get some sleep."

"Liam, please come with us," Kassandra wheedled.

Rolling on his side away from Kassandra, Liam mumbled, "Maybe next time."

Kassandra sighed and exited the tent. Konar and Vernon waited for her by the fire.

"Are we ready now?" Konar asked.

Kassandra nodded. "I guess." Then she smiled and added, "You know, it's you we've been waiting on?"

"My ass, you have," Konar countered.

The three of them walked through the large camp and made their way to Cedartown. Along the way they saw others heading there as well, even a few of the wounded who were able to walk made their way, eager to join the feast.

Kassandra glanced at Vernon. "Will your lady friend be here tonight?"

Vernon smiled. "I hope so. I haven't really had much time to spend with her lately."

Tossing aside the now empty jug of wine, Konar hiccuped as he said, "Well, Kassandra, it might just be me and you tonight."

Kassandra laughed. "I hope not. I can't carry you back to your tent by myself."

Soon they could hear music playing and people laughing as they danced around the large fires. They found Cedartown to be a small but welcoming town bursting with excitement. From paladins to resistance fighters, everyone around was having a wonderful time celebrating their victory over the elves. The smell of warm, cooked meat filled their noses and made their mouths water.

In the center of the village they saw a large, round table with many of their leaders seated around it, including the royal family and some village elders—even a pale and wounded Malum.

"I think that seat is reserved for you," Konar said as he pointed to the empty chair beside Kaia.

Vernon smiled at her. Kaia blushed and smiled back at him.

Kassandra nudged Vernon. "Well, go on. You wouldn't want to keep her waiting any longer."

Vernon made his way to Kaia, and she stood up and hugged him. Konar grinned as he whispered to Kassandra, "Look at how the queen is glaring at Vernon. I don't think she likes the idea of a man stealing one of her daughters' hearts."

Kassandra giggled when Alezzia's frown grew as Vernon placed his hand on Kaia's.

"Now that's what I'm talking about!" Konar exclaimed as he turned and walked away.

At first Kassandra thought Konar was talking about Vernon and Kaia. It took several seconds before she turned her head and saw Konar holding three plates piled high with freshly charred pork and what looked to be a hefty sampling of everything else on the tables.

Konar plopped down at a table full of Crixarian soldiers. Kassandra sat down beside him and reached for one of the plates, assuming the orc had politely filled one for her. Konar smacked her hand. "No, no, no," he said. "These are all for me."

Kassandra signed, then left to pile her own plate almost as full as Konar's with pork and bread and vegetables. She returned to her place beside Konar, but noticed how some of the Crixarians looked at them in awe.

She asked the Crixarians, "Is everything alright?"

One of the young men finally leaned over and asked, "Is it true you singlehandedly captured the elven Governess?"

One of the soldiers next to him punched him in the arm. "Of course they did."

"I just wanted to hear the story," the young man said while rubbing his arm.

Swallowing a large mouthful of food, Konar smiled and said, "I will be happy to tell you all about it."

Even the soldier who did the punching immediately leaned closer to listen. Just as Konar began his tale, a strong, handsome paladin walked to their table. He eyed Kassandra, then leaned on the table and said in a smooth, husky voice, "You're just as beautiful as I've heard. How about you and I go find someplace quiet?"

Kassandra barely glanced at the man. "No," she answered.

The paladin, and even Konar, was surprised by her answer, but as the paladin walked away, Konar returned to his story. "Alright, you're not going to believe this, but there I was, left out in the freezing woods for the whole damn time. Things started to get interesting when I got cobra venom in my veins—" The soldiers looked disappointed with the story, but then Konar added, "But, if it wasn't for me, they all would have been killed in Bakea."

Over the course of an hour, Konar regaled the troops with the story of how they captured Phyra. Two more young men approached Kassandra with offers of spending some quality time together, but each time she sent them away. The Crixarian soldiers sat transfixed by Konar's tale. "And then, out of what seemed like thin air, 30 Wraiths of Colubra ambushed me. It was just me and the wolf, but we held our own. Blaster killed a few of them, but I killed at least 25 of them."

An open-mouthed Crixarian soldier exclaimed, "Twenty-five?"

"Twenty-five." Konar confirmed.

Kassandra giggled to herself and shook her head, recalling the old saying, *the difference between a fairy tale and a war story is, a fairy tale starts off, Once Upon a Time, while a war story starts out, You're not going to believe this, but there I was.*

A young gentleman, this time from Cedartown, strutted his way toward Kassandra. She groaned and rolled her eyes, and turned to him before he could even speak and said, "No. I don't want to. Go away."

The young man walked past her, pretending he never intended to talk to Kassandra. As Kassandra returned her focus to Konar and his story, Konar placed the back of his hand against her forehead. She slapped it away.

"What are you doing?" she asked

Konar raised an eyebrow. "The Kassandra I know would have left with the first young man to pass by here. You must either be deathly ill, or an impostor!"

"I'm fine, thank you for your concern."

Konar laughed as he turned back to finish his story. Kassandra allowed a secret smile to crease her face. She couldn't explain it to herself or Konar yet, but she hadn't stopped worrying about Liam, even though she knew he was safe now with Blaster resting beside him. Her thoughts always returned to Liam, and she couldn't figure out why. Never in her life had she felt this way, and it began to both agitate and scare her.

She stood to her feet and proclaimed, "I have to go."

"But I'm almost done with the story," Konar protested.

Kassandra ignored him. Leaving the feast without anyone seeing her, she walked back to her tent. She wanted to lay down and fall asleep, but she felt like she needed to check on Liam. Sighing in the cold night air, she walked to Liam's tent and peeked in. She could tell he was still having nightmares.

She took a step back, but then stopped and looked at Liam on the ground. She tiptoed into the tent and crouched above Liam, wondering how she could ease his pain. She glanced at Blaster and whispered, "Why don't you comfort him?" Blaster puffed air at her.

She sat down by Liam's head and gently lifted it onto her lap. Softly she stroked her fingers through his hair and in a whisper sang the song she knew comforted him, *"My darling, My dear, Only death can keep me from thee, Though the enemy may be near, My love for you shall set me free, I will be waiting for you, Now and Forever, We will be together, Now and Forever."* After some time, his thrashing ceased. She smiled and decided to stay a little longer. Nearly an hour passed, and she started to doze. She tenderly placed Liam's head back on the ground and slipped out of the tent, smiling as she made her way to her own.

47

In the dawning hours, The Unbroken hustled to pack up their tents and belongings to get ready to move with the army as they pursued the elves.

General Izak called out, "Vernon! I need to speak with all of you. The elves have changed direction again."

"Again?" Konar questioned as he poured water onto their camp-fire. "First, they moved south, away from Roughstone, and now where are they going?"

Izak pulled out a small map. "They are now marching toward Roughstone pass, but I can't fathom why they would have moved south in the first place. It added two days to their journey, and they gain nothing out of it."

Kassandra glanced at the map and asked, "Have you asked Malum or Makay if they know?"

"They have a hunch," Izak answered. "They are looking through old maps right now."

Vernon was confused. "Why would they need to look at *old* maps?"

Liam, who had been silent all morning, answered from the smoldering fire pit. "The elves changed a few things on the maps once they took control."

Nodding his head Izak said, "I know it's only been two days since the battle of Cedartown, but if you are all able, I need scouts I can trust. Ever since what happened on Cedar Hill, everyone in authority, even Malum, has been reserved about using resistance soldiers for sensitive missions. With what is going on with those masked soldiers from our side, you are the only ones I fully trust right now to give us the best report on why the elves might have suddenly changed directions."

Vernon looked at each of them. Kassandra and Konar both nodded in agreement. Liam remained silent and studied the map.

"Are you alright Liam?" Vernon asked.

With his eyes still on the map Liam answered, "I don't think I'll go this time."

"Liam please. We need Blaster's nose and he will only go if you do."

Liam looked down at the wounded wolf and reluctantly nodded.

Izak rolled up the map. "Go then, and be quick. We can't afford to waste any time. If you think it's a trap, don't draw attention to yourself and get back here as quickly as you can.

Each member of The Unbroken donned their armor and grabbed their weapons. In moments they had mounted their horses and were riding off into the barren forest. Kassandra asked, "Vernon, what do you think we will find?"

Vernon shook his head. "I have no idea, but keep your eyes and ears sharp. We could be running into anything."

They rode for several hours following the elven trail before Vernon silently raised his hand for them to stop. He pointed ahead of them and whispered, "They set up camp there last night. And I think I can see an old road up ahead."

"An old road?" Konar questioned, "What do you mean by that?"

Glancing back to the campsite Vernon whispered, "Old, as in one that hasn't been traveled on in a long time. Small trees have grown up on the path."

Kassandra dismounted, slung her bow and quiver over her shoulders, and asked, "Do you want me to go have a look?"

Vernon ignored Kassandra and focused instead on watching Blaster sniff the air. Liam also watched Blaster. Once the big wolf began to wag his tail, Liam said, "Blaster doesn't smell anything or anyone."

Vernon got off his horse and said, "The elven army marched to Roughstone Pass to the northeast, but I want to see what's down that old road. Konar then dismounted and followed Vernon and Kassandra. Liam hesitated for a moment, then sighed and slid off his horse. He and Blaster followed the others.

Not far from the old elven camp they came to a clearing and stopped. Ahead of them they saw the ruins of a village, one that was burnt a long time ago.

Liam stepped forward and gave a short glance at the ruins. Before anyone could say anything he took off at a dead run toward the ruined village with Blaster on his heels.

"Liam, wait," Kassandra called after him, but he either didn't hear her or he ignored her. They all followed a few paces behind Liam and Blaster toward the village, which was long overtaken by foliage and weeds hearty enough to withstand the winter. Trees had also begun to sprout in the small village.

They lost sight of Liam and Blaster at what looked to be the entrance to the village. Vernon called out in a loud whisper, "Liam! Where are you?"

Liam didn't answer.

Kassandra's foot nudged against a charred board. She noticed that there appeared to be letters on it. She rubbed the cold mud off and read the sign, Jonesburg.

She felt as if she should know that name. Then it hit her. Dropping the board, she said, "There are no elves here." She then darted into the village shouting, "Liam! Liam, where are you?"

Vernon yelled, "Kassandra get back here. You don't know that for sure." Groaning at both Liam and Kassandra, Vernon nodded at Konar and the two of them ran into the village chasing Kassandra.

"Liam!" Kassandra cried out again and again, but received no reply. Her concern increasing by the minute, she ran throughout the village until she finally found Liam several buildings away, standing silent in front of a small, burnt house.

Kassandra watched as Liam and Blaster walked through the

burnt door, then followed. Peering inside, she saw that all that remained were old and burnt plates and cups on a table broken in half. Liam stood in the center of the room with his back to her. Softly knocking on the doorframe Kassandra asked, "Are you alright?"

"I'm fine," Liam, said but Kassandra could tell he was lying. He was holding a burnt straw object and that might have been a toy soldier before the fire.

"What is it?"

"Nothing," Liam answered. "Just something that belonged to a boy who no longer exists."

Liam threw the toy against a wall across the room, then turned and walked out. Kassandra started to follow him but glanced back at the toy. She walked over, picked it up, and tucked it into her cloak.

Back outside the building, Liam and Blaster were walking away, back to the horses, while Vernon and Konar finally caught up to her.

"What's going on?" Vernon asked her.

Kassandra answered, "This is Jonesburg. This is where Liam grew up."

Konar said, "Why would the elves waste time traveling here?"

"I don't know," Vernon answered. "But we need to go back to our forces and let them know nothing was here. I think it's for the best however if we don't mention to anyone what was here. If they figure it out, fine. But for Liam's sake I don't want anyone giving him a harder time than they already do, particularly Zafrinia and her troops."

"How far until we get to Roughstone Pass?" Kassandra asked.

"Six days from here, I think," Vernon replied. "Then we can finally give Xanica its freedom back."

48

A calm winter snow blanketed the ground as Tauriel strolled through the trees under a moonlit sky. With her army setting up their tents behind her and Roughstone Keep ahead of her, she contemplated how they would set up their defenses to hold the humans at bay. With the full moon reflecting off the snow, she could see the layout of the area well and began to formulate a plan she was confident would work. With the pass itself being only half a mile wide with sharp jagged rocks climbing hundreds of feet all around, she would use the terrain to her advantage and even dig a few trenches to slow the humans down. She turned around to start giving orders and was startled by Isila.

"Do you have to keep doing that?" Tauriel complained. "You don't have to sneak up on me every time you need to tell me something."

With her icy demeanor unflinching, Isila stated, "Domatin requests that we meet him in the command tent immediately."

Brushing past Isila, Tauriel said, "Let me give the orders and—

Isila stepped in Tauriel's way, "I don't think we are going to stay here."

Tauriel snickered, "Seriously? What good reason could anyone, especially Domatin, have that could possibly make us leave the pass?" Pointing at Roughstone Keep, Tauriel continued, "Look at that. Its stone walls are sturdy. It has three towers we can build trebuchets or ballistae on. We could build trenches to bog the

"

humans down while we rain arrows on them. This is the best spot to hold out until another elven army arrives. This keep was specifically built by the Xanicans to keep orc hordes out. If Imperator Bodesa hadn't have sent several spies into here and opened the gates, then we very well might still be trying to get into Xanica in the first place!"

In a calm but forceful tone Isila insisted, "I know, but we need to listen to what he has to say. Maybe he knows something we don't."

Tauriel groaned, "There's nothing else to know. We have 20,000 troops to the humans' 10,000. And even when the humans send a larger army against us, we can hold out."

Gently placing a hand on Tauriel's shoulder, Isila tried to explain, "I know. But remember, Domatin is going to care for you mother just as he cares for my son. We both owe it to him to at least listen. Sometimes he wants me to do things I think are unnecessary, and if I feel like I can talk him out of it, I do. Just don't be rude, like Leontina was, and I promise you can have your say."

Isila headed back to the command tent. After a moment to meditate on her mother, Tauriel followed her footprints in the snow.

Entering the tent behind Isila, she saw Domatin sitting in a chair twiddling the yellow ribbon in his fingers.

Domatin smiled. "It's good to see both of you again." Then he directed his attention to Tauriel, "I know, Imperator, that you must be itching to begin preparations for the defense, but I think it best if we leave Xanica all together."

"What?" Tauriel snapped, "That is insane! Why, we could—" Tauriel stopped herself, remembering Isila's advice. After a few deep breathes and in a calmer tone she continued, "Why would we do that?"

Storming into the tent in a furious rage Phyra blurted out, "Yes! Why would we leave my country?"

Domatin grimaced, "Go back to your tent cousin. Let the grownups talk."

"No!" Phyra screamed at him and stomped her foot. "This is *my* country, and these are *my* people. I will *not* abandon them just because you want to. You forget, *I* am the Governess, and what *I* say is law here."

Domatin replied, "It is pointless to stay here. Even if most of the humans in Xanica accept you, they won't stop the Crixarians or Tarians from kicking you out. We were never going to keep control of Xanica forever. Why waste more elven lives holding out for an army that won't be strong enough to defeat the combined forces of every human country?"

Her face glowing redder, Phyra argued, "You are wrong. Both the humans and the elves that live here will aide us. They love me. I brought peace and stability here. Humans and elves lived in peace until you had to come a ruin it for me, burning my city to the ground for no good reason."

"Cousin listen to me. For the first time in recorded history the humans are united. We united them, and we can't stop them here. We must wait and let the deserts of the Eacru Wastes take their toll on them. And then we will strike. Just go back to your tent, pack your things, and get ready to leave."

Unflinching Phyra took a step forward and shouted, "Oh, I'll pack my things alright. And then as soon as we get back to Azara I'm going to tell Auntie Julianna and the entire High Council about how you are solely responsible for losing Xanica. You are the reason Imperator Leontina is dead. You are the reason more humans are helping the resistance than ever before. Oh, and I bet everyone will be delighted to hear that Tantabus is still alive. I saw him with my own eyes. We'll see how long your mother can protect you once everyone knows."

Realizing there was no reasoning with Phyra, Domatin looked at Isila and ever so slightly nodded toward Phyra. Isila hesitated at first but as soon as Domatin stood up straight and gave her a forceful look, she knew she had no choice. Quicker than the blink of an eye, Isila drew one of her daggers and slit Phyra's throat.

"Oh, shit!" Tauriel exclaimed as Phyra grasped her throat, spewing out blood in all directions. She reached for Phyra and watched in horror as the Governess gasped for air. Phyra's trembling, bloody hand reached up and rested upon Tauriel's icy cheek, before sliding off as Phyra passed into death. In shock, her face and armor covered in blood, Tauriel sighed and she closed Phyra's now sightless eyes.

She looked up at Isila and saw the remorse in her eyes. Tauriel turned her gaze toward Domatin and saw no remorse in his. "Why did you do that?"

Taking a deep breath Domatin answered, "She was going to undermine everything we have accomplished here."

Gently placing Phyra's head on the ground, Tauriel glared at Domatin. "How are you going to explain this?"

Domatin glared back at her, the hint of a smile turned the corners of his mouth. "We will blame it on the humans, obviously. You are to leave her body in this tent, and once we get back to Azara we will tell them the humans assassinated her without mercy. She is to become a martyr. Her death will enrage our people. Just think about it—not only the death of the Governess, but of an Ophidian as well. It will make our soldiers fight harder the next time they fight the humans."

Domatin tossed a moist towel at a shaken Tauriel and said, "Get yourself cleaned up. We are leaving. The humans are less than an hour away, and we need to get going before they catch up to us. If I were you, I'd order the humans loyal to us set up camp as our first line of defense. We will take all our elven soldiers, pass through Roughstone Keep and then cross the Eacru Wastes. Do you agree?"

Struggling to wipe Phyra's blood off her white armor Tauriel nodded, fearful of what might happen if she disagreed. Isila cleared her throat and asked, "What about Liam? You said you were going to kill him before we left Xanica. Is that still the plan?"

Domatin regained his normal arrogant smile and replied, "Without a doubt. All it will take to break The Unbroken is for just one of them to die. I am sure Liam has visited his childhood home by now. I have him right where I want him. I told you that I used to put him in his Tantabus state of mind before a difficult fight, but that is not when he is most vulnerable. For about a week after the fights, I would notice how upset and distracted he would be. And now that I made him go back to where it all started, he won't listen to anything anyone says and, given the chance, I will lure him to me. He will be alone and unfocused. That is when I will kill him once and for all."

"How will you lure him to you," Tauriel asked.

Domain's sinister grin grew as he looked to his hands, holding the yellow ribbon.

49

The human army stood silent in the snowy night air of Roughstone Pass. With the full moon shining high, Queen Alezzia, followed by Benjamin, Kaia, and Tori, rode to the front to discover why the army had stopped. They found General Izak, Captain Harrison, Sofia Lati, and Malum discussing their next step.

From atop her horse Alezzia asked, "Why have we stopped? We need to catch the elves before they have time to set up defenses."

A still-wounded Malum glared at her and replied, "We are stopping because we are blind to the elves strategy and position. We sent The Unbroken to scout ahead."

"Scout ahead?" Alezzia barked. "We know where they are and what they are doing. Why do you need to scout?"

"Roughstone Pass is 50 miles long with Roughstone Keep directly in the middle at the thinnest part of the pass. Right now, we are only five miles away from the pass. We need to make sure the elves don't have any surprises waiting for us. Even a child could understand why we need to scout ahead," Malum replied.

Alezzia shot an ugly glance at Malum before she looked to Benjamin and asked, "What do you think?"

Benjamin looked at the barren forest ahead of them and replied, "If the elves have time to set up proper defenses, it could mean a long siege ahead of us. But if we could catch them by surprise we could win before the sun dawns."

Hearing multiple footprints crushing snow they all turned to see The Unbroken running back from the pass. Captain Harrison walked forward and asked, "What did you find?"

Kassandra panted, catching her breath. "It's rather confusing."

Izak looked to Vernon, who said, "From what we could tell the elves are not going to defend Roughstone Keep. They seem intent on leaving Xanica completely."

"That makes no sense," Malum said

Vernon continued. "We saw all the humans that fight for them grab their weapons and armor and start to set up a defensive line, but the elves were pulling out."

Some of the resistance members started to smile, thinking that after 16 years they might finally have their homes back.

Having remained silent, Kaia decided to ask a question. "Why are the elves sending the humans loyal to them back here to fight? They have to know without the elves' help that they are vastly outnumbered."

Malum answered, "My guess is that the elves are using the humans to buy them time and are just using them to slow us down. I doubt they told them how close we were."

Nodding his head Izak said, "Then we must seize the advantage."

"How?" Malum asked.

Looking around him at the army assembled, Izak offered, "What if, while the main army engages the human line and defeats them, at the same time we could send a force of volunteers to try and capture anyone of note from the retreating elven army? Perhaps one or both of the Ophidians, or even the new Imperator?"

Malum nodded in agreement and even with his side hurting yelled out, "Who will go?"

Immediately Liam said, "I will."

"As will I," Kassandra said.

"Don't forget about us," Konar said as he motioned to Vernon.

Dozens of men and women, from paladins to resistance fighters, also volunteered, nearly 200 in all. Sophia and Captain Harrison offered to lead the raiding party. Kaia hopped off her horse onto the snowy ground and said, "I will go too."

"Oh no, you won't," Alezzia countered.

Kaia confronted her mother, "I came to Xanica to help. I can do things no one else here can. Give me one good reason why I shouldn't go. And don't say because you told me so. That is no longer a good enough reason."

Leaning down from her horse toward Kaia, Alezzia answered, "Because you do not know how to fight."

"You let me fight at Sternz," Kaia objected.

Shaking her head, Alezzia continued, "No. Your father allowed it. I didn't."

Before anyone said anything they might regret, Benjamin spoke up. "Your mother is right. Fighting in a siege is different than in a battle. In a siege, the enemy comes at you from one way, over the walls. In a battle however, you have to be careful from every direction. You saw at Cedartown how messy and chaotic it was. Perhaps in time you will be ready—after someone teaches you how to fight."

Taking a moment to reflect, Kaia realized Benjamin had a point. She nodded and got back on her horse.

Limping on wooden crutches, and leaning on Jenna, Makay shoved his way to the front. Even with his back in pain he smiled. Malum said, "What are you two doing here? You both need to be resting."

"Just wanted to come say hello, it's getting quite lonely and boring just sitting down all the time." Makay then spotted Sophia dismounting her horse. "Hey there pretty girl."

With her sad smile Sophia chuckled. "Persistent, aren't you?"

Makay's smile spread across his face, "Well of course."

Sophia causally walked to Makay and gave him a gentle kiss on the cheek. "It's cute," she said, causing Makay's face to turn bright red.

Taking charge, Harrison gave the command for the raiding

party to sneak along the base of the mountains to the left of the pass. While everyone followed him, Liam knelt to Blaster and said, "You need to stay here."

Blaster whined and puffed air at Liam. Liam pointed to Blaster's shoulder, still wrapped in bandages, "You are still too hurt to fight."

Whining again Blaster raised his wounded arm and placed his paw on Liam's knee. Liam placed his hand on Blaster's paw, "Scouting and fighting are two entirely different things. You know that." Liam then motioned to Kaia and said, "You can stay with princess Kaia. You like her, and she will make sure you are alright." Giving one last scratch behind Blaster's ear, Liam then hurried off to join up with the rest of those ahead of him as they began their trek toward to Roughstone Keep.

For a time, all they heard was the wind and the sound of snow under their feet. But after about two miles, Captain Harrison raised his fist in the air and motioned for them all to lower. Without a sound, they all crouched and waited. Not long after, they heard the chatter of voices. They soon saw the humans who were loyal to the elves marching down the pass. Holding their breath, they watched like statues, praying not to be seen by the 3,000 strong force. After the enemy had traveled out of sight, Harrison stood and once again led the way.

Through the barren trees they could now see the towers of Roughstone Keep peering over the icy mountains. Harrison motioned for them to stop, but this time he quietly called out, "Archers to the front."

As anyone with experience with a bow quietly made their way to the front, Harrison looked at Kassandra and said, "I need you to be at our foremost point. We are going to hit them hard and fast. We cannot afford to engage a force that large, so once we reach the camp, archers will shoot anyone they could see. Once the alarm is raised the rest of us will run in. We need to be in and out before they even know we are there. Vernon, how far is it between the elven camp and Roughstone Keep?"

"About one mile."

Nodding, Harrison continued. "We will need to find the Ophidians before they have a chance to run. If you see anyone of importance, try and subdue them, but do not risk your life in a vain attempt of glory. Understood?"

Kassandra counted the arrows in her quiver—21. She took point and led them toward the elven camp. Seeing sentries walking outside of the camp, Kassandra reached for two arrows, and in quick succession she brought both guards down. With the archers around her releasing arrows as well, they quickly and silently began to inch closer to the camp. To their surprise and consternation there were very few elves in the camp, rather than the thousands they were expecting. Once they reached the edge of the camp, an elven distress arrow screeched over them. They had been spotted.

"Go, go, go!" Harrison yelled. Screaming and yelling they charged into the camp, striking down the unsuspecting elves.

Vernon looked to Konar and said, "This isn't right. Where are all the elves?"

Konar stopped and took a quick glance around, noting how few elves were there. Shaking his head, he replied, "I don't know, but we need to focus on capturing the Ophidians."

Within moments they reached the command tent. Harrison charged in, mace at the ready, then stormed out, anger and frustration written on his face. "They aren't here," he cursed. "They must have left after they sent the humans down the pass."

Konar rummaged through the tent, pushing open one of the flaps. He turned to Vernon and muttered, "This isn't good."

Vernon joined him and saw Phyra's bloody corpse on the cold ground. Stunned, Vernon called out, "Harrison! You need to see this. Why would the elves kill an Ophidian?"

Rubbing his face, Harrison answered, "They are going to blame us for it. They will go back to Azara and say we killed her without trial or ransom. She will become a martyr for their cause against us."

Disheartened, Vernon took one more glance at Phyra before realizing something was missing. "Where are Liam and Kassandra?"

At the far end of the camp, Liam and Kassandra brought down five more elves before Kassandra asked, "Where is the rest of the elven army. Do you think they've already left?"

Liam didn't answer. He just peered down the path to Roughstone Keep.

"I hope so," Kassandra joked. "I only have four arrows left."

Liam glared into the woods at something that shattered him. In the center of the pass, no more than 100 yards away was an elven banner, its white background blended in with the snow ground, its blue cobra emblem taunted at him. But what caught his eyes and pierced his heart was a small yellow ribbon wrapped around the midway point of the wooden shaft, fluttering in the evening breeze, illuminated by the bright moonlight. As he stared, Liam's hatred grew. Through gritted teeth he muttered a name, "Domatin."

Liam began to run as fast as he could into the forest.

"Liam," Kassandra yelled. "Where are you going?"

She spotted the banner and the yellow ribbon. She realized it must have been the yellow ribbon Maggie wore. Domatin was baiting Liam.

Kassandra started after him then stopped at the sight of the moonlit forest. She could feel the weight of the forest pressing in all around her. She began to shake. Her breathing quickened. The moon faded behind a passing cloud, and the darkness intensified her fear. All she could do was stand frozen as tears filled her eyes.

She gazed in the direction Liam had gone and silently begged, "Liam, please don't leave me here. Please come back."

50

Tauriel hurried her army into the entrance of Roughstone Keep. "Let's go everyone! We need to be in the Eacru Wastes by morning."

As her army pushed into the keep, Isila walked past her with all of her wraiths in tow. Grabbing Isila by the arm she asked, "Where is Domatin? I haven't seen him since we left."

Signaling with her head back toward the camp, Isila stated, "He is waiting for Liam."

"Damn him," Tauriel mumbled under her breath. "We need to go immediately. I can't risk losing another royal family member right now. I'm going to get him. I don't care about his personal vendetta. Maybe if the humans weren't already in the camp, then sure, but not right now."

Tauriel drew her sword and hurried into the woods, back toward Domatin. One of Isila's wraiths stepped forward to follow, but Isila quickly dismissed him. "No. Prince Domatin made it clear that he has everything under control. She will have to listen to him, for her mother's sake. He will send her back."

Rushing into the woods with the ten soldiers behind her, Tauriel hurried to find Domatin. She wanted to yell out for him but knew that if the humans had already advanced this far, they could also find him. Gesturing for the soldiers behind her to spread out they began to cover a wider area, passing through the trees and searching for any sign of Domatin.

The snapping of a branch forced them to stop. Peering into the area where the sound came from, Tauriel breathed a sigh of relief as Domatin walked toward her, followed by two praetorians.

With a cocky, satisfied smile he approached her. "Imperator, what a surprise to see you here."

Scanning the woods behind him, she answered, "We need to go now. You heard the distress arrow. The humans are at the camp and will be chasing us soon."

Snickering once Domatin replied, "I appreciate your concern, but everything is going according to plan."

"What plan? Liam?" she muttered pointing to the woods. "I fear you are over-confident in what you expect from him."

With a sly smile Domatin leaned in and said, "I'm not. In fact, he is chasing me right now. Alone."

As Tauriel peered nervously into the woods, Domatin assured her, "I have him right where I want him. Now, go back to your army and get them moving. If you like you can wait for me at the keep, and I promise I will be back shortly."

Knowing she didn't have a say in the matter, Tauriel sheathed her sword and gave one last look into the moonlit woods. As she turned to go, Domatin said one last thing. "Imperator. If it's not too much trouble, could you leave the 10 soldiers you brought with you? I may have use for them."

Tauriel nodded, though she knew that they would not come back alive.

With Tauriel escaping from sight, Domatin smiled and took a long breath of the cold night air. He relaxed as the air tingled his body. Shivering the cold away, he turned to the 10 elven soldiers behind him and said, "There is going to be a young human man running toward us in a few moments. What I need for you to do is lead him to this spot. You don't have to engage him, just lead him here." Domatin extended his arm to where they needed to go.

Hearing the rumors about who Liam might be, the soldiers drew their swords and crept into the dark woods. As they disappeared one of the praetorians looked to the other and chuckled. "How many do you think will come back?"

"A few might," Domatin answered. "I doubt it, but a few might. As long as they lead him to me it doesn't matter."

Scanning the area in front of him Domatin pointed to two large trees 15 yards away and said, "I want one of you hiding behind each tree. When Liam spots me he will run between them. I will talk to him first, focusing all his attention on me. When he charges, whoever is closer, kill him."

Nodding, the two praetorian's moved into position. Domatin gave each a glance to make sure that their entire bodies would be hidden from Liam's sight. As silence overtook them Domatin closed his eyes and smiled in excitement. Leaning his head back he opened his mouth to catch a few snowflakes on his tongue. Even in his dark blue, scaled armor he shivered slightly as a winter breeze blew across his face.

Looking back to the snowy woods he waited patiently, his devious smile never leaving his face. Then a noise—a noise he knew all too well—echoed once off the trees around him. He waited, hoping to hear it again. He didn't have to wait long. The sound of steel clashing against steel grew louder. "That's it Liam. Just a little bit closer."

Deep into the woods Liam chased down another elven soldier. The three that remained ran away as fast as they could with Liam directly behind them. Liam realized they were doubling back as he ran past footprints recently made. He slowed to a stop, examined the footprints to confirm his deduction. When he looked back up the soldiers were nowhere to be seen. Liam's grip on his swords tightened in frustration. Then he saw him—the man he had been searching for—Domatin.

From 30 yards away they stared at each other—Domatin, with his head slightly lowered and smiling maliciously, and Liam standing firm with anger blazing in his eyes and heart.

"Liam, my boy," Domatin greeted. "It's so good to see you again."

Liam shook his head at Domatin. With fresh elven blood dripping off his swords, he growled, "Don't start."

Domatin chuckled. "Don't start what? Can I not greet someone I have seen grow from a scared little boy to a scared young man?"

Liam began to walk forward, but Domatin raised his hand. "No, no. Not yet. I want to speak to you first. It's been such a long time since we've had a good chat. So, tell me, was it good to get to see your home again? I know it had been a long time."

Liam stopped walking, and his hands began to shake. All he wanted to do was kill Domatin, but some instinct warned him something was wrong.

"Of course," Domatin continued. "That never really was your home, was it? Your home was always with me."

"I'm going to kill you."

Domatin laughed. "No you won't. You will never be able to bring yourself to kill me. What purpose would your life have after you killed me? How long has it been since you've thought about doing anything but? Face it, Liam. You *need* me. Without your drive to kill me, you are nothing. What would you do without me? Become a farmer? No, I forged you into a killer. Without me to focus your rage on, you are nothing. I complete you. That was something all the other slaves understood—they needed me. Especially that one girl. What was her name? Mary? No, that's not right. Margie?"

"Maggie."

Clapping his hands and grinning, Domatin replied, "That's right! Maggie was her name. A sweet girl. Too bad she died protecting you. So sad. Then again, everyone you've ever been close to has died to protect you. I can remember your father's squeals as he begged me to spare your life."

Domatin's grin widened as he could see the rage about to overtake Liam. "You know, in a weird but logical way, I'm the closest you'll ever get to having a father."

"Enough!" Liam yelled as rage consumed him.

Smiling wider Domatin continued, "How long before you get your new family killed? It'd be a shame if I were the one to kill them as well, wouldn't it? Perhaps I'll start with the orc—or maybe the girl."

His hands shaking, his vision narrowed solely on Domatin, Liam roared in anger and charged. In his blind rage, he did not see the praetorian step out from behind a tree to his right.

The praetorian swung a heavy branch at Liam, breaking it in two as it connected with Liam's head. Liam's swords dropped from his hands as he spun around and fell to his back, knocked unconscious by the heavy blow.

The praetorian laughed and tossed what was left of the branch to the side, but Domatin, furious at what he has just seen, scolded him. "What are you doing? Why didn't you kill him?"

Surprised, the praetorian shrugged his shoulders and replied, "I thought you wanted to be the one to kill him."

Domatin pointed at Liam and shouted, "I don't care who kills him, I just want him dead! Kill him. Kill him, now!"

Bowing to Domatin, the praetorian picked up one of Liam's swords and raised it high the air. As he started to bring the weapon down, an arrow pierced his neck and he fell dead to the ground. A second arrow struck the other praetorian in the chest as he rushed out from behind his tree. Domatin ducked in time to dodge a third arrow, which barely missed his neck.

Domatin scanned the woods and saw Kassandra stepping from the shadows, her bow raised and another arrow ready to release. With passion in her voice she declared, "You will not take him from me."

At first Domatin's face was a mask of pure anger, but as their relationship began to dawn on him, he smiled. Standing up straight he said, "Oh, this is just precious. I didn't think Liam would ever get close to anyone again. I always thought he would push everyone away, but I guess you've just pulled back harder."

With Liam on the ground between them, Kassandra took an assertive step forward and pulled back on her bow.

Domatin laughed and pointed to her empty quiver. "You're not going to shoot me. That is your last arrow. What if you miss?"

"Test me," Kassandra challenged. "I'll show you what I can do with just one arrow."

Domatin mockingly raised his hands to his chest and exclaimed, "Oh, I'm so frightened. But we both know you aren't going to risk it."

Kassandra steadied her arm as she stared at Domatin.

Domatin glanced behind him before saying, "If you shoot that arrow there is no guarantee that you will kill me. I dodged the first one you shot at me, and I didn't even see where you were. If you miss, both you and Liam will die here tonight, and judging by your face I don't think you want that. On the other hand, if you were to lower your bow, I will simply walk back to the keep and leave you alone with Liam."

"You're lying."

Domatin sighed, "If I charge you right now, you'll wait to shoot me until I'm too close to dodge. Instead we are at an unfortunate impasse. But I am going to let you decide. Either I can leave here tonight, or all three of us can leave. Your choice."

Kassandra glanced at Liam and then back to Domatin. Back to Liam and again to Domatin. With the cold winter wind blowing she knew she would need to aim slightly to the left. Once again, she looked back to Liam, then back to a smiling Domatin. She knew she needed to kill him. *But what if I miss? What if my arrow hits him but doesn't kill him? What if he even wounded he is a better fighter than me?* Forcing those thoughts out of her head she narrowed her vision on Domatin.

Confident he knew what she was going to do, Domatin slightly bowed as he looked her in her very soul and said, "I'll be seeing you soon." Giving one last glance at Liam, Domatin turned and walked into the woods toward Roughstone Keep.

Kassandra took another step forward, readying her shot. With her eyes narrowed solely at the back of Domatin's neck she took a deep breath, pulled the arrow as far back as it would go, but then lowered her bow. She couldn't take the risk. Watching Domatin walk out of her sight, Kassandra hurried to Liam. Setting her bow beside him she wiped the snow off his face before shaking his shoulders. "Hurry and wake up." Liam was out cold, but he was breathing.

Relieved that he was alive, she smiled at him before looking around her at the moonlit forest. Feeling the weight of it closing in on her she looked back at Liam, and her fears subsided. "I told you I won't leave you alone. I've got your back, now and forever. I saved you this time. I guess this means we are even for Sternz."

As light from the dawning sun began to peek over the mountains, Kassandra sat beside Liam keeping him warm with her body heat, waiting for him to wake up. She started humming the soft tune of *Now and Forever*. She hummed through the song several times before finally Liam opened his eyes. Dazed and confused he looked around him and rubbed the side of his head. Laying eyes on Kassandra he asked, "What happened?"

She smiled at him and said, "I'll tell you about it later, when your head isn't hurting."

Liam slowly raised himself up to his feet and began looking for his swords. Kassandra had already set them near at hand. She said, "You know, you really should get some sort of sheath for these, just so you don't have to carry them all the time." Studying the blades, she said, "I could make you one like mine if you want."

Grabbing his swords, Liam smiled back at her, "I'd like that."

Kassandra pointed to the towers of Roughstone Keep. "Shall we go scout ahead and see if the elves have left or not?"

Liam agreed, and they made their way to Roughstone Keep only to find it empty. Not a single elf was inside, and the castle appeared abandoned. Kassandra grabbed Liam's hand and led him into the tallest of the towers. Hurrying up the stairs, Liam questioned, "Where are we going?"

"You'll see."

Reaching the top of the tower they could see everything around them. Overcome by the breathtaking view, they both stared in awe as they watched the morning sun rise over the desert of the Eacru Wastes. Crimson and auburn clouds glowed overhead, and they could see the elven army retreating.

From down below, Konar cried out, "Hey! What are you two doing up there?"

Looking down, Kassandra and Liam saw the entire human army approaching Roughstone Keep. Kassandra yelled, "Well, someone had to capture this castle. Might as well be me."

Turning her eyes back to the horizon, she nuzzled close to Liam and wrapped her arms around his.

"What do we do now?" he asked.

As the morning sunlight glistened off the snow around them, Kassandra smiled and said, "We forge our own paths, full of hope and happiness as we challenge the unknown."

"That was slightly poetic," Liam joked.

Kassandra giggled, "I try sometimes."

Pulling herself closer they watched the sun rise, happy that Xanica was finally free, and both ready to cross the deserts of the Eacru Wastes.

About the Author

Luther Salyers has studied battle strategy from his childhood, and he was introduced to the fantasy genre while still in elementary school. His literary encounter with King Arthur and the Knights of the Round Table opened the door to whole new worlds of imagination and adventure.

With his knowledge of history and military strategy—combined with his love of fantastic stories—it was inevitable that Luther's debut series, *The Unbroken*, would be High Fantasy, paying homage to the masters of the genre, such as Tolkien, Lewis, Howard, and Jordan, while creating his own unique, dangerous, and often unpredictable world.

Luther lives in southern Kentucky. When he is not creating new worlds, he enjoys spending time with his playful dog Caesar.

Connect with Luther online at:

http://theunbrokenbooks.com